I0717062

Portals: Book 5 – Towers & Trolls

Portals: Book 5 – Towers & Trolls

Portals:

Book Five

Towers & Trolls

Travis I. Sivart

Travis I. Sivart

Portals: Book 5, Towers & Trolls

Copyright © 2024 Travis I. Sivart

ISBN: 978-1-954214-39-2

Talk of the Tavern Publishing Group

Portals: Book 5 – Towers & Trolls

Portals: Book 5 – Towers & Trolls

Dedication

For Andrea who saved me from a broken world and helped me live my dreams. Also, to Cuddlefish for all the hours on my lap. Mister Bitey Otter for insisting I take sink breaks. Zazzles who constantly interrupted to be let into the executive washroom. Gobblin for the mysterious hellos from dark rooms. G-Raff for a twenty pound snuggle. Skwerl for coming out of hiding just for me. Hairy Hausenkat for singing at my window. Noodle for not heavy breathing as much as he once did. Steve Purr-win for attacking the wily freshness seals. And last, Tom Meowaton for joining our little family and singing the song of his people every night for the first year.

Table of Contents

Portals: Book 5 – Towers & Trolls

Travis I. Sivart

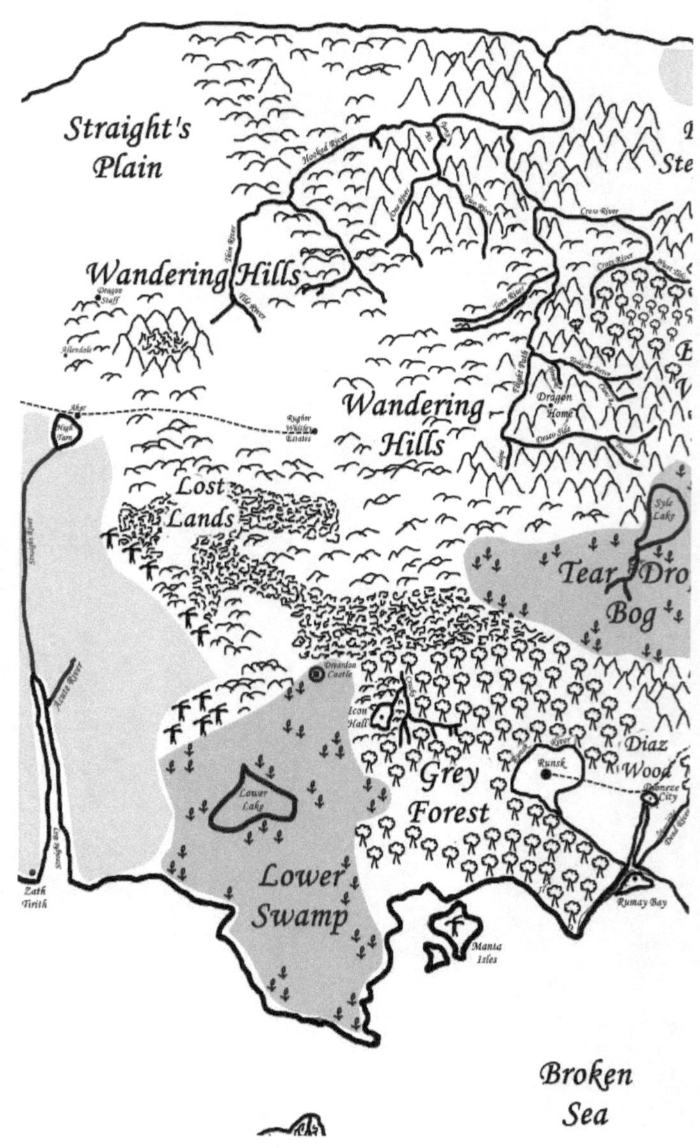
Straight's Plain
Wandering Hills
Dragon Staff
Allendale
Wandering Hills
Akar
High Tarn
Rygher Whaley Estates
Lost Lands
Tear Drop Bog
Syle Lake
Dragon Home
Desto Side
Dreadon Castle
Icon Hall
Grey Forest
Diaz Wood
Runsk
Lower Lake
Lower Swamp
Manta Isles
Zath Tirith
Rumay Bay
Broken Sea

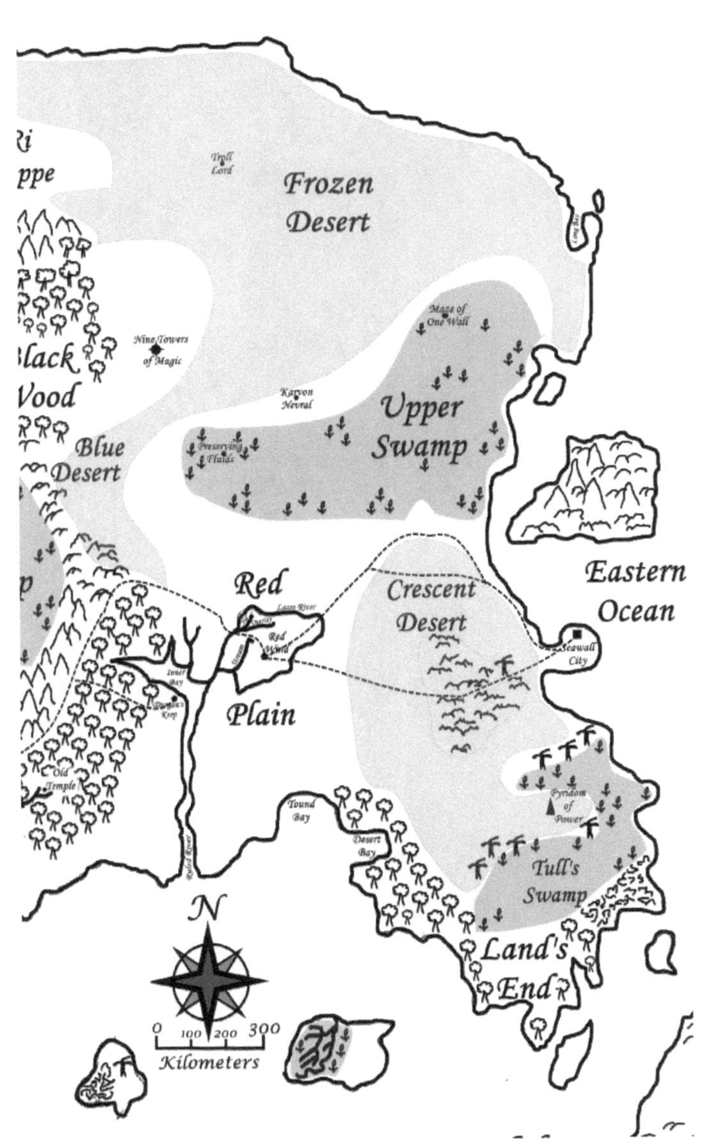

Frozen
Desert
Troll
Lord
Ri
ppe
Black
Wood
Nine Towers
of Magic
Blue
Desert
Kayvon
Nevral
Preserving
Fluids
Upper
Swamp
Maze of
One Wall
Eastern
Ocean
Red
Crescent
Desert
Lasso River
Red
World
Inner
Bay
Dragon's
Keep
Plain
Seawall
City
Pyridom
of
Power
Old
Temple
Tound
Bay
Desert
Bay
Gold River
Tull's
Swamp
Land's
End
N
0   100   200   300
Kilometers

Travis I. Sivart

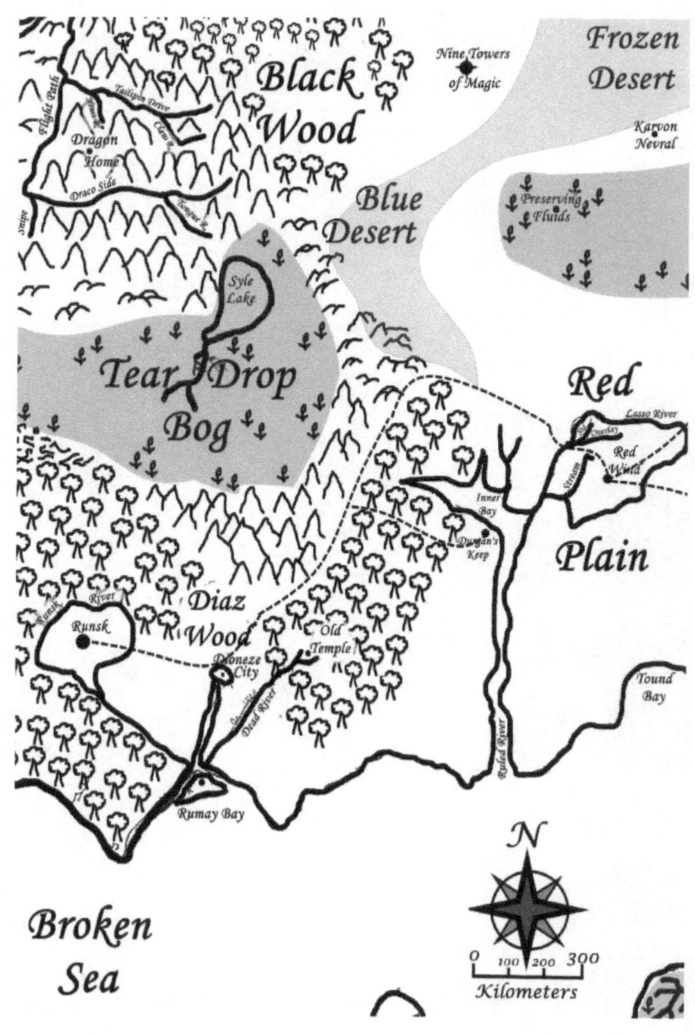
Black Wood
Frozen Desert
Nine Towers of Magic
Karvon Nevral
Flight Path
Tailspin Drive
Dragon Home
Draco Side
Snipe
Blue Desert
Preserving Fluids
Syle Lake
Tear Drop Bog
Red
Lasso River
Overlay
Red Wind
Stream
Inner Bay
Durgan's Keep
Plain
Diaz Wood
Runsk River
Runsk
Old Temple
Dioneze City
Dead River
Tound Bay
Ruled River
Rumay Bay
Broken Sea
N
0   100   200   300
Kilometers

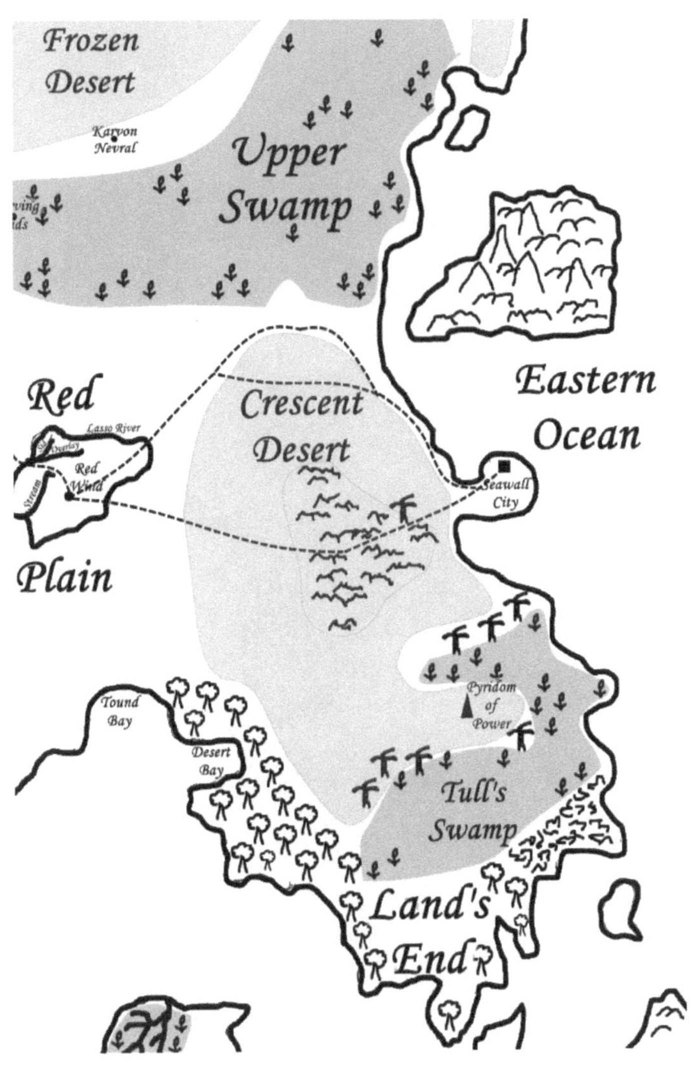

Frozen Desert
Karvon Nevral
Upper Swamp
Eastern Ocean
Red
Lasso River
Overlay
Red Wind
Stream
Plain
Crescent Desert
Seawall City
Pyridom of Power
Tound Bay
Desert Bay
Tull's Swamp
Land's End

Prologue

Cogsley wiped at the hard water speckles on his giant, inverted pear-shaped glass head with a clean cloth held firmly in his white gloved hand. The automaton sprayed himself in the face with cleaning fluid and jerked his dome back, then wiped again. Looking around the empty common room of The Traveller's Inn, he heaved a mechanical sigh that sounded like a pneumatic printing press winding down.

"Sir," Cogsley said to the only other person in the room, "The tavern has been bereft of most of its regulars for weeks now. You've sent each of them on a mission, using the term loosely. The upstairs rooms are quiet, the extra clothes and items they didn't need make little noise. Though sometimes I do hear odd sounds from Wanderly's room."

The proprietor, Jack Tucker, paced back and forth between the booths along the front wall and the seating area in the center of the room containing two rows of double-long, picnic-style tables. The windows flashed with blue-white light, indicating the establishment was flickering through different timelines and realities.

Jack stopped pacing and looked up, as if surprised to hear someone speak. He ran a hand through his medium length hair and down his neck to rub it.

"Cogsley, you're still here," Jack smiled absently. A raven croaked from the wooden beams overhead.

Jack looked up, squinting into the murky shadows overhead. "Yes, you're here too, Captain Farrell."

"Well, sir," the automaton said, "I have nowhere else to go. You have said that my appearance would draw too much attention if I were to go elsewhere. Is it the tuxedo or the top hat that you feel would stand out?"

"Neither, Cogsley, it's your…" Jack trailed off, grimacing sheepishly. "You got me. Okay, what can I help you with?"

"I think perhaps it is what I can help *you* with." Cogsley picked up a rocks glass, set it on the bar, and uncorked a bottle of whiskey. Pouring two fingers of amber liquid into the glass, he went on, "It appears you have something on your mind, and keeping it restrained is only causing you frustration. Perhaps speaking it aloud would help. I'm all ears, as the saying goes."

"Why not?" Jack shrugged. He moved across the room to the bar, climbed onto a stool, and picked up the whiskey. "Here's to problem solving." Jack raised the glass towards Cogsley, then took a sip and smacked his lips. "Cogsley, thanks to the various reports from the people I've sent out as eyes and ears, I've caught wind of a few problems on Aetheria. They're huge, too. The problems, that is, not our conscripted spies. Someone is hunting the last known Troll Lord. I've also heard whispers that someone has set their sights on taking control of the Nine Towers of Magic. Nothing good ever comes of that."

"I see, sir," Cogsley's dome nodded, his top hat jiggling, "and if this mystery person succeeded, what would happen, and why does it matter?"

"Well," Jack paused and held up a finger, he took a larger drink then continued, "if they capture the Troll Lord, they'll have direct access to a major conduit of magic in the world of Aetheria. If they kill him, it may destroy the magic in the land, or the power may shift to them. No one is sure exactly what the repercussions would be. If they gain control of the Nine Towers, it means it may shift the entire pantheon of gods, potentially killing some gods and usurping their power."

"And why does that matter?" Cogsley picked up a clean mug and began polishing it with the cloth he'd used on his head earlier.

"That's a lot of power in the hands of one person. From my experience, that's rarely a good thing. The whole 'power corrupts', etc."

"Is that why you sent away Nomed, Croaker, Wanderly, and the others?"

"Yeah," Jack nodded, spinning his glass in a small circle by the rim, "and that world has gone through enough problems in the last few decades. The ecosystem still hasn't settled down since their apocalypse. Its entire equilibrium is still finding balance. The weather is whacked, the animals are mutating, and people are barely able to rebuild on top of their collapsed societies."

"You do have your limitations, sir," Cogsley said, "and you made a vow about directly interfering."

"Yeah," Jack looked up at the automaton, "I'm partly at fault for breaking Aetheria, and I just want to help fix it."

"Stand and deliver!" Captain Farrell croaked from the rafters.

"Yes, what the raven asked." Cogsley set the mug down and picked up another to polish. "What solutions can be had in this situation? Can you use the two remaining people you brought to the planet to help resolve this kerfuffle?"

"Aiyana is an incredible wizardess, one of the most powerful the continent of Teurone has ever seen," Jack sighed, "but she's single-minded. Reginald does a pretty good job of keeping her balanced, but he's an old man in a young man's body. An archaeologist turned swashbuckler. He has the magical artifact, Marcid, but other than that…just his mind and his words."

"And his mind is enfeebled from age?" Cogsley asked.

"No, not at all." Jack shook his head. "He's sharp as a tack, and patient. I'd even call him wise."

"That's good, then." Cogsley stopped cleaning and tilted his head. "You usually bring in a third person for these situations. Will you be doing that again, sir?"

"I want to, but I need someone strong." Jack paused, studying his glass. "But not just of body, though that would help. I need someone stubborn, who isn't afraid of powerful magic and won't back down. Someone who can't be intimidated, and who will stand up to Aiyana, and whoever it is that's trying to take over the world."

"You need a machine," Cogsley drawled, "someone from Earth who knows magic and combat, but won't quit when facing impossible odds. Someone who is so hardheaded, when faced with being deposited into a world of magic, dragons, trolls, and zombies…they won't flinch."

"That about sums it up," Jack nodded, slowly raising the glass for another drink of whiskey.

"If only there was a training program," Cogsley said absently, "where someone constantly faces insurmountable odds, over and over, but never doubts for a moment they will win."

Jack sputtered into his glass, jerking his head up to look at the bartender, spatters of whiskey speckling the automaton's recently cleaned glass head.

"That's it!" Jack said. "A training program! I need a gamer! I need someone who's young enough to feel immortal, but old enough to think critically. A person who's always craved adventure and excitement but disciplined enough to stay on track to beat the bad guys!"

"Very good, sir," Cogsley said drolly, wiping at his face with the cloth. "And do you have someone in mind?"

The windows of the inn slowed their magical pulsing, the blue-white lights dimming and settling into the ochre glow of early morning daylight. Jack's eyes went distant, his face slack as he stared at the window.

"Yes," he nodded slowly, the sound of morning traffic coming from outside. A stuttered cacophony of distant horns, the surge of an engine, and the whine of tires drifted through the walls of the time travelling inn. "I've got someone. Griffon, the monster masher."

"The winged cat-bird creature?" Cogsley looked over the edge of the towel in his hand.

Captain Farrell fluttered down from the rafters, cawing, and landed on the bar. He waddled forward and pecked at the jar of peanuts.

"You agree, Captain?" Jack asked the raven, who gave the man the side-eye in return. "Then it's settled. I'll bring in a basement-dwelling gamer who's never left home. He should be perfect for this."

"I believe he was indicating nuts, sir." Cogsley opened the jar, scooped up a handful of peanuts, and dropped them on the bar for the bird. "It's a state of mind you get used to in this place."

Chapter 1

"I'm confident I can help bring freedom to these people." Aiyana's tone was stiff, and she stamped her foot, her platinum blonde ponytail bouncing. "It's all I wanted to do back on Earth. It's the reason I marched and protested. It's the reason I died on that world. That's all I want to do here, for those who don't have the power to free themselves."

The aeifain woman paced the large chamber, white marble walls towering over her small form. She ran her finger along one of her pointed ears, her almond-shaped eyes lost in thought. Morning sun pushed through the trees outside and poured through the long-slit windows to dapple the floor. The design of the room mirrored the elegant architecture of the Torck city outside.

"They're not really enslaved, Aiyana." Reggie sighed, a small smile rippling his features, changing his face. His eyes shifted from serious to curious, crinkling at the edges and forming the trident of crow's feet of someone who smiled a lot. The intense and determined line of his mouth became the crooked and amused look of someone who appreciated humor where others may not even realize it existed. "They're just poor and struggling. And no one is doing this to them. It's just how the world is right now. It's broken, and everyone is merely trying to survive."

She glared at the human, his wiry—but muscular—arms moving with graceful precision to brush unseen dust from his dark breeches. Rolling her eyes and looking up at the balcony circling the room and the dome above it, she raised her hands in supplication to the circle of blue sky in the center of the ceiling.

"Don't do that, Reginald. You know what I mean. With knowledge and accessibility to resources, they can change the world. I just want to offer that to them. I learned that in college. I was someone who never struggled, but I thought I did. I was never cold or went hungry. I was sheltered from those things. My worst experience before I went to college was not getting the dress I wanted for a dance. I—"

"There's a lot of 'I' in that for someone claiming they want to help others. But what if they don't want it?" Reggie pulled out his pipe and tobacco pouch, leaning back in the chair by the fire. "What if they don't care at all? When I was an archaeologist—back in our world—I discovered some amazing things. Lost knowledge of history or how to make concrete that lasted thousands of years. References to history that was already dozens of centuries old when it was written down, and almost triple that by the time I found it. But most people never cared. It was teatime chat, and then forgotten."

"Don't be a pemtie," Aiyana used the native word for idiot or stupid, dropping into a seat across from the man. "This is different, Reginald. This isn't some ancient, wrinkled mummy or faded parchment. This is real stuff that changes their lives!"

"Ouch," Reggie held a hand to his chest, showing over his open white shirt and unbuttoned navy doublet, feigning hurt. "Look around, Aiyana. We're in a newly discovered civilization of rammen, the Torck. Because of this encounter, the world changed. Without them, we wouldn't have been able to beat the armies of the warlord, Manalo Maqsher, and his pet alchemist, Tymere. You would have never found clues of where the aeifain went and what happened to their city of Icon Hall."

"I don't know if Tymere was the pet in that situation," Aiyana's eyebrows rose and her forehead wrinkled, "Tymere was a master planner. Alchemists are like that by nature, because the very essence of their magic is planning and being prepared. And meeting Kajuun and her people isn't the same as discovering a lost temple. They built this entire civilization in the past few decades. We didn't discover something ancient, instead, we met something new. But you're distracting me from my point. My point is: you're not an archaeologist anymore. You're a rogue and a swashbuckler. You're a gambler who lives by your sword and wit. And frankly, you're doing the same thing as me."

"What does that mean?" Reggie looked up through his eyelashes as he packed his pipe, the corner of his mouth quirking again. "I'm not trying to force anyone to accept things they don't even know they want or need, things they can't even understand."

"You want to help the world and make it a better place." Aiyana stabbed a finger towards the man. "We just have different methods. You want adventure and to make a difference, leaving a legacy that spans far beyond your years. Just because I'm fifty years younger than you—well, in the old world, a couple centuries older in this one—doesn't mean I don't see what you're doing."

Reggie watched Aiyana, pulling a small flame on a piece of straw into his pipe, lighting it. He shrugged, then asked. "And?"

"You're a good man," Aiyana said. "Kazzek Tel Virian and Reginald Betancourt are both good men. And whatever name you choose to use, you try to help with the wisdom of your seventy plus years, or your experience with a blade. Just because you're in a young man's body now doesn't mean you can ignore the lessons you learned in your other life."

"Very well, Donna Russo or Aiyana Riandell," the woman cringed at the mention of her other name, "we both want similar things, but go about it in different ways. So why are we arguing?"

"We're not arguing," Aiyana gasped, mimicking his previous gesture of holding a hand to her chest in a wounded movement. "We're discussing passionately. You know I get…enthusiastic about what I'm trying to do—"

"More like obsessed with a one-track mind," Reggie muttered around his pipe between puffs.

"Don't interrupt when I'm complimenting you and pointing out my flaws," Aiyana said seriously, then grinned and continued. "I know people are put off and taken aback by my bluntness. I know many don't like me and think I'm mean. I just want to help, and I'm not worried about what they think about me if I can accomplish the impossible."

"She is not being wrong there," said an accented voice from the marble archway that led from the room to the diplomatic antechamber outside.

The two looked over to see Kajuun leaning on the doorway. The woman wore a maroon outfit with wide sleeves and pant legs, a dark leather corset across her midsection. She had two sets of horns that swept back from her the top of her head, just above her dark bangs. The front set thick and pointed, the rear set curled until they pointed back at her ears.

"And how long have you been eavesdropping?" Reggie asked.

"Long enough to be knowing you were fighting," Kajuun smiled, "and to know you're both right. You did incredible things and will be doing more if I am knowing you both."

"Well," Aiyana breathed, "thank you, I think." She paused, tilting her head. "Is it time?"

Kajuun nodded. "It is. We will be to talking to the gathered council, then I will be accompanying you both to Dargaon's Hole to begin a diplomatic mission of friendship and trade. I am thinking that this will be the beginning of beautiful things. We are all being makers of a new world."

"But we still have a meal waiting…" Reggie blushed to the roots of his light brown hair as the women looked at him. "It's a long trip, and I'd hate to leave on an empty stomach. And I do love those green, leafy wrapped things filled with that stuff that makes me think of couscous. They're so spicy and full of garlic. I burp for hours after, but I can eat a dozen."

"Men," Aiyana sighed, "always worried about their stomachs."

"It is good, though, no?" Kajuun watched Reggie with soft eyes. "He deserves, no, you both be deserving a good meal before we go. There are being reports of bands of trolls in the lands to the east. The council are being to send patrols of minotaurs out to be helping to make sure we are not having too many troubles. They will even be one to be meeting us at Dargaon's Hole."

"I'm sure we can handle a few trolls," Aiyana laughed.

"Be careful," Reggie pointed at her with his pipe, "remember what overconfidence brought in Icon Hall."

Aiyana's face hardened, her pale blonde brows hooding her eyes. "I will never forget what I lost, Reginald. And I will not make the same mistakes again."

Silence fell over the three, Aiyana staring at Reggie as he tamped at his pipe. Kajuun cleared her throat. "Shall we get on with our diplomatic duties—and break our fasting—then be leaving?"

"I need to get my notes." Aiyana moved to the side table where she'd spread her notes across the surface and started organizing them into neat piles.

"What is it you're researching?" Kajuun asked. "We are a new society, and our libraries are being woefully bare." Kajuun leaned to peer at the sheafs of parchments. She stared for a moment, then picked up a sheet and squinted. Her eyebrows rose, and she let out a surprised gasp. "This is what you have been trying to do?"

"Yes, exciting, isn't it?" Aiyana grinned and looked over the horned woman's arm to see which paper she was reading. "I thought if I can send a person from one place to another, why not something less…physical?"

"Care to fill me in?" Reggie asked from his seat, waving his pipe in front of him. "You've been recalcitrant to tell me about this secret project, but now you're bubbling over with—"

Aiyana turned; her face flushed with enthusiasm, her words rushing out. "I can make portals, moving myself and others from place to place. But I've been thinking about Jack, and how he can move through time…apparently. Anyhow, I've been exploring that. I've even tried sending things through time and space and failed. Nothing big, just a quill or an apple. When it didn't work, I attempted to send them from the same place to across the room. They portalled, but instantly rather than a minute or so later."

She stopped to take a breath, collecting her thoughts. She pulled her shoulders back and went on.

"I began thinking about words," she said, "wondering if I could send a message. And…it worked. But still in the same time. I couldn't send a message into the future or the past."

"That would be handy," Reggie smiled. "You could tell me what poker hand beat me so I could fold instead of staying in."

"Reginald," Aiyana huffed, "that's amusing, but I'm pretty sure you're teasing me. You must be able to see the endless uses of this. If I could send myself, or you, a warning of danger—for example, the invasion of Icon Hall—then disaster could be averted. Nathan may not have had his hands cut off, and he may have chosen to stay."

Reggie studied her, his face growing serious.

"I know, I know," she waved away his concern, "I don't think I can send a message into the past, because it already happened. But maybe into the future. But then again, if Jack can travel to the past, why can't I send a few words to myself or someone else? I don't have his skill with portals—he's way beyond my abilities—but I've been inside whatever is in between here and now and then and there. The ether or the phlogiston, whatever you want to call it. We travel through it when we portal. Sending a few words should be possible. I just need to find the research, the key to this, and I think it should be possible."

She stopped and looked back and forth between Kajuun and Reginald.

"Maybe…" Kajuun said slowly, sifting through the notes, "the Nine Towers of Magic has something to be helping you? It was once the greatest of schools for the magical arts, and if anyplace has something that be for helping, it is that place?"

"But what if I fail?" Aiyana said quietly, her hair falling across her face as she bowed her head. "I could mess things up."

"Or you might not," Kajuun patted the wizardess's shoulder. "It cannot be hurting to try and learn more."

"Aiyana," Reggie said, standing, "if anyone can do this, it's you. The amazing thing about you is that every time you fail, you learn from it, and then do better. But right now, I think you should gather your research, stuff it all into those endlessly deep magical pockets of yours, and we should go talk to the dignitaries."

Chapter 2

Griffon groaned, opening his eyes, and staring up from his back. Everything hurt, a dull ache across his entire body, but especially his head. The dense jungle foliage waved far above. The breeze moving the leaves was little more than a sluggish, humid caress on the jungle floor. Insects buzzed around him, and sharp, little stings and itchy welts made him aware of their feeding on him.

The fetid smell of the trees and rotting plants clung to his nostrils, and the coppery taste of blood was in his mouth. Muscles rippled in his belly, threatening to cramp at any moment.

"I'm Griffon, the monster masher," he mumbled out his gamer title and chuckled, staring up at the canopy. The movement made him wince. "And, omfg, a bus crushed my ass. TPK, total party kill, and here I am…wait, where the hell am I?"

Another thought—so different from what Griffon had experienced on the busy downtown street—rose to the surface. The memory of a dark, magical ritual and the gore of a gladiator ring came to his mind, and something underneath his surface thoughts screamed of danger.

Something went horribly wrong in more than one place. He remembered dying—twice. He remembered being hit by the bus, but also remembered the goblins, kobolds, and green-skinned, pig-faced warriors he'd fought and killed moments before he died.

A flock of colorful, long-tailed birds burst from the trees above, distracting him. He looked towards the treetops, smiling and wondering if they'd drop a dookie on him. A dark blur leapt across the space and snatched a bird mid-flight.

"Oh, yeah!" he muttered, his mind returning to what he'd been doing before he woke here. "I was playing that game…wait, no, I wasn't. I was out picking up Doritos and Mountain Dew. But if this is the game, wow! They really did a VR graphics upgrade on this week's patch!"

A different memory flooded his mind, making him flinch. The thought of being a sacrifice, and a wavy kris knife gutting him—first across his rippled, muscular stomach, then up and down from his ribs to his junk.

His hand shot to his belly. It wasn't what he expected. His usual flabby gut that bulged over his sagging jeans was gone. His abdomen was taut and tight, and he thought it felt like a human version of braille. Melody, his cousin, was blind, and he'd messed with her books to figure out how she read anything with those tiny bumps when he would barely figure out where the light switch was in the dark.

It's so funny that her parents named her Melody, he thought, his mind still muddled. *How does that make sense when she's blind? They're so stupid!*

Sound clicked back into his awareness, like he'd unmuted his game. Chanting surrounded him, blending with the screams of the hunter and the hunted in the branches above the clearing.

He bolted upright, his head jerking left and right. His vision blurred, and it felt like his skull was in a martini shaker.

Twelve witches stood in a wide, rough circle in the surrounding clearing, and a thirteenth stood over him. She gyrated like a pop diva on XTC at a rager rave, her arms thrust up. Beyond them were dozens and dozens of people in the stands, an audience of the arena in which he was the prime attraction. The crowd cheered and the women's chanting grew louder and more intense. The witch above him had a wavy-bladed knife in one hand, and her other hand was covered in blood.

His blood.

She brought her hand down and smeared a crimson streak across her face, from one ear, across her mouth and nose, to the other ear. She brought her fingers to her mouth and thrust three of them in, licking and moaning loudly.

Griffon couldn't quite put together what was going on. This had to be the game, right? He was the hero of this game, and he'd just barely survived a killing blow. That was the only thing that made sense.

Everything was so crisp, detailed, and real. It felt surreal. He struggled to wrap his mind around the situation and scrambled to remember the events before the crosswalk.

Conflicting memories fought for attention: a Doritos bag popping along with his leg and hip, a two liter of Mountain Dew exploding, and also killing a dozen monsters with a hundred gathered creatures in the rough wooden stands around the arena.

"Crowd?" he muttered and looked around.

The surrounding valley rose, the spectator stands ringing the natural depression. Bent trees jutted up in the middle of the partially scraped logs that made the rough bench seating. Hundreds of forms writhed and undulated, matching the woman standing over him and her companions, which formed a ritualistic summoning circle. Most seemed to be caught up in the fervor, but a few spotted his movement, and were pointing and shouting.

How do I know this arena is a ritualistic summoning circle, also? He thought. *And am I healing super-fast? This is the coolest! Better than boring graphics and a flash of light. I really feel my body pulling itself together!*

He fingered his healing abdomen.

"They sacrificed me!" he mumbled under his breath. "They meant for me to be the last thing in their magical…"

Magical what? he thought. *What game is this? The graphics are great, it must be VR.*

I don't have a VR unit, was his next thought, *so I must be at Tony's house, using the console he just got! Let's see if I can level this bitch up!*

Griffon reached out, snatched up his two-handed sword from the sand next to him, and jumped to his feet. He hunched his shoulder, slitted his eyes, and glared straight ahead to lock his menacing gaze on the woman's…

"Belly button?" Griffon sputtered, looking down, then up. "Where's the rest of me?"

The witch noticed the small man standing in front of her, the top of his head barely reaching her midsection.

"Are you feckin kidding me?" Griffon whined. "Hey lady, are you a giant? Please, please, please, tell me that you're some sort of huge amazon warrior! I'd never make a short toon! I hate dwarves, halflings, and especially gnomes. Just hold on a second!"

Griffon held out his sword crossways, and the pointer finger of his other hand up, to indicate he wanted the woman to pause, to give him a time-out. He began exploring his features with his free hand.

He patted his face, starting at the jaw and moving up.

"Uh oh," he said, "a short beard, a long moustache, and huge sideburns, a big bulbous nose, bushy eyebrows, and anime hair…oh, no."

He looked at the base of his sword, where blood hadn't covered the blade, and studied his features on the polished surface.

"Oh, no. Oh, no!" his voice rose to a shrill scream. "Imma fricken gnome, aren't I?"

The woman in front of him—who a moment ago was performing a sinuous dance, her ankle length loincloth swaying—stared at him, her eyes flooded with the threat of death. She screeched and swept her wavy blade down.

His blade came up instinctively to block the blow, the tip of her dagger a finger-width from his eye.

The witch pulled the blade back and slashed side to side, stepping forward with each stroke.

Griffon stumbled backwards, unable to get stable footing or predict the rhythm of the attacks. He fell onto his butt, leather briefs pulled tight between his nether cheeks, leather straps and metal buckles biting into his chest and arms.

"What the hell am I wearing?" Griffon glanced down at himself, taking in his outfit for the first time.

He wore all leather. Sandals with ties wrapping around his calf. Greaves strapped to his thighs protected the front. His wrist and forearms had bracers, one shoulder a pauldron, and his chest and back had a half cuirass that met the girdle across his midsection.

Knitting scars showed where she'd gutted him just below his wide belt and right above his…

"Leather underwear? And I'm a gnome? Really?" Griffon moaned. "And who designed this? I'm barely covered, and things are hanging out all over the place! Is this meant to protect me?"

The last words trailed off as he looked up to see the woman who'd been trying to kill him moments before leering at him. Her eyes tracked along up his shapely legs, across his muscular thighs, and paused at his leather pouch, which had nothing to do with holding coins, but held his family jewels.

"Hey, lady!" He shouted, waving a hand back and forth across her line of sight. "My eyes are up here!"

"I've always liked the short ones," the woman hissed, her voice thick and gruff. She wiped the corner of her mouth with the back of her hand, smearing more blood across her lips. "You make me feel powerful when I'm smothering you with my…feminine wiles."

The women in the outer circle watched the commotion in the middle of the arena and looked back and forth between each other. They continued chanting, though, never missing a syllable of the incantation.

One woman pointed at their leader standing over the gnome, and flapped her hands at a second woman, indicating that she should go in and see what was going on. The second woman shook her head vehemently, refusing to move from her assigned spot.

Slapping his thighs together, Griffon swung his sword at the leering leader's midsection. She stepped back, and he missed.

She laughed.

"Aw, does the poor wittle man feel uncomfortable?" The witch mocked, drawing the words out. "Who do you think dressed you in that? Who do you think cast the spells so you couldn't take it off?"

"Um, you?" Griffon mumbled, looking around for something to distract her.

There wasn't much out here. His steel buckler lay to the side, next to a circle drawn into the sand with silver dust, runes marking points inside of the arcane ring. The magical markings glittered, the metallic symbols shining as the ritual pulled power into them.

"No! I'm not a chuzzing servant!" the woman screeched, using the local swear word that Griffon recognized as being equivalent to the 'f-word.' "I made a novice do it. Touching filth like you is below me!"

Griffon's mind slipped, fear and anxiety creeping forward, and another consciousness flooded into the empty space. His fingers dug into the sand under his hand, and his face lit up.

"Oh, you like the idea of the eunuchs undressing you, bathing you, putting on this adorable wittle outfit, and then an acolyte running her fingers across your taut and tight body to seal the armor to your flesh?" she asked, her voice thick and lustful.

Griffon's hand shot up, and a handful of sand sprayed across the woman's face. The woman screamed and frantically clawed at her face, trying to dislodge the grit from her eyes.

He rolled to the side, snatching up his shield. Acting on instinct that wasn't his own, he slid his left arm under it and into the waiting strap and gripped the second strap. He lurched to his feet. Turning his shield parallel to the ground, he dropped the flat of his blade atop it, clanging the two, and stepped forward. Pulling the weapon sideways, he pushed with his shield arm to give it more momentum.

The sword cut along the woman's midsection, and she screamed again, her hands dropping to clutch her belly.

Stepping back with his right foot, Griffon bent his elbow back and lifted his weapon to eye level for a thrust. He angled it up and pushed it forward. The tip of the blade caught the woman on the solar plexus, unbalancing her, making her tumble backwards, splaying across the outer circle and the magical runes.

She screeched and writhed, one hand on her face, the other on her belly. Silver and sand scattered around her. The women at the outer circle began gesturing furiously at Griffon, crossing their waving arms above their heads.

Placing the tip of the blade at the throat of the witch on the ground, Griffon looked to the crowd in the age-old expectation of the onlookers choosing the fate of the fallen.

Griffon shook the buckler up his forearm, freeing his hand. Lifting his arm, he clenched his hand into a fist with the thumb jutting out parallel to the ground. He waved it, bobbing the thumb up then down, indicating that the crowd should choose the woman's destiny.

Spare her…or kill her?

The crowd went wild, leaping to their feet, screaming. The screams slowly morphed into one word: kill.

"Kill, kill, kill," the mob chanted.

The gladiator inside of Griffon came out, and he smiled. He'd done this dozens of times. He was one of the best. His small size made everyone underestimate him. Though his reach was short, he was quick and clever.

He leaned sideways; the blade slid easily into the bumpy length of the woman's neck, piercing her larynx and sliding deeper. With a jerk of his wrist, he cut the woman's throat, slicing a line across her neck. Her head tilted back, blood spurting as the gap widened.

The spectators rose to their feet with a roar, clapping and shouting and stomping. The women at the edge of the arena stopped chanting, watching their leader's lifeblood drain onto the sand inside the arcane circle of runes.

Griffon tugged the sword out of the woman's neck and held it aloft, spraying a line of blood across himself and the sands.

Then he danced.

"Oh yeah, oh yeah," he shouted in a singsong voice, wiggling his hips and dipping his knees, "I kicked your boss's ass, oh yeah, I'm the best!"

He laughed as the women at the rim of the arena turned and ran, pushing and shoving through the spectators to get away. The crowd grew quiet and stared as Griffon—now back in control of his own body—did his victory dance.

He hammed it up, throwing in classic dance moves he'd learned from Fortnite and other bits from touchdown dances in football games. Griffon closed his eyes, holding his sword above his head, and spun in a circle, throwing his head back and howling.

The silence of the crowd grew eerie, and the sound of shifting and sliding sand behind him grew louder. Griffon slowed to a stop and opened his eyes.

A single shout from a man in the stands drew the gnome's attention. The lithe man dressed in purple, with long silver-blonde hair and almond-shaped eyes, pointed at something behind Griffon, who slowly turned to look behind him.

Foul smelling, grey tinged with green, oily smoke, filled the circle in the center of the arena, seeping out from where the witch's body broke the magical ring.

The sand was pouring off something inside, a shadowy form rising to the height of two men. A long, scaly snout topped a massive set of shoulders that wound down to a tapered waist. Three tentacles writhed on each side of its torso where arms should have been. A guttural hiss came from the beast, sounding like a volcano in a teakettle, a rumble with an underlying angry whistle.

The creature took a step forward, showing thick legs with backwards bending knees. Two tentacles shot forward, extending well past where they should've been able to reach, and snatched up the dying witch.

The woman's head fell backwards, ripping her throat further. The beast lapped at it with dual forked tongues, tasting the blood offering. Its open mouth showed multiple rows of dozens of pointed teeth in a spiral pattern that led deep into its maw.

"Oh, bidj," Griffon stumbled backwards, using the native swear word without realizing it, "looks like it's time for a boss fight! But I gotta say it again; these graphics are insane!"

The summoned monster glared over the body of the witch and eyed the tiny gnome far below it. Leaning down, it pushed the woman's head into its mouth and bit down. Shaking back and forth, bones crunched under the pressure of its jaws.

The woman's body jerked and twitched, the arms severing and falling to the ground as the beast tore off half her torso.

The monster threw its head back, jerking its neck up and down, choking the bitten off portion down. All the while, it stared at Griffon.

"Wow," he gasped, "that is *intimidating!*"

The abomination threw the corpse to the side and looked down at its clawed feet, which were halfway out of the magical circle.

"I-I am not," each guttural word came out separately, as if it had been a long time since the creature had used words, "restrained."

It did something with its face, which Griffon guessed was a grin. The sight made him shudder, and he felt the sudden need to pee.

The beast stepped forward, out of the circle, and turned its head to inspect its surroundings.

"So, many, morsels," it growled, pausing after each word, watching the panicked crowd turn and run. "But a little snack first."

The creature looked at Griffon, and its face split again, the edges of its mouth twisting in unnatural ways. It bent to leap, and shot forward, mouth wide, and tentacles flailing.

Griffon's world swooned, the edges going blurry and the center misting. This didn't feel like any other video game he'd ever played. Other video games didn't have that weird sensation of sweat trickling down your spine and into your butt crack. Other videos games didn't tell you, let alone let you feel, when your bladder released.

Something shifted and clicked in Griffon's head, and he let go, maybe even fainted. Something else took over, and he was merely a passenger in his body.

Shoving the buckler into the beast's maw, the gnomish gladiator swung his sword upward, cutting through two of the tentacles on one side of the monster's torso.

The creature jerked back, but the gladiator pushed forward, keeping the buckler in the thing's mouth, its two tongues dancing across his forearm and leaving red welts wherever they touched.

The monster rose to its full height, and the gnome's feet came off the ground. Pushing off the beast's torso, the gladiator swung away. Coming back in, he thrust the sword in front of him, and the tip pushed into the beast's chest.

The thing roared, opening its mouth wider, and jerked its head to the left. The miniature warrior flew across the sand, landing on his side, the wind knocked from him.

His exercises told him to breathe, and he'd exhaled as he hit, so his body was ready to inhale. Getting his feet under him, he rose as the monstrosity came at him. His sword severed two more tentacles, this time from the other side of the beast's body.

The monstrous maw of many miniature marrow mashers shot at him again, and he barely raised his bucker in time. The shield flicked flat, and dozens of teeth sunk into his arm.

Gritting his teeth, he glared into the snake-slit eyes of the attacker, reversed his grip on his weapon, and jabbed it sideways into the thing's eye socket. It burst out on the other side with a splash of viscera and gore.

The thing screamed and pulled away, jerking the blade from the gnome's hand. Falling to the sand, the gnome watched the creature shuffle backwards, clutching at the weapon with its two remaining tentacles.

The gladiator pulled twin dirks from his wide leather girdle, and stepped forward, blades slashing and cutting the tender inner thighs of the beast. He ducked under its crotch, and came out by its tail, sliding each blade across the hamstring of a different thigh on the monster.

It collapsed backwards, and the gnome rolled to get out from under it before it came down on him. Coming up on his feet, one dagger fell from the numb fingers of the arm the beast had bitten, but the gladiator brandished the remaining blade.

The abomination thrashed in the sand, legs useless, sightless, with a gushing wound in its chest.

This battle was over. The only thing that remained was showmanship for the crowd. It was time to grow his legend. Auric, the gnomish gladiator, was once again triumphant.

The crowd had stopped its panicked exodus, and he looked at them. He raised his one good arm, and a weak cry came from the spectators. He raised his weapon again, and the cheer was stronger. A third time brought a defending thunder of clapping, whistles, stomping, and shouts.

He strutted around the flailing enemy, taking his time to stab his thin-bladed dirk into sensitive areas, hitting arteries when he could.

He knew he'd won, but he'd have to make the closing quick. Whatever venom this beast had was getting into his bloodstream, and if he didn't tend to it soon, he'd be the final loser of the arena today.

Possibly ever.

Throwing his blade into the back of the monster's neck, he ran up the thing's back to grip his sword, still piercing the creature's head from one side to the other.

Griffon pulled it free, wobbling precariously on his perch as the thing went into death throes, and thrust his blade down into the creature's skull. He hit the crease that he knew would be there, and the well-cared-for weapon slid into the thing's head, the tip burying itself in the sand.

The crowd went wild, and the gladiator leapt from the back of the beast and held up his good arm in victory, the wounded one hidden behind the buckler.

Wiping his sword on the remains of the dead woman, he slid it into its sheath, then snatched up his dropped dirks, cleaned them, and put them away.

Turning to the crowd, he made the universal sign of wanting a drink, spreading his pinky and thumb apart while leaving the rest of his hand in a fist, and tilted it at his mouth. He then pointed at the crowd.

Dozens of people jumped into the sands and rushed towards him and the creature. His adoring fans, coming to lift him up after his victory.

They rushed past him, a few tossing wineskins or flasks at his feet. The mass of people fell on the creature, slashing with knives and tearing off hunks of scales and meat. They shoved gobs of bloody flesh into their mouths, devouring the monster.

Inside the gladiator, a slight urge to vomit fought against his sensible thought to grab the strongest liquor at his feet and use it as anesthetic, orally and topically.

Snatching up a metal flask, he popped the corked and sniffed it. Powerful spirits tickled his nose, and he jerked back. Pouring the contents over his arm, he saw the mass of people turning on one another.

A few turned towards him, murder in their eyes. He stumbled backwards, then turned and ran as the mob set their sights on him. He paused for a moment at the witch's corpse, snatching up her belt and pouches, hoping for some sort of healing potion before he headed into the wilds.

The mob fell upon each other, giving him a precious moment that would save his life. Griffon—trapped inside the mind of the gladiator—thought of his grandmother's Precious Moments collectibles and began weeping silently as the truth about this world washed over him.

Portals: Book 5 – Towers & Trolls

Chapter 3

Aiyana sighed. She'd traveled with Kajuun, Reginald, four dasism, and a dozen of the Torck from the marble city of the satyrs, fauns, and minotaurs. They made their way through the jungle north of the Grey Wood, skirting the Tear Drop Bog to the east, into the Wandering Hills. The journey would end at Dargaon's Hole, the ancestral home of the dragons, in the thin mountain chain connected to sprawling hills.

Torrents—the barbarian she'd worked with a few years back—had mentioned the place when she'd seen him a month ago in The Traveller's Inn. He told her to ask for Rose or Axle, the leaders of the new community established there with his help.

Dargaon's Hole was once—hundreds of years ago—a grand, thriving place where dragons and humans worked together. The former provided protection; the latter raised cattle for food. Dragons weren't what Aiyana had expected. They weren't the destructive brutes that stories made them out to be. They were cultured, intelligent, flying creatures with a talent for magic. Only one remained in this mountain range, the Wandering Hills, and she was named Trinity.

Aiyana liked the dragon, even without having met her. Trinity made it her personal mission to explore strange new lands, to seek out new friends and new dragons, to boldly go where, well, she had to go to make this happen in hopes of rebuilding what they once had.

Being a Star Trek fan—a new television show that came out last year—she thought of the dragon as a starship and its captain all in one. Aiyana hoped one day there could be a lady captain of a starship, or better yet, a woman astronaut in the real world.

Aiyana looked around The Citadel—the spacious, magical tent she called home when on the road. It held all the amenities and, when taken down, folded up as small as a bedroll. It was divided into different areas: a cooking area, a sleeping section, and a research space where her work was spread out. It could also camouflage them from people outside, though she'd disengaged that feature since they were traveling with others.

She gripped the edge of the table, stiffening. The feeling of a rush of portalling magic washed over her. It came from somewhere to the southwest, and from someone else. The person felt lost and scared but had an inner core of strength hidden below a life of ease.

She'd felt this just before she'd met Reginald. Someone had come through from her world to this one, and they weren't far away.

She shuddered.

Reginald looked up from the shards of pottery on the table in front of him. Puffing on his pipe, thin clouds of smoke moving across his face as he observed the wizardess.

"What?" Aiyana glared at him, her tone scolding, though he hadn't said or done anything.

"It just amazes me you were once human," Reginald said, setting his pipe aside. "I mean, your body language and physical nuances are so completely different from mine or other human peoples. You've completely adopted the mannerisms of a race you've never met in person. You've only seen them through the eyes of someone else's memories, or your research."

"You think having a couple hundred years of memories in my head would be enough to give me credit for knowing? Besides, how would you know what my people's mannerisms are?" Aiyana snorted.

"Well…" Reginald paused, leaning back in his wood and canvas director's chair, an addition he'd made to the magical domicile. Puffing on the pipe clenched between his teeth, he steepled his fingers and studied the aeifain. "For one, the fact you said, 'my people's'. And if you recall, back home, I was an archaeologist for decades. I've encountered, interacted with, and analyzed a dozen or more cultures never before seen by civilized man. If we compare Italian idiosyncrasies to Americans, there are differences. If you take a tribe that has never encountered the modern world, there is a…world of differences."

The two stared at one another. Reginald folded his hands across his midsection and gave a small smile.

Aiyana folded her arms under her breasts, scowling. "What's your point, old man?" She leaned into the last two words, her tone indicating she didn't like him very much at the moment.

"You move, speak, and even interact differently than humans do," Reginald plucked the pipe from between his teeth, using it to point at her as he adopted his professor tone, something Aiyana also did when explaining things to others. "You have diverted from the standard social style and have something different. Now, since I haven't directly encountered any aeifain—other than yourself—I can't speak to how true it is to them, but I do know it's not human."

The woman glowered at the man and his explanation.

"You asked," he spread his hands apart nonchalantly, "but, more to the point. Why did you shudder?"

She glared at him for a moment, then sighed, her shoulders relaxing.

"Someone else has arrived," she explained, shrugging. "Another one of us."

"Someone from our world?" Reginald leaned forward in his chair, the wood creaking. "You can feel this? Did you know when I came here? How do you do that?"

"Whoa, calm down." Aiyana held up her hands to stop the questions. "Yes, I feel it. I felt it when you came and felt something when Nathan left this world to go back home."

Her eyes grew distant as she mentioned her missing friend. She trembled again, but differently than before.

Reggie popped his pipe back into his mouth. Relighting it, he waited for her to go on.

"Anyhow," she continued, locking eyes with him, "I attuned a part of my mind mage magics to the…wavelength we're on. I guess you could call it that. And now I feel something whenever someone from our world comes into, or leaves, this one. Happy now?"

"I see…" Reginald said, hesitating, "…and should we seek this person out? Are they important to something to come?"

"I think so," the woman's forehead creased, "but it's just one more way Jack, our little mystical host, manipulates us."

"I see…" Reginald said.

"Stop saying that!" Aiyana snapped, stomping a foot.

They stared at one another for a long moment.

"Alright," Reginald nodded, "so what's our next step?"

"We find him," she sighed, "or he finds us."

"He?" Reginald cocked an eyebrow. "Do you have information about this person? Can you describe them?"

"Yes, and no," she huffed. "I know he is a he, and a powerful warrior. I've seen him, sorta. He has a beard, and is clothed in leather, I think."

"Well," Reginald looked up at the ceiling, "it's not much to go on, but it's something. Do you have a direction?"

"He's…" Aiyana's focus turned inward, her eyes growing distant, "south, southwest of us, and running for his life. That's it. That's all I got."

"Very good," Reginald stood, putting both palms flat on the table. "Let's send out scouts in that direction to find him. That should—"

Aiyana huffed, threw up her hands, and stormed out of the tent.

"What did I say?" Reginald looked around, confused.

Reggie caught up with Aiyana a few minutes later. She was talking to the torck leader, Kajuun. The woman was in field clothes—as Reggie thought of them—her usual great sword slung across her back, and leather pieces of earth-colored clothing.

Reggie marveled at Kajuun's double pairs of horns. The front set swept back from behind her bangs, and the second set curled back from behind them. She moved with practiced grace on her hooves, with a confidence that couldn't be taught, only learned through experience.

"I can to be doing that," Kajuun nodded at Aiyana, her thick accent warm. "I shall be sending my minotaurs. They can be running the longest, are the strongest of my people, and quite able fighters. What should they look for to help to be finding this man?"

"I don't know!" Aiyana threw her hands up. "Someone short! Oh!"

Aiyana stopped, surprised by her words. She drew in a deep breath, then went on slower.

"A short, leather-bound warrior with a beard," she spoke with care. "He seems lost, confused, and speaks in a manner that is not from this place."

Reginald watched the girl.

Girl, he thought, scoffing internally. *That girl is hundreds of years my elder in this world, but fifty years younger in the world we came from. It's like she's in a high stakes poker game without understanding the odds.*

Reginald—Reggie in his head—played poker most of his life. It was his third passion, archeology being the first. The second was a blend of family and teaching others that could be summarized as duty.

Poker came third place and was something he did in his downtime.

To him, gambling wasn't gambling. It was knowing the odds and reading people. Counting his chips and weighing them against others. Reading the other players and knowing if they were calculating or careless. Poker wasn't about luck, and neither was life. It was about knowing what came before, so you could predict what was likely to come next. Knowing when to stay in, and when to get out.

Dealing with people was like playing cards in that manner. So many thought they were unpredictable, or on the other hand, solid and steady. But there were always patterns, set against random chance throwing things off. Reggie balanced the two, but most people never considered both sides of the coin.

Aiyana was the second kind. She believed she always thought everything through, leaving nothing to chance. She was rigid and didn't like bending. It was like the old saying about the oak and the willow reed. One stood strong against the storm, the other bent in the wind. The oak did well until it broke when it could no longer handle the wind, instead of flexing with the storm.

Reggie worried about the girl—woman, he had to stop using that word for her—because she wouldn't bend. She was strong, smart, and driven. That was a powerful combination. But she couldn't do it alone. She needed people and needed to understand and accept that. Otherwise, one day, her stubbornness would break her.

He'd be there, though, and he'd pick up the pieces, or protect her while she figured out how to adapt.

His daughter, Victoria, had been like Aiyana. Victoria didn't want to marry for position or lifestyle, insisting on studying medicine. He'd supported that, even though her mother had fought against it. Her mother, Veronica, said their daughter should settle down, have babies, and be a socialite—like a proper society lady. Victoria persisted, though, and not on being a nurse, but to be a doctor.

Reggie couldn't have been prouder. But he had to placate his wife, bluff her, telling her to humor Victoria and let her go to medical school. By the time his daughter graduated and fought her way tooth and nail into a respected position, even her mother was proud of her, and fiercely protective of her progress.

Of course, he'd made it seem like it had been Veronica's idea all along. It was easier that way, and when the cards were shown, he'd won the hand.

But he didn't know if he could play this particular hand in the same manner. There was too much at stake, and he needed his partner at the table to be on the same page.

"Shall we pack up and move on?" Aiyana asked, surprising Reggie out of his reverie.

"Don't we want to wait here for our newly arrived companion to join us?" Reggie asked.

"No," Aiyana spoke with authority, "he'll find us, no matter what we do. I found the others. You found us when you came here, and this new person will, as well."

"When the others found you, weren't you right in front of them, having been hung by the town guard?" Reggie asked.

Aiyana glared at him.

"So," Reggie drew the word out, "we just head for Dargaon's Hole and see if this man catches up?"

"Yes," Aiyana nodded, "that sums it up nicely. Either he finds us, or he doesn't. But I have every confidence he will."

The autumn winds cut through cloaks, lifting them in the breeze as the procession walked between the lofty peaks of the Wandering Hills. Leaves scuttled along the trails, swirling and dancing. The smell of fall was strong, and the chill of artic ice was in the air. It would be an early winter.

The group walked because the people of the torck didn't ride horses. Their hooves didn't do well with stirrups. The dasism didn't mind riding, but they didn't mind walking or running, either. Kajuun was something between a satyr and a faun, and a respected warrior and leader of her people. She'd been out in the field for a long time—longer than most of her race—but recent events placed her in a position that demanded she stay in their city. She'd joined this outing to the dragon community against the council's wishes.

Kajuun convinced them by pointing out that establishing a healthy rapport with the newly reestablished human community—as they had with the dasism—would be important to their future well-being. And with her experience, she was the one to do it.

What her people didn't know was that she was one of the first to come here from another world, guided by Jack Tucker, the man who ran The

Traveller's Inn. He'd brought a homeless man along too, PepperGarten, and later others, such as Reginald and Aiyana.

When she'd met the two, they'd been traveling with Nathan, a rokairn priest of Jonath. The dwarf-like man of the mountain folk had left this world to return home, which he'd left at the moment of his death. He'd been shot in the gut with a double-barreled shotgun, and Reggie didn't know if he'd survive his return.

Aiyana had grown attached to Nathan, and Reggie didn't know how well the woman was handling his departure, especially if he returned to their native world only to die.

Signs of civilization crept into the road. A more level path, some small structures along the side, and the aroma of cooking food wafting on the wind, carrying smells of stews and roasting meats. The sound of anvils and people echoed off the canyon walls, joined by the smells of sheep, horses, and other livestock, showing that they were close to their destination.

The high canyon walls—a perfect place for an ambush—were directing all the activity of Dargaon's Hole towards the approaching group.

Stepping out from a rock blind, a group of four guards moved to block the road. They didn't look threatening—their swords still in their scabbards—but the way they held themselves spoke of their duty. These were the guards tasked with watching the pass, so no undesirables entered the village. This was frontier territory and bordered on wilderness. But it wasn't the local flora or fauna that was the biggest danger. That was always people.

As the spokesperson of the group, Kajuun stepped forward. She bowed slightly at the waist, her huge two-handed sword shifting on her back.

Staring at the group, the guards gaped at the curled set of double horns on the sides and on top of Kajuun's head. Wide, thick horns of the four minotaurs towering over the humans also drew looks. The other satyrs and the one faun that completed the diplomatic contingent hardly received a glance, overshadowed by the leading five. Leaning on short spears or unstrung bows, the dasism stood out with their terracotta skin and buckskin clothing.

"Good day, friends," Kajuun said, her voice firm, but friendly. "I am being here with my delegation to be meeting with your people and making a formal alliance. May we please to be led to where your leaders are?"

One man leaned to the side, looking around the spokesperson to see who else had come along with the odd group. His eyes lingered on the aeifain and the human, his brow creasing.

"You two okay back there?" the young man called out.

"Are you kidding me?" Aiyana sounded off, and Kajuun could only step to the side and roll her eyes. "Yes, we are fine, I assure you. But we have traveled for weeks to get here, and we'd love to just have five minutes to sit in a chair, or pour the pebbles from our boots, or have something cooked that doesn't have flakes of ash from a campfire stuck in it. So, do you think, just maybe, you can go find out if they'll speak to us, rather than you four gaping at us here in this canyon, like you've never been separated from your mother's teat and still need your ass wiped for you?"

The man looked over his shoulder for support from the other three, flustered.

"Perhaps," Reggie said, leaning around a massive minotaur, "send a runner back. We sent a missive letting the council know we were coming. They should be able to verify the purpose of our visit."

An hour later, the group sat around a stout dining hall table in one of the many side rooms of the Grand Cavern. The table easily sat thirty people on stone benches carved directly from the stone floor, conversation-pit style. Steaming food was being laid out in the center of the table using long poles with metal looped bands supporting the lip of the dish. Once the platter, bowl, or trencher had been set down, they'd drop the loop and jiggle it out from under, pulling the pole back over the heads of the diners. People passed other dishes down, giving the whole gathering an informal feeling.

Seven council members sat opposite the visiting dignitaries, and of the seven, four were human.

A dasism woman smiled at the visitors, her hair shaved along the side of her head and tattoos on her upper arms showing she was from a tribe from the Straight's Plains to the northwest. A ruddy-complexioned rokairn dragged an urn of wine over and poured himself a goblet, sweeping his braided moustaches to each side before taking a drink. A slim aeifain man—the first they'd ever seen—watched Aiyana with interest, absently brushing at his dark purple vest that almost appeared black. He smiled at something and shook his head, his pale, radiant hair pulled back into a ponytail, shimmering in the lamplight.

"Thank you for coming," a woman said, smiling. "I'm Rose, and we're thrilled to have you here."

Etched with life, the woman had lines around her eyes and mouth that deepened when she smiled. She wore a plain, woolen gray dress that matched streaks in her hair.

Kajuun liked her immediately.

To the woman's right was Axle, who looked slightly younger and impatient to get on with the matter at hand. He wore a white shirt, brown breeches, and a dark unbuttoned waistcoat.

The other council members dressed in a similar fashion, and it felt odd to the diplomat. She was used to the leaders of a community greeting her in their finery. These folks looked like they may have just come from the kitchens, preparing the meal, or outside chopping wood in preparation for the cold months.

"It is being our pleasure," Kajuun answered, "and delighting us you are by agreeing to speak. Our community is new, only a few decades old, and we'd like to be finding allies against warlords, or just being to discover someone to trade with. In the Grey Wood we are having many resources we can share, from wood to crops, and much more. We have been hearing that you are having excellent stone workers and have even been to mining iron from the mountains. Also, you are having extensive herds of cattle and goats, something that the forest doesn't allow us to be having in large numbers."

"She gets right down to business, doesn't she?" Axle smiled at Rose. "I like her style."

"Yes, dear," Rose patted the man's hand, "but we should eat first. Everyone is more agreeable on a full stomach. And it's hard to focus when you're tired and hungry, let alone have clear thoughts."

The matronly woman turned back to Kajuun.

"Would that be alright with you and your people?" Rose asked politely. "Can we get to know one another a bit while we break bread and share wine? Well, mead and ale, but we're hoping for wine soon. What we've grown, harvested, and bottled is still aging."

"Yes," Kajuun smiled, nodding, "and I am pleased to be seeing many vegetables here, because most of my people are not eating meat. Our mouths are not being made for it."

"Then why the interest in our herds?" Axle picked up a bowl of fried potatoes and scooped some onto his plate.

"For milk and cheese," Kajuun waved at the table, looking at her entourage and encouraging them to eat, "and also the leather. These things are scarce when you are hunting deer and not wanting to over-hunt the area."

Everyone reached forward, choosing one dish or another, serving themselves, then passing it to the next person.

Aiyana sat at the far end of the table, arms crossed, a sour look on her face. She took in each person individually, appearing to weigh and measure the council and the additional settlement officers who joined them.

Reggie sat beside her, forking some brisket onto his plate. As far as Kajuun could see, he was in his element. He chatted amicably with anyone near him and asked casual questions, setting others at ease. He should be leading this, not her.

"How did you come to travel with a human and an aeifain?" Rose inquired of Kajuun.

"Torrents sent me," Aiyana interrupted.

The council froze, staring at the woman.

"Torrents?" Axle laughed into the awkward silence. "How's the big guy doing? He was so lost when we first met him, but he really came through. How's the Kid? They still hanging out together?"

"He warned me of trolls gathering, and heading to the northeast," Aiyana said dryly.

"Ah," Axle traded looks with the other people of Dargaon's Hole, "yes, we've heard they're massing in the southwest and heading this way."

The dinner went on, each side offering recent events to the other, and trading information regarding the warlords in the south and east.

Afterwards, everyone adjourned to a high-ceilinged room, a carved stone bench circling the wall. They broke into small groups, chatting casually with mugs and goblets in every person's hand.

The silver-haired aeifain approached Aiyana, smiling and looking her up and down. He moved with an air of importance and confidence, his body swaying slightly like he was walking as a waltz played. His outfit was simple but impeccable, cut in an antiquated style. From his waistcoat to his knee boots, everything was pressed and polished. He wore a silver ring on each hand; one with a blood-red garnet, the other in the shape of an ancient reptilian beast. An ornate torc hung around his neck, silver with sapphire inlays at each end, and the body carved with a pattern that resembled Celtic knotwork, or maybe Nordic.

"Zykrite," the man introduced himself, giving a little bow, "and it's a pleasure to meet another aeifain. You're from Icon Hall, aren't you?"

She nodded her head, looking around to see where Reginald was. She spotted the human, a ring of women around him, laughing. But he caught her eye and gave a small nod.

"Yes," Aiyana replied to the stranger, bowing her head slightly, "and you? Are you also from Icon Hall?"

The man laughed, a light and tinkling noise.

"I haven't walked those streets in the light of day for centuries," he said, "but I know it well. Dealt with the politics there at one point, but was never a citizen. Before I came east, I was from the Twin Mountains, and before that from Aeifa, the aeifain lands across the Southern Seas, though I doubt you'd have heard of the places from our ancestral lands."

"Try me," Aiyana said, her voice cold and hard, "I've heard of many things that others haven't."

The man laughed again, and Aiyana wasn't sure if he was mocking her.

"Of course," he said, "I meant no offense. I can see you have experience beyond your years. But it's a delight to meet another aeifain. And you're the one who's opened the portal network again, isn't that correct?"

"Yes," Aiyana narrowed her eyes, "why do you ask?"

"I ask because that was one of the keys to our people's greatness," he smiled, "and I'm thrilled with the work you've done. I look forward to the full network being open again. That's how I was able to travel to all these places, back when I was young."

She looked at him closer, trying to gauge his age. It was hard to guess an aeifain's age once they were over two or three centuries old until they were closer to eight or nine centuries.

"Please," Zykrite said, "allow me to share some of my knowledge with you. Especially regarding opening the portals at points of power. The Highest Spire, Pantageas, The Nine Towers of Magic, Seawall City, Silver Castle, The Olde Kingdom, and so on operate on a certain wavelength. Well, it's more of a double wavelength, like they put another layer on top of the first, to make it harder to use for the uninitiated. Would you like to know about that?"

Chapter 4

Griffon stomped through the jungle's underbrush, petulantly whacking at branches blocking his path with his sword.

"I wish I had a coat or jacket or something," Griffon mumbled. "It's super chill out here, but not in a good way. And I'm starving."

He forced a laugh over the idea of freezing or starving to death. After he'd gotten away from the bloodthirsty mob screaming for his blood, and flesh, and bones, and entrails…he'd spent over an hour curled in a fetal position under a bush, crying. Whatever had taken over his body for the fight was gone, and he felt abandoned, scared, and didn't know what to do.

"It's not fair," he muttered, "games are supposed to tell you where to go next. It's not like real life where you have no idea what you're supposed to do."

In school, the other students always picked on him. He was too fat, too sensitive, too serious. Then a teacher would rescue him, coddling him—which was nice, but never helped once they were gone—so he learned to not show his feelings. Never express became his personal mantra (though he didn't know what a mantra was, and wouldn't for another ten years), and he emulated the cool kids, the tough kids, the popular kids.

Mocking others became his defense mechanism, and once he'd discovered online gaming, it dominated his online personality. He was strong physically—at least digitally—and in chat and voice. He called out the weak ones, telling them to quit crying. 'Stop QQ-ing,' he'd say, teasing them about being pussies. It wasn't his natural instinct, but it was what others expected from the hero.

Heroes were tough. They never broke down and cried. They were alphas, controlling, and didn't take bidj (Griffon knew this word in this world meant dookie, and naturally translated it), from anyone. They were alone at the top of the food chain.

Griffon never wanted to be alone, but with his parents doing their own thing when he was at school or at home, he learned to hide in a group when gaming. Behind a screen, no one saw his red face, pimples, and choking sobs.

But that other stuff—the person and memories in his head, whatever it was—made him get up and continue on. He ran along a game track, following the curve of a small stream. Tilting his head up, he gazed at the thunderheads forming above. It wouldn't be a warm spring or summer rain. It was one of those dark autumn rains that made everything grey and hard to see more than a hundred paces away.

Griffon couldn't remember the last time he'd been caught out in the rain…on purpose, at least. It might've been second grade when he went out to play in a downpour. His parents didn't even notice he was gone until he came back in, dripping wet and tracking mud through the house.

Griffon's father had been on the computer, playing some FPS—which newbs called a first-person shooter—racking kills with his guild. His mother had been surfing social media. She did it all, and he meant all of it: Facebook, TikTok, Snapchat, Instagram, Pinterest, Twitter, and a half dozen other ones. She was on everything, and spent hours swiping one way or the other, scrolling and clicking, finding all the things to keep her entertained for hours.

He'd picked up his computer habits from them, though he'd never realized it before. By the time he was six, he had a smartphone. By the time he was nine, he had his own MacBook Pro. He'd been playing online games for nearly a decade now, and this world wasn't too far away from the tech level of those digital fantasy worlds.

If he could build things, he'd have thought he was playing Minecraft or Fortnite. But those games didn't make his legs ache from walking or make him feel the chill from the autumn air. The leather harness—he couldn't think of a better word—wasn't much protection. He doubted the realism of the MMOs—Massive Multiplayer Online—games he'd played previously. Sure, he looked cool, but it didn't mean he had any real protection.

The arena with the witches came back to mind. Were they really witches? They were definitely doing some sort of magic, but that didn't mean they were what he thought of as witches.

His stomach rumbled. He hadn't eaten since, well, before his failed execution and sacrifice.

That was something else he never had to worry about when gaming. His toons—or characters—never got hungry. They just ate to recover health. He had used grain alcohol on his arm and found one bitter healing potion in the witch's belt he'd taken. It was still red and throbbing. This was so much more real than any other game he'd played before, and he wasn't sure if that was a good thing.

And he was being tracked and hunted.

He wasn't sure how he knew, but some new, internal instinct told him it was true. It also told him he could turn those tables and become the hunter. He couldn't be sure if it was that, or the weather that caused it, but his skin rose in goose pimples, and he noticed other things, too.

"Turgid nipples," he giggled, thinking of some cheap adult fiction he'd read on the internet at some point.

His hand moved to his left buttock—the urge to surf for pics of bewbs pressing down on him—looking for the phone that was normally there. His father kept his wallet there, but Griffon kept his wallet in his front left pocket. He didn't have pockets now, he had small pouches and a gunny sack thing with a shoulder strap.

Other things were different now, too. His nose was huge and rounded. He had a nicely trimmed beard; was significantly shorter and weighed a lot less. He was a fricken gnome, and nothing could be worse. He shook his head and mentally changed the subject.

The grey sky suggested bad weather was rolling in. Cloying humidity—oppressive and making him sweat—shifted with the temperature drop. He shivered, wanting to curl up on a warm couch with a wireless controller, and his mother to bring him a soda and a sandwich.

Griffon whimpered. The sound turned to a choking noise in his throat, his body locking up on the self-pitying reaction. Impulses flooded him, pushing aside his whiny nature.

Facts, plain and simple, filled his head. He was being hunted. He was cold. He would need food and shelter before it grew dark. He was in an unknown area and needed to remove the threat before resting.

The other side of his brain argued with the survivor inside him. The whiner inside of him said he was in a VR game, or dreaming, or something. He was a twenty-two-year-old gamer who rocked the games and didn't go walking through jungles—or outdoors at all if he could avoid it.

He sulked, mentally crossing his arms, and refusing to go on.

His body kept moving, like it was on autorun and auto-other-stuff. When Griffon let go of control, his body stopped hacking at branches, ducked low, and moved into the underbrush next to the game trail he'd been walking along.

He slid the two-handed sword back into its scabbard on his back and crouched, dropping his gunny sack to the ground. Digging through it, he pulled out lengths of rough cloth, wrapped them around his forearms, and tied them down with a length of rawhide cording. He repeated this with his calves.

Pulling out the short sword he'd found in the arena stands and a dirk from a sheath on his waist, he tilted his head one way and another, trying to catch the noise from his pursuers. The smell reached him…trolls, the swamp and jungle sort, not the northern or mountain ones. These would be tall and wiry, with moss patched skin to help them blend into the greenery. Their northern cousins were shorter and covered head to toe in short, matted hair.

But Griffon knew, or at least his body did, that they'd all have certain characteristics in common. The ability to resist magic for one. Something about them repelled it. But that wouldn't matter to him, he was no mind mage who could cast illusions, or an elementalist who could call down lightning or summon fireballs.

He was a warrior, and he made his way with his blades. But that threw another wrench into the works. Troll hide was thick and hard to cut. They were also incredibly hearty and could recover from injuries three to four times faster than most races. It wasn't like magical healing, but it meant if you didn't kill them, they'd come find you within a week.

Bidj! He thought. *They have an incredible sense of smell, close to that of hunting dogs. Just hiding and staying quiet won't be enough. They'll smell me.*

He looked around, trying to find something to mask his smell. Nothing helpful stood out in the immediate area.

Raising his prodigious schnoz to the wind, he sniffed. A sour, rotting stench wafted past.

"Ging-ging fruit!" Griffon whispered, and then was up on his feet, running in a crouch in the direction of the odor.

Gnomes weren't the best at moving quietly, but they weren't the worst, either. Trolls weren't sight hunters or sound hunters—some argued that those two senses were muted in trolls—so Griffon wasn't too worried about making a little noise or his movement being detected. It was confirmed that their sight was better at dusk or dawn than during daylight, proving trolls were twilight hunters.

In short order, Griffon found what his nose was tracking. Coming into a small clearing, tall, thin trees with wide leaves, far above, lined the edges. Scattered across the jungle floor were large seed pods, yellow with green stripes, and about the size of Griffon's head.

Even as his mind rebelled, his body swung the dirk down into the husk of the ging-ging fruit, splitting it open. Scooping out the orange, stringy pulp of the seed pod, he slathered it along his upper arms, belly, and thighs to cover his scent. It smelled like rotting meat mixed with feces, and he gagged, swallowing as his gorge rose. It was nature's way of making sure animals didn't eat the fruit, so it had a better chance to root.

What? His brain screamed. *I know about plants? And I just rubbed some bidj-stinking fruit all over me?*

Staring down at his hands, he considered popping some into his mouth. It would help hide his scent when he peed or took a dump, which would be helpful hiding from any predator of the Lost Lands and wouldn't hurt his digestion, either. It was full of nutrients and would give him a burst of energy.

Scrunching up his face, he stuffed gobbets of the plant's meat into his mouth, chewed a few times, and swallowed quickly. His stomach and nose argued against the plan, trying to force it back up, but he shoved another double fingerful into his mouth and stood up to move on.

He was the hunter now.

Wiping his hands on the cloth on his forearms, he bent and recovered his sword and dirk. Moving into the underbrush, he circled around the way he'd come, searching for the creatures stalking him.

The wind shifted, and the dank, musty smell of trolls swirled around him. He was close.

Griffon crouched, insects buzzing around him, and waited for his quarry to come to him.

A few minutes passed before he heard the rustle of movement along the animal track he'd been on earlier. Then he saw the branches shift and trolls came into view. It wasn't just a couple, either, and for a moment he thought he'd run across a whole hunting party. But they kept coming, dozens of them. This was an entire tribe on the move.

Trolls weren't migratory, at least, not that Griffon knew. And even if they were, they wouldn't be heading north when the weather was changing to cold. This was something else.

The human Griffon, inside the brain of the gnome body, froze like an opossum in headlights as they passed within two paces of his hiding spot. Head and shoulders taller than a grown human, even with their hunched posture, they were huge. Wiry and slim, ragged loincloths covering their junk, carrying stone knives with wood and stone spears.

They loped past, not noticing the crouched gnome, and he counted at least thirty. He felt confident he could take out one, maybe two. With luck, he could outsmart a hunting party of five. But this was more than an entire village could handle, and even with his skills, he knew he wouldn't be able to fight them.

And they were hunting him!

The last one moved out of sight, and he rose to follow them.

What am I doing? He thought, panicked.

I'm gathering intelligence, he answered himself. *This is something weird, not normal. I won't attack them, but it would be best if I found out what's going on. Besides, they have bedrolls and cloaks. Maybe I can swipe one of them to keep warm tonight.*

The trolls stopped moving, and Griffon ducked into a thicket. Trolls weren't bright, but they could have a rear-guard circling back. It was basic reconnaissance, and something any hunter would know to do.

In front of him, there was a flurry of movement and the scream of an animal.

Griffon hunkered down.

Something large broke through the trees, bolting past him. A huge pig-like creature with an elongated snout, a short spear jutting from its shoulder, ran into the canopy.

The trolls spread out. Using a series of calls, whistles, and clicks, they communicated to the others where their quarry was heading. The jungle came alive with movement. Flocks of birds launched into the sky, and small tree monkeys screamed and darted through branches overhead.

An arrow shot across a sliver of blue sky, catching a monkey in mid-leap. The little guy fell, landing an arm's length from Griffon.

Something large moved through the thicket, and a pair of dark-green and grey legs appeared in front of the gnome. He could reach out and pet the short, coarse hairs on the troll's leg if he wanted.

The monster bent over, scooping up the simian, and twisted the wounded monkey with both hands. With a pop, the simian went still.

The troll pulled out the arrow, opened a sack, and stuffed the morsel inside, a dark liquid staining the bag.

The gnome breathed through his mouth, so he didn't have to smell the predator's musk, but also to keep as quiet as possible.

Another troll joined the first, speaking a scratchy, guttural language that Griffon didn't understand.

Slowly reaching up to his ear, the gnome pinched the small pearl earring there. Magic from the jewelry settled around his awareness and the language burst into clarity.

"…don't find this gnome, but at least we'll eat something tonight, right Grunter?" the second troll was saying.

"Yeah, Wheezy," the first troll huffed, "more meat on a tapir, anyway. Tastes better in the stew, too."

The two set down their wrapped bundles, pulling out thick twigs that Griffon recognized as anise, and rubbed them on their teeth.

"It'll take weeks to get to those Nine Towers of Magic," the first troll grunted. "We're going to need food to keep going."

"Yeah," the second troll had a nasal whistle, and the name Wheezy was fitting, "and once we join with the other tribes, we're going to end up overhunting the whole land."

"Doesn't matter," Grunter said. "Once we get what we're going for, we'll be able to summon food using magic like our aeifain cousins."

"Ugh," Wheezy shivered, "as long as we stay strong and don't become broken like them. Using magic made them weak."

"The One of Legend says we'll be the best of both," Grunter laughed.

Griffon's attention wandered to the two bundles on the ground. He saw a wool cloak shoved into one of them. If he could just cut the straps, he could grab it so he wouldn't freeze tonight.

The trolls continued to discuss what was to come, watching the younger hunters running down the tapir in the distance. Now would be the only chance Griffon would have.

He went for it.

Reaching out of the bushes, he slipped the tip of his dirk under the first strap, the well-honed edge of the blade cutting through it easily. It made a small popping noise as it split.

He froze, his eyes moving up to see if they'd noticed.

They hadn't.

Grunter was picking his nose with enthusiasm, as Wheezy leaned back against a tree, rubbing the stick along his gums.

"We've got a few human places marked out to raid along the way," Grunter was saying.

"Yeah," Wheezy nodded, "that'll be fun. It's been years since I've done that."

Griffon slid his weapon to the second strap, cutting it with another pop, and the bundle unfolded with a flop.

The squeal of the tapir came at the same moment, pulling the attention of the two trolls away from what was going on right under their noses.

"There was that farmstead three moons ago," Grunter pointed out, proudly inspecting the hard-won booger on his finger, "and the men who came looking for us afterwards."

"Yeah," Wheezy said, his nose whistling as he breathed in, "but there was only a handful in each of those. It doesn't really count, does it?"

Griffon grabbed the corner of the cloak, pulling it towards him. His inner gamer was ecstatic! He was doing something you couldn't ever do in a game, and he was going to win!

"You're right," Grunter popped his finger into his mouth, scraping at his prize with his teeth, "but it's good to keep in practice during the lean times."

"I guess…" Wheezy trailed off, "what's that?"

Griffon turned his eyes up to see what Wheezy was talking about and saw the troll staring down at the open bundle at Grunter's feet.

The gnome jerked his hand back, still gripping the cloak, and the bundle spilled open, tumbling across the ground and Grunter's knobby toes.

"Hey!" Grunter yelled, dancing backwards.

Wheezy strode forward, bent over, and pulled back the branches of the bush hiding Griffon.

The gnome stared up into the surprised faces of the two trolls. Grunter's and Wheezy's ohs of shock changed to wicked grins of triumph.

"It's the damned gnome!" Wheezy said. "And it's stealing your stuff!"

"Bonus snack," Grunter grunted, "get it!"

Griffon thrust his dirk past Wheezy's leg and drew the razor-sharp edge back across the troll's calf, slicing through muscle and sinew. The troll toppled with a cry.

Bundling up the cloak under his arm, Griffon leaped to his feet, turned, and ran.

Grunter made a grab for him, claws raking down his spine, and he felt his flesh tear. Warm liquid ran down his back. His belly twisted and nausea rose inside his guts.

Dodging around trees and ducking under bushes, the gnome put on all the speed his small legs could muster.

The long strides of the troll kept pace, though because of the monster's size, it couldn't catch the smaller gnome as he weaved around obstacles.

"Get over here," Grunter yelled, "and get in my belly!"

Griffon's knees went rubbery and buckled at the shout, the realization washing over him that he may have given up his life for a wool cloak. His tummy rolled over again, and the ging-ging fruit threatened to come back up.

He burst out of the dense foliage and into a clearing. Putting his head down, he pumped his legs for all he was worth. The troll crashed out behind him, closing the distance.

Passing into the shade of the tree line ahead of him, he looked up, searching for a way to get into cover and away from the troll.

Four huge, wide humanoids stepped from the shadows of the jungle and into the clearing. They were wider than three of Griffon side-by-side and rippled with muscles. Looking up at their bodies, he realized they weren't trolls, though they were almost as tall.

They wore billowing pantaloons, and dark fur covered their arms and bare torsos, and atop their shoulders were bull heads with wide horns curving outward over their shoulders.

"Holy chuz," Griffon swore, his feet sliding out from under him as he tried to stop and backpedal, "chuzzing minotaurs!"

He slid to a stop at the hooves of the giants, and that's when his stomach lost the fight with the ginging fruit. He spewed chunks all over the shins and hooves of the man-beast standing over him.

Chapter 5

Lightning flickered in the distance, silhouetting the jagged outlines of the crags, the crisp air saturated with static. Aiyana looked up, her attention drawn by the tempest, and listened to the thunder tumble across the mountain peaks and canyons around Dargaon's Hole. The ethereal forms of elementals haunted the broken range, conducting electricity from the seething clouds into the valleys. The smell of ozone permeated the area.

The Wandering Hills suited its name, meandering across more than a thousand kilometers east to west at its widest point, and over two thousand north to south. It was a land of rolling hills in the west, and a line of broken ridges in the east. The southern portion cradled the Tear Drop Bog, a salty marsh that was the shallow grave of an inland sea.

Dargaon's Hole was in an immense bowl valley—like an amphitheater of the gods—in the center of the range.

When the humans of Hope's Hollow first returned to the abandoned community, the only scraps of the long-lost civilization were a cave system with an immense, domed central cavern and a warren of passages running in all directions. The main chamber was enormous enough to house the entire community.

The architecture wasn't like that of the great Rokairn halls she'd read about, but it was impressive.

Two balconies ran the circumference of the main chamber, ramps leading up to each. The builders carved rooms into the rock, along with pillars, tables, alcoves, and design accents of scrollwork mixed with blocky maze-like elements. The rooms had various uses, from dining halls to barracks, from kitchens to storage. Eye-catching scrollwork, carvings, and statues of men and women cut into the worked stone of the mountain displayed centuries of forgotten history and lore. Aiyana wanted to stare at the displays of lost heroes, like a child, making up fanciful stories in her head, and wondering if one day someone would make a statue of her.

The craftsmen—probably dragons and humans working together—had built privies into side chambers. Holes drilled down to an underground stream carried waste away. They drew fresh water from it upstream. The designers of the refuge were smart enough to not pull tainted water for drinking, bathing, and cooking.

Up the mountain's steep slopes were the dragons' caves, connected to the lower caverns by tunnels. Jagged cavern mouths, visible from the valley, dotted the mountainside. A concave plateau—rounded by centuries of the massive reptiles sunning themselves—jutted out in front of each like a giant's porch.

Torrents had told her the people of Dargaon's Hole explored those caves, hoping to find some forgotten scraps of treasure, but found nothing. That which once housed dozens of the noble beasts now lay empty.

The town grew outside of the main cavern's mouth, expanding in two rows perpendicular to the rock face, jutting outward from the maw of the mountain like pincers. The buildings were simple compared to the older construction, functional rather than decorative. Within a year, and with many fresh faces showing up, there was a second row of businesses behind both original rows. People built houses and farmsteads in the valley, necessary for their crops, expanding herds, and growing families.

After the contingent of Rammen, led by Kajuun, departed to return to their city a week ago, the settlement returned to its normal pace and rhythm. The smell of fresh-baked bread hung over the village nestled in the hills outside of the cave. The ring of the blacksmith's hammer and anvil competed with the sawing and planing of wood from the wainwright and cooper. Neighbors gossiped by the town well in the newly bricked courtyard, marveling over the new three-story town hall being built near the Grand Cavern entrance.

Many glanced nervously at the sky, muttering guests arriving with foul weather brings foul tidings. But most went about their daily lives. The town council had sent a message to Trinity, warning her of the danger, and asking if she could return to the valley with haste. They'd also sent riders out to the other nearby settlements.

Aiyana knew from her studies that Rugber Whitley Estates, a week west, was the closest community, with Allendale and Akar almost five days past it. Allendale was the gateway to the west, and Akar was on the lake known as the High Tarn, on the border of the Great Desert. Dragon Staff had once been an outpost of Dargaon's Hole, used to recruit new families and merchants to join their mountain community.

Rugber Whitley Estates, known for its mind mages, wasn't a place with any specific schools or teachers for that branch of arcane power, but many of that sort of caster were born there. The most recent was Cite, the bard. He'd traveled south into the Great Desert where he'd met Rogen the Plague, the infamous slave master of the Desert Empire. The two had traveled west, meeting others and together had changed the world during the Downfall under the glaring gaze of the comet called the Talisman. Aiyana had made a trip there, spending two days in their libraries searching for information about communicating through portals.

Aiyana now paced back and forth in her chamber above the Grand Cavern, muttering to herself. She glanced southwest through the thin windows. They were just wide enough to stick an arm, bow, or sword through. Angled down, the builders had designed the narrow openings so weather would pour out instead of in, and defenders could aim bows and crossbows towards oncoming invaders. She thought about closing the shutters to block out the coming storm.

She'd been thinking about the heroes—or villains, depending on who you asked—of the Downfall. The ones who'd changed the face of the world, bringing people together who would have never survived if it weren't for the influence of the small band of…of what? Misfits? Power-hungry monsters?

But there had been an artifact, the voice in her head whispered again, drawing her back to her earlier train of thought, *a long-lost relic of power. If you could find it again, then you could be the one who changes the world and brings together the new order and ushers in a new age.*

A knock on the door made Aiyana jerk and bump into the high washstand between the windows. The water pitcher wobbled back and forth, then toppled to the ground, shattering.

"Miss Aiyana?" a matronly voice came from outside of the closed door. "Are you alright? May I come in?"

"Y-yes," Aiyana answered, shaking the thoughts from her head, "come in, it's open."

The heavy door creaked, swinging wide. The plump woman from the council stood there, holding a cloth-covered tray. Smells of food wafted into the room.

"Hello," Aiyana tried to smile, her lips pulled into a tight line across her teeth. "I thought you were a council member, not a serving woman. Your people here are so casual with how they allow others to just come and go. There's hardly any social hierarchy. It's very refreshing." The aeifain turned away from the older human woman. "Everyone should allow equality," she continued, "and to be what they want to be within a society."

The matron set the tray down, nodding and making agreeable noises as the young aeifain went on about social issues, and then stood with her hands interlaced in front of her, facing Aiyana.

Aiyana turned back to the woman, cocking her head.

"Oh, you're still here," the aeifain smiled indulgently, "is there something else you needed? Are you also picking up laundry or something?"

"No, I was just letting you talk," the woman spoke slowly and patiently, "or more that you needed someone to listen. But since you stopped for a moment, allow me to introduce myself again. I'm Rose, and I'm the co-leader of this community. I'm the one that led them from Hope's Hollow under the advice of the Kid. And yes, I was at that table with you, but as the one who runs this place, not some serving wench. I brought you some breakfast if you're hungry."

Rose gestured at the covered tray.

Aiyana's face flushed, then went pale as the woman spoke, and she shifted from foot to foot as Rose finished.

"Oh!" Aiyana jumped a little, realizing the woman was waiting for her to speak again. "Yes, thank you. Very kind of you to wait on me personally and, um, bring me something."

Aiyana moved towards the small table where the food sat, and Rose strolled to the window slits, glancing at the broken pottery and puddle of water on the floor.

The aeifain slid into a high-back chair and pulled the cloth from the tray. A small, chipped, mismatched tea set was in the center, two cups and saucers on one side, a little pitcher of creamer and a covered bowl of honey on the other. Pastries with nuts and a bowl of butter, hot oats, and slices of roast fowl covered the rest of the tray.

"Use the cloth as a napkin," Rose fluttered her fingers in Aiyana's direction, "and the tray as a plate. I'll be joining you for tea in a few moments, but I need to pace a bit to get this next part to come out right. You ever do that? Just walk around a tad, and it helps your thoughts form. It's like churning butter, isn't it?"

"Um, yes," Aiyana's face was neutral, "I've done that, and I guess it may be like churning butter. I've never churned butter but understand what you mean."

Rose leaned against the wall, crossing her arms under her bosom, studying Aiyana.

Aiyana tore a pastry open, buttered it, and paused; the woman was watching her. She appraised the woman who'd brought her the food, and who'd sat across the table from the leader of the Torck—a battle-hardened warrior, and a spellslinger of notable ability—Kajuun. They'd spoken as equals, and though Axle was also part of the talks, as well as the rest of the council, they'd all listened to Rose.

The older woman smiled, showing a grin with fewer teeth than Aiyana had expected.

"You remind me of someone," Rose said. "Did Torrents ever mention Esperanza?"

"Oh, maybe?" Aiyana felt like she was in front of the kindly school marm from primary school, a gentlewoman who also knew how to swing a switch when children misbehaved.

Rose nodded and walked forward, her hand reaching out.

Aiyana flinched, then blushed as Rose took the teapot and poured two cups of tea, one for each of them.

"Cream or honey?" Rose asked.

"Ah, yes, cream please," Aiyana smiled up at the woman, and the aeifain's cheek twitched.

"Esperanza was a powerful priestess of Latress who was in Hope's Hollow when Torrents arrived there, dragging Axle back with him," Rose said with a fond expression. "She'd already been in our village for a few weeks, healing the sick from some plague or malady that had fallen upon us. She died there, doing that."

"Oh," Aiyana said, her spoon of oatmeal almost to her mouth, "I'm sorry. She sounded very nice."

"Oh, she was kind, but not very nice," Rose chuckled. "But her story wasn't done yet. After she died, she came back. And it changed her. Her voice was different, she carried herself differently, and I swear even her height, hair, and skin had changed a bit, though no one else ever seemed to notice. Too busy adoring the amazing healer, I guess."

Rose shrugged and sipped her tea.

"But, yes, she came back from the dead," Rose continued, wrapping her hands around the warm teacup. "She was scared and didn't seem to believe in her goddess anymore. Until a necromancer showed up, calling for her head. Louis, the necromancer, to be specific."

Rose laughed a good belly laugh.

"Well, Esperanza suddenly changed when he threatened the entire village," Rose went on, "and Esperanza charged out of my little mud hut and showed that fat, little bully what's what, and how things work. She really put him in his place!"

"So," Aiyana leaned forward, "she chased him off?"

"Oh, no, dearie," Rose looked a little more serious, but still amused, "she turned his enslaved zombies against him. They ate him, right there, in front of everyone."

"That's horrible!" Aiyana gasped.

"Is it?" Rose took a thoughtful sip from her tea. "She did to him what he'd done to many others, and what he intended to do to dozens of others that night. After that, she fought against another necromancer who'd been hiding in the town, and who I suspect had released the disease among us, so she'd have more bodies to add to her army. And then Esperanza, Torrents, and the Kid hunted down the necromancer and her army.

"Even though she was constantly scared and confused, she did all these things to help others," Rose continued, "and she looked at me the same way you are now when she met me. She looked through me. When I touched her, she pulled away, like the dirt under my nails and smeared on my clothes was catching. She looked at me with pity when she saw how little I had to eat. When she combed her hair or washed her hands, she looked superior. I could see her wince when she looked at the people of Hope's Hollow. And you remind me of her."

Aiyana's face shifted through emotions: embarrassment, flattery, confusion, and then annoyance.

"And which parts are you reminded of?" Aiyana asked, her tone biting.

"All of it," Rose raised her eyebrows in challenge, at the same time raising her cup for another sip of tea.

"Do you care to explain?" Aiyana pressed.

"One thing I've learned, dearie," Rose said, setting her empty teacup down, "is no one listens to someone else's advice unless they want to avoid responsibility. And with most people, when I've given open, honest, and free thoughts on something and how to fix it, others make excuses or give reasons it wouldn't work, or doesn't apply, in their situation. So, instead, I've told you a story, and my feelings about something. I leave you with this gift, and you may toss it aside, or look deeper into it. After all, it's yours now."

Aiyana sat there, staring, unsure what to say, her jaw working in tiny little motions.

The most powerful woman in hundreds of kilometers trundled to the door, opened it, and looked back over her shoulder at Aiyana.

"Hope you enjoy and find it fulfilling," Rose smiled, pointing, "and everything digests well."

The older woman left the room, closing the door behind her. She'd pointed at the food and tea, but Aiyana didn't think—not for a second—that was what the woman had meant.

Aiyana's human side wanted to pout, stomp its feet, and say none of it was true. She wasn't anything like that other woman, Esperanza. But her aeifain side wanted to listen to the wisdom of her elders and consider the lesson within what Rose said. Or maybe it was the other way around, and the aeifain side was being petulant, and the human side thoughtful.

Picking at the tray, Aiyana's mind wandered as she pulled apart the pastries and popped bites into her mouth.

She wondered what Nathan would have said, thinking of her old friend who had gone back to their world.

Then she laughed.

"That story could've come from Nathan," she mused. "He used to tell me little parables, as well. He never gave direct advice, just little things I could mentally chew on until I came to my own conclusion."

She grunted, sipping lukewarm tea, considering and rolling memories of her rokairn companion through her mind.

Aiyana didn't know how long she'd sat there thinking—only that the sun now came in through the southwesterly facing arrow slits—when there was another knock on the door.

She stood, tossed the linen over the remaining food, picked up the tray, and walked to the door. Opening it with her free hand, she thrust the dishes at the person waiting outside.

"Thank you, I'm finished, you may take my dishes…oh, Reginald," she trailed off.

The swashbuckler leaned against the wide doorframe, a small smile playing across his lips.

"Thank you, milady," he said with an annoying little bow. "It would be my pleasure to clean up after you."

"Oh, stop it," Aiyana huffed, turning back into the room.

"Wait," Reginald said, a hand on her arm.

She turned back to him, and he lifted the tray from her hands, bent over, and set it on the floor in the hall next to the door.

"They'll get it from there," Reginald said, then grinned and continued, "otherwise you'll have to carry it down to the kitchens, like the rest of us peasants."

"Ugh," Aiyana turned and retreated into the room, leaving the door open, "why are you here? Just to bother me? Or is there some higher purpose in your visit?"

"Of course, your highness," the man followed her into the room, closing the door behind him. "I've spoken with what is essentially the quartermaster—or the equivalent—and found a chamber where you can set up a permanent portal."

"What?" She spun to face him. "I didn't ask you to do that."

"I know, but you were gone on your brief trip to Rugber Whitley Estates," he grinned, "and I do have a mind of my own, free will, and the ability to observe your modus operandi. And…"

He trailed off, and Aiyana looked at him, annoyed.

"And what?" she asked.

"Shush." He held up a hand to stop her.

"Don't hush me!" She took a step towards him.

"No," he said, walking to the window and tilting his ear towards it, "hush. Don't you hear it? They're ringing the bell. Someone has sounded an alarm."

Chapter 6

Griffon and his band of hairy brothers—that's how he thought of the minotaurs he'd met—raced past the outermost Dargaon's Hole guard post. One of the massive rammen, Tory, scooped Griffon up and swung the scantily clad warrior onto his shoulders. The gnome grabbed the minotaur's horns, stood up, and bounced on the bull's muscular shoulder.

"Woo-hoo!" Griffon yelled, pumped a fist in the air, and laughed.

They call the men bulls, he thought, *and the women heifers! They don't even get upset when you do it. I must've said heifer fifty times last night, and not a single one of them tried to beat the bidj out of me.*

A shout behind Griffon made him look over his shoulder. The panicked guards were running after them but weren't trying to catch them. Instead, they were desperately trying to keep up. They looked like they were running from the Devil himself, hot on the heels of the three minotaurs and the gnome. Apparently, they'd seen what Griffon knew was coming.

The group turned a corner in the canyon and saw a small town in front of them. People lined the porches and streets in front of the rows of wood and stucco buildings, curious why the alarm bell was ringing.

"Villagers!" Griffon crowed. "Actual to gods, real-life villagers!"

He was getting used to this super video game he'd entered. He'd read some manga and some isekai and understood what the books meant to be in a very real-feeling video game with ultra-VR capabilities.

It must've been because I'm such a kick-ass player, someone recruited me into this new game. I'd probably agreed to it but hadn't bothered to read the TOS. But really, who ever read the Terms of Service?

He hadn't figured out how to display up his stats box, though. He also wasn't sure where—or if—he'd reappear in the game if he died.

This is the most realistic game I've ever played, he thought. *But I'll have to put in a trouble ticket concerning taking a bidj in the woods without paper, and the damned mosquitos. You'd think that a high-end game like this wouldn't include bug bites and hunger pains. And the food is nasty, and I'd actually had to physically eat it. That's ridiculous! Somebody's gonna hear about this when I finally figure out the interface.*

"By Torr's smokey breath," Griffon yelled, slapping Tory on the head, "put on the speed of his lightning falcon, and blaze the trail to glory!"

The minotaur carrying him let out a snort. The gnome wasn't sure if it was amusement or annoyance, but it didn't matter. Whether this guy was a player or NPC—which is what anyone who wasn't a newb called non-player characters—it didn't matter. He'd get over it.

The minotaurs all had very gruff names, full of grunts and stuff. Griffon had given them nicknames that were easier to pronounce: Tory (short for minotaur), Tower (short for mino-tower), and Fred. They'd lost one minotaur yesterday, when the troll horde caught up with them. The fourth had been

Ted, but he'd changed it in his head to Ded since the guy had died.

A claxon bell went off, and the town erupted into a flurry of activity, like someone had kicked an anthill. *Not that I really know what that looks like since I never really bother to go outside.* Dozens of people ran in his direction, while others ran towards an immense set of double doors built into the mountainside.

He wondered if dwarves had built it. He cocked his head, studying it as he bounced up and down on Tory's shoulders.

There aren't a bunch of decorative columns, gigantic statues, or steampunk-looking tanks, ballista, and catapults, so I don't think it's dwarven. And all the people running around are human. Maybe I saw an elf or two but couldn't really tell with everyone running around like idiots.

Then he noticed something odd. The people who'd run towards him were forming defensive lines. The first row dropped to their knees, planting tall shields in front of them. The second line jammed spears into the dirt, so they stuck out over the shield line. Another dozen with bows shoved quivers on spikes into the ground, grabbing arrows and setting to their bowstrings. Behind them were a dozen people on horseback curving out and around the others, coming towards Griffon.

That seems like, well, like they want to kill me, he thought. *This is supposed to be a checkpoint, or a save point. Somewhere I can be safe, not attacked!*

The minotaurs slowed, raising their huge hairy hands above their heads, not reaching for their axes and swords.

"What are you doing?" Griffon screamed, slapping Tory on the head. "Draw your weapons! Kill them! Defend me!"

The last two words came out as a squeak.

Tory reached up, grabbed Griffon by his shoulder, and gently lowered him to the ground.

The calvary swept around and past them. The panting town guards caught up and ran past Griffon and his meaty guardians, heading for the shield wall.

"Get back, get inside! Something's coming!" one shouted at the assembled defenders, waving her arms. The four skirted the group and continued to run past.

A slim man with blonde, greasy, shoulder-length hair jogged up to intercept the fleeing guards. The faint sound of sharp words reached Griffon, and he saw the exhausted guardsmen gesturing wildly towards him and the minotaurs, then beyond them.

Nodding, the newcomer slapped the man on the shoulder and pointed at the huge wooden double doors embedded in the mountainside. The guards moved towards it, slower than before.

Turning back towards the group, the slim man studied Griffon and his companions for a moment, then jogged towards them.

Griffon drew his mighty two-handed blade, almost as long as he was tall. Looking at the sword slapping against the approaching man's thigh, Griffon realized their weapons were the same length.

A giant hand came down on his shoulder. The gnome looked up into Tory's watery brown eyes. The minotaur shook his head.

"Put it away," Tory chuffed, still catching his breath, "these are not enemies. They are allies of the Torck."

The three minotaurs, though stoic, were exhausted from running from an enemy for hours. They stood panting, a sheen of foam on their barrel chests and thick arms.

Flanks? Griffon thought, remembering the term from some horse stuff he'd read once, but didn't know if it applied to cow-dudes. *Cowboys? I wonder if they live on dude ranches.*

The man from the mountain jogged up, stopping a few paces in front of Griffon's group.

"What's going on?" he asked.

"We're here to…" Griffon started, his voice shrill, then a huge mitt covered his mouth, stopping him.

"Trolls, sir," Tory said, "about a score and a half, maybe more. They're armed with spears mostly, but skilled in combat. I don't think it's wise to face them in the open."

"I understand," the man said, nodding. "Let's get you inside."

The newcomer turned, leading the group past the defensive wall at a fast walk.

"I'm Axle, and I'm kinda in charge of Dargaon's Hole," he explained.

"Kinda, my arse," one spearman shouted. "He runs this place!"

Other men laughed, calling out their agreement and support.

"Ignore them. They're just grunts." Axle rolled his eyes. Noticing the concern on the minotaurs' faces, he added, "Your ambassador, Kajuun, is gone. She and her entourage returned to your city. I'm pretty sure she left in time to avoid the trolls."

The minotaurs exchanged relieved looks with one another.

"Aren't we going to fight these things?" Griffon asked, running to keep up with the group. "I took one out all by myself! They can't be so tough that we can't beat them down with fifty men armed with bows and spears."

"You made one limp, little one," Tory scoffed and patted the gnome on the head, causing him to stagger. "The hunting party as a whole is almost an entire tribe and will use group tactics that'll shred the defenses."

"He's right," Axle said, looking back at Griffon, "and we can better defend from within the mountain. There, we can pick them off without risking the lives of our people. We don't have enough skilled fighters to take them on, on their own terms."

"But I…" Griffon said.

Axle spun, knelt, and grabbed the gnome by his leather harness and pulled him close to his face.

"Look, I'm sure you're tough," Axle said with a tight grin, "but you smell green to me. *You* can stay out here and fight them, but I'm pulling *my* people back to safety."

He pushed the gnome away, turning and walking away in long strides.

Griffon stumbled, falling into the dirt on his leather clad butt. Getting up, he had to run to catch up.

Tory lingered behind, waiting outside the massive doors, and placed his massive hand on Griffon's chest.

"Put away the sword, little one." Tory said. "You're fierce and determined. Almost to the point of a berserker. We all acknowledge that and admire your fire. It's Torr's own drive burning inside you. We respect that. But know the time and place. We follow the command of the one who is the leader, or we die alone instead of living as a herd. Understand?"

"Yeah, I guess," Griffon mumbled, sliding his blade back into its scabbard. "But I'll show this guy that I know how to kick…"

"Everyone!" Axle shouted, turning back to the lines of defenders. "Orderly retreat! Shopkeepers and families first, soldiers last. Watch for the farmers coming in and let them by!"

Men and women in rough uniforms took up the cry, taking charge of smaller groups. People hurried into the mountain, the soldiers holding the defensive line to give the civilians time to retreat.

Soon, the entire settlement was inside the barred doors and sheltered within the mountain. The ancient halls bustled with activity. Babies cried and small children clung to their parent's legs. Older children ran through the hall on errands, gathering arrows and other necessities to protect their home, from medical supplies to foodstuffs. Contingents of soldiers moved to the upper plateaus, arming the catapults and ballista.

Griffon stood to one side, sulking. He noticed a lady elf and a smug man heading towards him. The man caused bile to rise in Griffon's throat. He swaggered, gods damned swaggered. His white shirt had a deep V-shaped opening showing a muscular chest, and his dark blue doublet was unbuttoned and hung open. He wore knee-high boots with pants that puffed out of the tops, and a long, thin sword swung on his hip. The sword had delicate metal swirls in the shape of vines and leaves around the grip. A flat, pointed dagger hung from a wide leather belt on his opposite hip.

The woman wasn't dressed anything like the elves in the games Griffon had played. She wasn't half naked in a purple metal bikini with silver piping. She didn't have green hair or ears that stuck way above her head. She was like a poor man's elf.

She wore a brown laced corset over a deep red dress with two long slits up the front of her legs that showed dark brown boots that came up over her knees. Platinum blonde hair hung lank around her shoulders. She walked towards Griffon, a silver staff clunking with each step.

The weapon was the most interesting thing about her. It was a solid metal shaft shaped like a spine halfway up, a few curved ribs at the top that arched up to a bone hand with long, thin fingers clutching a blue crystal shaped like a flame. It was equal parts creepy and cool, and Griffon would bet his purple epic sword back home that it was magic.

"That staff rawks," Griffon said, trying to see the woman's minimal cleavage between the laces above the corset.

"Thank you…?" the elf said, the words neither a statement nor a question, but something in between. "And that's a lovely, um, what are you looking at?"

Griffon snapped his eyes up and stared into intense ice-blue eyes. They held him, and he thought they might be grey, like storm clouds, including little jagged bits of lightning darting through them.

"Earth, United States, Russia, China," the smug man muttered, cocking his head as he observed the gnome's reaction.

Griffon shifted his gaze to the man, who had a hand curled in front of his mouth as he coughed the words.

"Reginald," the woman's tone cautioned, "that'll be enough of that."

"What?" the man, Reginald, said. "Either he recognizes them, or he doesn't. But it will let us know if he is from home. And look at his face…"

The swordsman gestured at Griffon, who—after a moment of surprise—smiled and nodded.

"He knows those places," Reginald went on, "so we know we've found the correct fellow. He's the one you felt enter."

"Yeah, bae," Griffon said, turning back to the elf and dropping his voice to what he considered a deep, sexy tone, "you can feel me enter anytime you want!"

"You…little…pig!" the woman said, drawing her hand back to slap the gnome.

"Aiyana!" Reginald snapped in a whisper, reaching over and grabbing her wrist to stop her.

She jerked her head towards the peacock of a man, glaring at his hand.

"It's okay," Griffon said, breathing on his fingernails and buffing them on the leather strap of his gladiator's harness. "I'm used to that reaction. Women can't handle it when this hot hunk of man meat shows interest in them."

Reginald let go of Aiyana's wrist and they turned to look at the gnome, then at one another.

"Well, he's certainly not what I was expecting," the man said, then turned back to Griffon. "Listen, son, you can't just speak that way to a lady…"

"I ain't your son," Griffon huffed, "and you ain't my dad. So don't think you can tell me what I can do. Just because you're PC's, like me, don't mean you know me. I'm tired of you people trying to mod me when I'm just being nice. If she doesn't get it, that's her being sensitive. I didn't do nothing wrong here. I'm the victim!"

The two gaped at the gnome, mouths hanging open.

Aiyana recovered first.

"How old are you?" she asked, incredulous.

"And what is a PC, and how do they mod someone?" the man asked.

"I'm forty-seven!" Griffon snapped without thinking, then did a double take when he heard his own words. "Wait, what? No, I'm twenty-two! And a mod is one of the game controllers that people run to, to tattle on those that make them boo-hoo, que que, wah."

"I don't know what most of that means," Reginald said, glancing at Aiyana.

The woman shrugged.

"Look, s--" Reginald cut himself off, then continued slower, "sir. You're from Earth, right? And you died. And then you woke up here, in this body. Is that right?"

Aiyana looked around frantically, making sure no one was watching or listening.

"Oh, yeah," Griffon nodded, smiling, his fit forgotten. "This game is epic. I even had to poop. Did you guys have to poop yet? It's so real!"

"First," Reginald raised one finger, "this isn't a game. This is real. Second, we don't talk about that in front of a lady…"

"How do you know she's a lady?" Griffon interrupted, ogling Aiyana again. "I mean, she could be a dude who just rolled a chick toon. We don't know who's on the other side of the keyboard."

"What? Keyboard?" Reginald exhaled sharply, leaning back with wide eyes. "I don't understand what you're saying."

"He thinks this is some sort of game," Aiyana explained, "like those video games on television that Nathan told us about. Is that right, um, what's your name?"

Aiyana looked down at the gnome again.

"Oh, I'm Griffon," the little man hooked his thumbs into his leather harness—like they were backpack or overalls straps—and rocked back onto his heels, grinning. "But this toon had some other pemtie name, so I decided to stick with my real name. Did you guys get stuck with pemtie names, too? Oh wait, Reginald and Aiyana could be your pemtie names!"

"I'll have you know Reginald is my real name, but here I am known to some as Kazzek Tel Virian." Reginald sniffed, lifting his chin slightly.

"Really?" Griffon laughed. "And you stuck with Reginald? Reginald? I mean, come on, Kazzek is so much better! Reginald is like a grandpa name or some old guy who wears a toupee and drives a convertible to make himself not feel old."

"Aiyana is my pemtie name of this world," Aiyana interjected as Reginald sputtered, red blotching his face, "and I don't think I'd like to share my other name with the likes of you."

"It's that bad, huh?" Griffon asked. "It's all good, I get it. Aiyana isn't bad, anyway. Not as bad as Reginald."

"Maybe you should just call him Reggie," Aiyana suggested. "He likes it when people call him Reggie."

"Reggie?" Griffon burst into exaggerated laughter. "As in, it rhymes with wedgie? Reggie Wedgie? You really think that's better than Kazzek? Oh, no!"

The gnome dramatically fell to the floor, his weapons clanging loudly on the stone as he clutched his stomach.

People turned to look, and the three minotaurs he'd arrived with hung their heads and looked away from the scene, shuffling awkwardly.

"Oh, ah, oooh," Griffon wheezed, pushing back to his feet. "Maybe I'll just call you Kazzek Van Twinkletoes, or whatever it was."

"Tel Virian," Reginald said coldly.

"Reginald, Reggie," Aiyana said, patting the man's arm, "he's trying to get your goat. Don't let him. It's below you."

"You're right," Reggie puffed out a breath. "I normally wouldn't have even reacted to his juvenile jibes, but we're under a bit of stress right now, and, well, I'm sorry. I'm fine now."

"Wait," Griffon said, putting his fists on his hips in a heroic pose, "were you old where you came from? Sorry, old man, I was just trolling you. Don't get all emo on me. But it literally made me roflmao. That was priceless."

"Trolling me?" Reggie asked.

The line of stranglers from the outlying farms came in through a smaller door beside the enormous set. A thick bar slid into place with a dull thud, locking the enemy out and everyone else in.

Moments later, pounding assaulted the main doors, and the crack of axes on wood echoed through the hall.

"Speaking of trolls," Aiyana said, drawing herself up and hefting her staff, "I think all of Dargaon's Hole is about to be trolled."

Chapter 7

"I need to go to my room." Aiyana spun on her heel and headed for the ramp, calling back over her shoulder, "I'll need a clear view of the battlefield if I'm going to use magic to help."

"Oh, I bet she doesn't know that thing about trolls," Griffon giggled.

"Reginald, come," the aeifain commanded, "and bring the shrimp. It may have some useful information."

"Wait, what?" Griffon squeaked. "Did she just call me—urk!"

Reginald grabbed him by a shoulder strap, hauling him along. Reggie noted the minotaurs trading looks and moving to follow. The swashbuckler side of him noted the tender bits of the creatures' anatomy; inner thigh, midsection, armpits, and throat. These were the spots where Marcid, his magical transforming weapon, would do the most harm—or good—if it came down to an altercation.

Griffon complained about being dragged along, but Reggie ignored it, following Aiyana towards the spiraling ramp that wound around the edge of the cavern, leading to the upper levels.

"I can walk, old man," Griffon yelled. "Stop pulling on my thing!"

No one paid the gnome any attention.

The cavern was a beehive of activity. Men and women rushed to defensive positions along the walls, ready to defend their home, as civilians headed deeper into the tunnels.

Arrow slits, like the ones in Aiyana's quarters, lined the walls within alcoves big enough for two people. One person looked out across the valley, bow in hand, ready to fire. The other waited to assist with reloading, or to take over should the first fall.

The second level had places for pouring boiling oil, or water if times were tight, and the third level had larger openings with defunct ballistae within the niches that hadn't been restored yet. The community wasn't prepared for an attack and hadn't thought to build outer defenses.

Reggie would bet if the people of Dargaon's Hole survived the invasion, they'd erect a wall in the canyon, and perhaps towers above the burgeoning city.

The archaeologist winced, thinking of all the hard work these people put into their little town over the last five years. They'd built shops, homes, and everything that went with a peaceful town. But now, the reality of an attack and war had been brought down on them.

"You do know," Reggie said to the gnome trotting along beside him, "that the gryphon was a noble beast of mythology, don't you?"

"Yeah," Griffon shrugged, "I've seen them in games. They had a bird's head and wings, and a horse's body or something."

"No," Reggie sighed, "the hippogriff had a horse's body, and was a fabrication of Ludovico Ariosto in the sixteenth century for a poem that gained some renown. The gryphon had a lion's body.

It was Mediterranean, but also popular in western Asia."

"Yawn, grandpa," Griffon mimicked a long, bored yawn, "you sound like a teacher. Is this how you win a fight, by boring people to death?"

Reggie fell silent, letting go of the smaller man's leather strap. He didn't care if the gnome followed or not. He wasn't worth the time or effort of caring.

Griffon trotted along beside him, looking everywhere at once.

"This is just a snack stop for the trolls, you know?" Griffon said. "I heard them talking. They raid human places for food and fun. They're really headed for some place called the Nine Towers of Magic."

Reggie glanced down at the man but said nothing.

"These people are screwed, aren't they?" the gnome asked. "I mean, really, if they get stuck in here, they'll eventually starve. If they go outside, the trolls will kill them. They're tough. I fought one. Took him down, too. Would've killed a couple more, but Tory stopped me. Guess he felt sorry for them because he knew I'd totally pwn them."

"Did you say, 'pwn'?" Reggie couldn't stop himself from asking the question.

"Yeah, pwn!" Griffon nodded. "Like wreck, own, stomp them?"

"As in, defeat them?" Reggie glanced down to see the gnome nodding.

A rough guffaw burst from the human.

"You think you could beat these trolls in a fight?" Reggie asked.

"Yeah!" Griffon nodded again. "I'd totally rock their world. I can't be beat. You know, I took down a whole arena of witches and a demon when I first got here?"

"Did you, now?" Reggie scoffed.

With a troubled look on his face, the gnome nodded again, this time without any ego, as if the smaller man wasn't sure of something.

Reggie knew braggarts. He'd dealt with their type his whole life. Men who'd touted their deeds, expanding the story with exaggeration until they were the perfect hero.

This guy beside him looked like a scared little boy for a moment, full of doubt. And like sitting at a card table, he read the gnome in that split second, and knew the lad.

He wanted adventure but feared everything. He blustered to feel better about himself and hoped it made people like him. He thought that the only way to find acceptance was to be better than everyone else, and more important than he was.

Reggie decided to attempt a different tack. It wouldn't be easy, and it wouldn't be quick, but it would work. Eventually.

Griffon glanced up, his face scrunching up.

"What're you looking at, old man?" the gnome spat.

"You, my little friend," Reggie said with gentle kindness. "I understand now. You're going to be fine. You're with friends now."

Reggie dropped a hand to pat the gnome, who jerked away.

"Stop trying to touch me, creeper!" Griffon squealed. "Why are you always trying to touch me? You some kind of pedophile?"

"You're older than me," Reggie retorted, looking at the door they were approaching. "Perhaps it's you who is trying to tempt me with your clever reversal of roles?"

The gnome skidded to a stop, his sandals sliding on the thin layer of sand on the stone.

"Wait, what?" Griffon asked.

"We're here," Reggie said, gesturing towards the door that Aiyana had opened and passed through. "Why don't you invite your friends in and join us for the defense we shall mount?"

Reggie didn't wait for the gnome to answer but saw the gladiator looking back and noticing the minotaurs for the first time.

Griffon waved frantically at his traveling companions, then moved into the room, followed by the minotaurs. The chamber, though spacious, felt crowded once you put an aeifain, a human, a gnome, and three minotaurs into the space. The enormous fourposter bed, a table and three chairs, and the wardrobe usually seemed dwarfed by the cavernous chamber, but three massive bull-men towering head and shoulders over everyone else made it seem cramped.

Reggie stood beside Aiyana, who was peering through a slit in the wall. The minotaurs moved to other openings, pulling crossbows from their backs.

The swashbuckler felt useless in this situation, even with a magical blade that could transform into any weapon he needed. Any weapon, that is, except a bow or crossbow.

Nathan, a priest of Jonath, had gifted Marcid to him, and the artifact could become an axe, a sword, or even a spear. But he wouldn't throw the most valuable item he owned out a window, except as a last resort.

Looking over Aiyana's shoulder, Reggie peeked at the chaos outside.

The town was burning.

Trolls skulked between buildings, throwing torches at thatch and wood-shingle roofs. They chopped at the beams supporting porches and ran into shops, taking anything they wanted. It was full on looting.

Arrows whizzed across the space below, most falling short of targets. The Grand Cavern was designed to defend against an assault on it, not a haphazard series of buildings built up in front of it.

Reggie watched Aiyana lean against the opening in front of her, focusing her magics. What had been mild autumn clouds now roiled and churned, moving faster than a few minutes before, the storm heads flickering with bursts of electricity.

Clutching her staff—which Reggie knew brought the five primary magics together—Aiyana shifted left and right, trying to get a better view of the battlefield.

The minotaurs pressed to their vantage points, Griffon rising on tiptoes to look out in front of one behemoth. Aiming at the raiding monsters below, the rammen fired their crossbows.

Between the mist of rain, the gusting winds, the distance, and the limited degree of firing, they soon gave it up as hopeless.

Aiyana raised one hand above her head and pulled it down sharply. Lightning bolts erupted from the heavens, hitting the turf below, exploding. Shards of stone and sprays of dirt showered the trolls.

The blast threw the brutes into the air like rag dolls, arms and legs flailing as they flew higher than the rooftops and crashing to the ground. A few stayed down, but most got up, dusted themselves off, and glared towards the protective stronghold.

"You're going to do more damage to the buildings than to the trolls," came a voice from behind the group, making them jump.

Reggie spun, his blade halfway drawn, and saw the aeifain that had been talking to Aiyana last night standing in the center of the room, his arms folded across his chest.

"You've managed to set at least two buildings alight," Zykrite went on, "and it looks like you're doing the invaders' work for them."

"What would you suggest we do?" Aiyana snapped.

"I'd suggest icy winds, snow, sleet, hail," Zykrite pointed at the arrow slit, "things the buildings can withstand, but that would make the trolls uncomfortable and want to move on. Using fire will only aid their efforts. Lightning is the same, and earth would do more damage than good."

Aiyana grunted and turned back to the view.

"I wouldn't use any magic directly on the trolls," the aeifain council member continued. "Their species is resistant to it, so mind magic and other such tricks would likely fail. Though maybe you could come back downstairs and enhance the group about to go out into the town to defend it?"

"Oh yeah," Griffon chimed in, "I knew that thing about them being resistant!"

"You could've mentioned that earlier," Reggie said, "don't you think?"

"I forgot!" the gnome said defensively.

"He was too busy ogling the wizardess's goods, more likely," Tory said, and the other minotaurs chuckled.

"Oh yeah," Griffon agreed, "that too!"

"Perhaps," Zykrite's raised voice cut through the mirth, "you could open portals for the militia to move through, so they can come out behind the trolls and surprise them, instead of being slaughtered running out the main gates. Isn't that something you can do, something you've been working on for years?"

Aiyana turned to look at the man, wincing.

"Yes, it takes a lot out of me, but," she nodded with a sigh, "you're right. Let's go see what aid we can offer to them, instead of…"

She left the words hanging and strode towards the door.

Reggie fell into step beside her, like a bodyguard, and Zykrite moved to walk on her other side. Griffon and the minotaurs walked behind the three like a strange honor guard.

"Your name is an ancient gemstone, isn't it?" Aiyana asked the other aeifain as the group stepped into the hallway and moved down the ramp. "Isn't it green or yellow?"

Zykrite glanced at her, and Reggie wasn't sure if it was at the implied jab of envy and cowardice, or the fact that Aiyana knew the origin of his name.

"It's actually orange with lines of emerald green," Zykrite corrected, "and it was in very limited supply. The rarity comes from it being mined from fallen stars. But I'm impressed that you're familiar with it. So many young aeifain have no knowledge or interest in the old things of our people."

"I'm not your average aeifain." Aiyana sniffed. "I've seen more in my time than most see over their whole life."

"Not too hard to do," Zykrite quipped, "considering most of our people on this continent are dead or fled the land during the Talisman. But I am curious. What things have you seen in your life?"

The group rounded the ramp, moving down the second level, and heading for the ground level.

Reggie watched the man and Aiyana trade barbs, and wondered who was baiting whom, and to what end?

Aiyana's carrying herself differently, Reggie thought. *Not sure if she's trying to impress this man, intimidate him, or hide her insecurities. But she's got me here to watch out for her.*

Reggie coughed a laugh at his thoughts, causing the others to look at him.

He shrugged.

"A funny thought," he explained to their inquisitive looks, "should we stay and fight this fight by opening a lot of portals for the people here? Or should we open a portal and get to the Nine Towers of Magic to block them from their ultimate goal?"

Aiyana stopped, turning to look at Reggie, her head cocked.

"Admirable," Zykrite said, nodding, "but a few hours here could make the difference in these people having their homes remain intact or being destroyed by these marauders."

All eyes turned to the councilor.

"Yeah!" Griffon agreed. He continued, laying it on thick, "We could encourage all these people to run out into the storm—whether it's rain and lightning or a blizzard conjured by her majesty—and die quick deaths! That's a great idea! I got the feeling that these people are more of the farmer and shopkeeper sort of NPCs, but maybe they all secretly train with swords and bows at night, and are good to go to jump into combat with super warriors like trolls! Let's do that!"

Now everyone looked at the gnome.

"I'm ready to go out and kick ass," he explained now that they focused all the attention on him. "But I'm a gladiator, skilled in the way of the sword. I mean, I already took down two trolls, and would've got more if these guys—"

Griffon jerked a thumb towards the minotaurs.

"—hadn't pulled me off of them."

"Yeah, short stuff," Tower said, patting the gnome on the head. "That's exactly how it happened."

Fred laughed and punched Tower in the arm. The two chuckled together, nodding at one another.

"If I may," Tory said, "we met the wee warrior at the edge of a glade, with one troll chasing him. It took four of us to take him out. We ran, and they hunted us. We're all experienced in war, fought many battles, and we were facing twelve or twenty trolls. We were never sure exactly how many because they're skilled at guerilla tactics. We lost one of ours on our flight here."

The rammen took a deep breath and Fred put a supportive hand on his shoulder.

"Muerin was a fierce warrior," Tory continued. "Perhaps the best of us. He died covering our escape. We faced off against the trolls three times, each time barely escaping with our lives. As much as we know about combat, Torr preserve us, the trolls are more skilled. And resilient to boot, able to heal quicker, travel faster, and better than is in every way in a one-on-one fight. Sending these humans out to face them—no disrespect to their abilities—is sending them out to die. Just my two copper fleks. Take it or leave it."

A group of humans moved around the group on the ramp, carrying armfuls of arrows.

Zykrite scoffed and scowled.

"Yes," he said, "the trolls are experienced, but as the saying goes, 'one man defending his home is worth ten invaders'."

"Cool saying, elf guy!" Griffon slapped the councilor on the back, and the man stumbled forward. "Sounds like something you tell people who aren't hiding inside of a mountain. Sure, send them out to die on some pemtie old saying."

Zykrite opened his mouth to retort, but Aiyana cut him off.

"Thank you, all of you," she said. "Each of you—well, most of you—has offered wisdom born of experience, and I value the advice. You're knowledgeable and it shows. I think I'll go speak with Rose about this and see what she thinks."

Aiyana turned away, continuing down the ramp, not waiting to see if the others followed.

Atta girl! Reggie thought, taking up his place beside the wizardess.

Woman! He mentally corrected. *Is atta woman correct? No, but it doesn't matter right now. She's taking charge, and making her own decisions, while listening to others. She has the makings of a leader, if she could get that huge chip off her shoulder.*

At the bottom of the ramp, Aiyana looked around the immense chamber, searching for the leaders of the community.

Seeing Rose talking with Axle and others, she beelined for them. They looked up as she and her entourage came near.

"Rose," Aiyana stopped a few steps away and bowed to the woman, "I need to discuss your strategy and how I can assist."

Rose raised an eyebrow and looked at the group flanking Aiyana.

Reggie noted Zykrite had slipped away and was no longer with them.

"Of course, dearie," Rose nodded, "go on, then. Come, tell me what's going on."

"I can portal your warriors on the other side of the foe, allowing them surprise," Aiyana recapped the plan, "and also provide cover with a snowstorm. Would that help your current plan?"

Axle snorted.

"No," the blonde man said, "we're not planning to go out at all. We're staying right here and making sure the trolls don't take out the main gate."

Aiyana looked down her nose at the man, then returned her attention to Rose.

"He's fine, dear," Rose patted her partner's arm, "and what he says is true. We wouldn't stand a chance out there against them. We built this place from nothing, and we can rebuild anything they destroy."

"In that case," Aiyana said curtly, "Reggie mentioned an inner chamber that I can use to create a permanent magical doorway that can access other portals in a network that spans the land?"

A loud splintering noise echoed through the hall from the front doors, and there was a collective gasp from everyone within. The floor shook and a dull cracking noise split the stunned silence.

Aiyana turned towards the massive oak doors and saw light streaming through a split high on the wood and felt an icy breeze. A sheen of ice traveled from the aperture and expanded across the smooth floor, a tiny crevasse moving along it, heading directly towards her.

Zykrite watched from the shadowy recesses of the third floor, viewing the Grand Cavern like a battle map laid out before him. He lowered his hands with the rings attuned to the elements of water and wind. It only took a little push from him to set things into motion.

When he'd suggested ice as a tool to be used to Aiyana, he'd been hoping to get her to do what he needed done. But she was strong-willed and did what she wished.

He knew the wizardess was the momentum he needed to move his plan forward. Just a few more things for her to do, and he'd be able to proceed in saving this wretched land. And perhaps find the right person to rule at his side.

He smiled, watching Aiyana move into action.

Portals: Book 5 – Towers & Trolls

Chapter 8

"Damn all the fool gods and their minions!" Aiyana muttered, looking around the chamber.

And here I was, she thought, *thinking for a moment that Rose and Axle had some sort of strategy or defense plan, but they look stunned that the enemy got in.*

Well, her internal dialogue continued as she strode forward, *the trolls aren't inside yet, but they will be if someone doesn't do something soon.*

Aiyana mentally reached out, seeking the ley lines for wind and water, focusing on creating an ice storm to implement the plan she'd discussed earlier.

Stopping with a gasp, she let the energies she'd grasp dissipate.

There's already ice, she thought, *and it worked against us. From everything I've read, trolls don't have magic, not even shamanic magic, so shouldn't have been able to do this. Unless they've bonded with some new god that allows them to touch magic. Who did this then?*

Her mind flicked through options, discarding a half dozen ideas in the span of a breath.

"Fine," Aiyana said, spinning back to face the group, "Rose, get any who cannot fight to either the upper or lower chambers. If there's an escape tunnel, take them there. Axle, organize your soldiers in doorways. They're more defensible."

Not waiting for them to answer, she turned to Reggie.

"Reginald," she went on, "work from the shadows or overhead and command the units within the Great Cavern by word of mouth. Shout if you must. And if necessary, help where you can or must."

Her tone brooked no argument, and Reginald nodded. He moved away, scanning the upper reaches.

"Tory," Aiyana turned to the spokesperson of the minotaurs, "take your men—and the crumb-snatcher—and form a blocking wall. Whatever comes through that door, it's your job to delay them long enough for someone else to take them out or turn them back."

The rammen grunted, drew his weapon, and turned. The minotaur put a huge ham hand on Griffon, turning the gladiator towards the breached doors before the gnome could open his mouth to object. He trotted away, Fred and Tower following.

"Now," Aiyana muttered to herself, "how the hell do I make myself useful?"

She strode forward again, calling out directions to anyone who seemed unsure of what to do or who wasn't moving towards an obvious task.

She knew that leadership was seventy percent confidence, twenty percent experience, and ten percent success. Effectiveness was in the eye of the beholder, but you'd never be an effective leader if you didn't have those three things in some measure.

Racking her brain, Aiyana went through what she could do, clacking her staff—The Key of Aiyana—with each step to set the rhythm of work and give a drumbeat to everything the people did.

Elemental magic is out, she thought, *and so is mind magic. Alchemy initiated by my staff is possible, but it would be minor without the proper preparation time. It allows me to do holy magics, and I could reach out to Onyx, The Travelling God, or maybe Promethene…but the trolls would probably shrug that off as well. Damn their resistance to the arcane energies. I could try to summon something, but that could bring in the wrong element. I won't call in demons or undead, ever—*

Her thought trailed off as the entry cracked again—a sharp retort like gunfire in the expansive chamber—and a triangle of wood from the upper part of one door fell to the floor, leaving a gap wide enough for a troll to pass through.

A troll head squinted into the gloom of the Grand Cavern, clawed hands bracketing its cheeks. Aiyana marveled at its features, this being the first time she'd seen one up close. A receding hairline—more of a mane—framed deep-set eyes, which were shadowed by a sloping brow. The nose jutted out, almost like a snout, but flattened at the end, twitching as it scented prey.

The monster turned back to shout to its companions—a throaty, guttural sound—and four arrows sprouted along its arms and hands inside the door. The brute fell backwards with a scream, and a cheer rose from those in the chamber.

Four more heads appeared in the split.

A lanky form wiggled through and dropped to the floor, followed by another, and another.

Arrows flew, the twang of bowstrings followed by the whistle of the feathered flights. The first invader—already standing—turned away and hunched its shoulders, taking the shafts to the back.

"Aim for those coming through the crack!" Aiyana shouted to the archers. "Let the minotaurs handle those inside! Let no more come in!"

I need to remember that these are farmers, not soldiers. Aiyana thought. *I told Reginald to take this role, so I can focus on…what? What can I do?*

She cocked her head, considering. If she couldn't affect them directly with magic, then she'd have to affect them indirectly, but physically.

Drawing energy through her staff, she ramped up her mind mage abilities—her native magic, rather than the learned Dasism magics of elements. She drew from inside of herself, building her mental fortitude up, and psychically flexed.

The wedge of the broken door laying on the floor wobbled upward. The slim, awkward strip of timber reminded her of a super-spy plane that was developed in her time, the Northrop's Flying Wing. Her father worked with men planning the next generation of the aircraft.

Powered by Aiyana's telekinetic magic, the triangle of wood flew forward and pierced the troll, tearing it in half.

"Magic might not hurt you bastards," Aiyana growled, "but a wedge of wood will!"

She whipped the massive weapon around, but three trolls landed on top of it. They drove it to the ground and laid into it with axes. In moments, it lay in pieces on the floor.

Aiyana drew her magic into focus again, tightening her hold on the shattered wood. She lifted the broken splinters, pulling in the arrows scattered across the floor, and violently gestured with her hand. The detritus followed her movements and tore through the invaders.

More trolls dropped through the opening in the door, as others chopped and battered at what remained of it. They formed into squads of three and charged deeper into the cavern, attacking anyone they met.

Aiyana glanced around, taking stock. Reginald was commanding waves of soldiers forward in groups of five. Each group had a colored flag, which the swashbuckler used as their call sign when shouting orders.

Reginald was halfway up the ramp, between the first and second levels of the chamber. He shouted to the groups, organizing the archers above with the ground troops below. Directing the bowmen to provide cover fire, he issued the command for his mini regiments to move forward or retreat, to attack the invaders or to defend passages other villagers had run down.

Griffon and the minotaurs fought as one, syncing up attacks, wading into the small squads of invaders. The rammen were a force unto their own, moving in perfect rhythm with one another, a steady wall of muscle that was precise in its efforts. The gnome danced between the larger warriors, weaving in and out of them and the enemy, a short sword in one hand and a dagger in the other.

The door burst inward—murky daylight pouring through—with more trolls waiting to get inside. They poured forward with a shout of excited bloodlust, spilling across the floor in a surge. Aiyana directed her focus to them.

There's more than we thought! Aiyana gritted her teeth. *They must've joined up with another tribe or two! I need to do something else, something more. We need more defense, more people, more power!*

She mentally went through her options again, the summoning and conjuring sticking in her brain.

Calling in animals might work, but it's shaky at best. Unintelligent creatures tended to run when confronted with death, and creatures with intelligence usually want a reason to join a fight.

What can I summon that would be effective and willing to help? She wondered if that had been her thought, or the other voice she'd been hearing.

An idea popped into her mind, and she considered it, turning it over and over in her head in a few precious seconds.

"Yes," she murmured, "that would work."

Throwing the remaining debris at the charging horde crossing the threshold, she pushed her awareness out of the cavern and across the countryside, searching for the one creature who would protect this place. Her staff hummed with the effort, vibrating against the stone below her.

"Prepare yourself to defend your home," she said out loud, pushing the words onto the one being she thought would help. "I'm bringing you here."

Using the energy from the storm she'd created to power her summoning, she created a portal, then reversed the flow of the phlogiston. Instead of propelling herself or others somewhere else, she pulled something massive from hundreds of kilometers away to the Grand Cavern.

Trolls pushed deeper into the cavern, blood rage driving them. A dozen ran down a back corridor that led deeper into the mountain, where the families had hidden. The clash of sword and axe, steel and stone, rung out across the cave.

An axe cut into Aiyana's shoulder, pulling her focus and concentration back to the here and now.

"No!" Aiyana shouted, thrusting her will back into her magics, mentally scrambling to maintain her portal.

The room erupted into a blue-white explosion of light and energy, and a massive white scaled beast burst into existence above the battle.

A dragon, flapping its wings to stay aloft, looked around, taking in the scene of carnage below it.

"I am Trinity," the dragon roared, fixtures and fighters shaking with the words. "How dare you attack my home!"

The beast landed, four taloned feet splaying to pin four different trolls, and her tail swept in a wide arc to cut through three others. Her massive jaws came down on two more, ripping them in half, and throwing their torsos towards the door.

The people of Dargaon's Hole rallied at Reginald's command, following the experienced warrior, surging forward to join the dragon and minotaurs in close combat.

Aiyana fell to her knees, and the swashbuckler was suddenly beside her, wrapping an arm around her. She clutched his shoulder. Then the gnome was there also, both struggling to support her and defend her.

She slipped from their grips and fell face first to the ground. She tried to lift her head and her vision swam, then everything went dark.

Zykrite watched the dragon decimate the trolls, his lips quirking upward. It was a small price to pay and well worth the cost. A thousand lives would be a small price compared to the return he expected.

From his vantage point, Zykrite watched Grunter, Wheezy, and the hand-picked group of trolls break away from the fighting and move into the back caverns. Once Aiyana established a portal, something this attack would expedite, he'd find the hidden trolls and send them through. He knew Axle and Rose would ask him to help attune the portal—after all; he was a member of their little council—and that would allow him to thread his own magic into the portalling system. The control he'd have would allow him to use the portal without detection, sending the trolls through to the next stage in his plan, and he'd transport to his destination.

Upon arrival, he'd re-attune the magical doorway to send Aiyana and her lackeys to the next task he needed them to complete. If they could do that, it would take a lot off his shoulders, and allow him to escape the notice of some powerful beings that he didn't want to reveal himself to at this point. They would come later.

With the temple being opened, that would set up their final task and allow them to move forward for the next step in the plan: opening the major points in the portal network.

He'd told Aiyana the truth. Most portal points were easy, but there were ones built into potent magical structures or points in the world. The locks on the arcane strongpoints were too intricate to just burst through with raw power. They required finesse and skill. If the wizardess and her minions played their parts correctly, they'd all open at once instead of having to be opened one at a time.

His plan had lain fallow for much too long because his own people had decided he shouldn't be free. Too ambitious, they'd said. But now he could move forward, and the world would tremble at his success.

Aiyana woke to noises around her; soft shuffling and murmured voices echoing off the tattered remnants of a dream. It was a sweet, but brutal, dream of being back with someone she loved, right as they died.

Do wake up, the voice whispered in her head. *We have much to do.*

Shaking off the cloying cloth of sleep, the aeifain forced her eyes to open. They were gummed shut, and she raised her hand to wipe away the crust. Her shoulder throbbed under the effort, and she let that arm drop. Trying her other hand, she found it worked.

"Hold on, take it easy," a masculine, but gentle, voice said.

A rough, warm, wet cloth wiped at her eyes, and she blinked them open.

Reginald sat above her, smiling.

"Did we survive?" Aiyana asked, her voice thick and her throat scratchy.

"We did more than that!" Griffon appeared in her line of sight, smiling down at her.

From her lower vantage point, she noticed things about the gnome she'd never seen from above him.

The wide gap between his two front teeth, the strand of meat wedged between his lower teeth, and his breath smelled of onions.

"I single-handedly killed a bunch of them!" Griffon bragged.

"Yes, you did," Reginald nodded his agreement, "after Trinity tore off their arms and other various and sundry body parts."

"Still counts!" Griffon whined.

"The dragon helped, then?" Aiyana wheezed.

"She did," Reginald nodded again. "Was her arrival your doing?"

"Yes," Aiyana whispered.

"Then you're the hero of the day," he smiled. "You saved everyone."

"The town?" Aiyana grunted and tried to push to a sitting position.

"It's wrecked!" Griffon offered cheerfully. "Mostly burned and looted, and lots of people died, but it'll give the NPCs something to do for a while."

"You're a horrible little man," Aiyana breathed, falling back down to the cot with a pained groan, and passed out.

Chapter 9

"It's taken three days," Aiyana said, her hands on her hips, "and I think that's long enough. We need to move now, otherwise we won't beat the damned things to the Nine Towers!"

"Take a breath, sister," Trinity said, her gentle voice gentle echoing in the massive cavern, "we're getting to that, and it will happen today. I just wanted to talk to you about a couple of things before you left."

The two were in Trinity's private quarters in the upper reaches of the mountain, the dragon eyeing the early morning sun across the plateau outside of the cave's mouth. She was hoping to get out there and warm herself on the rock later today. With winter coming, there wouldn't be many warm days left in the year, and she wanted to take advantage of prime napping spots before time ran out.

Looking around her 'room', Trinity felt a surge of comfortable contentment. It was home. She knew it had been before, but she'd been all alone until the humans had returned. It was nice to have the company, but the short-lived races—like humans, rokairn, and even dasism and aeifain—rarely bowed to patience, and almost never cultivated wisdom. It happened, but rarely.

Even Zykrite was impatient, and he was old. Really old, if Trinity's nose was telling the truth. He didn't look like he'd been around for more than a millennium, but maybe that was some of his magical ability hiding it. But that aeifain hid a lot of things, probably because he felt humans were impatient and impulsive, just as Trinity felt he was.

Since she'd returned—well, since she was summoned first by message, then by magic—Trinity had fought trolls, argued with the council on how to best rebuild the town, been approached to carry rocks from the quarry, given a dragon's blessing (whatever that was) to two newborn babes, and asked to inspect the most magically attuned chamber to build a permanent portal.

Trinity knew magic—all the intelligent dragons did, to some extent—but it wasn't her forte. That was more Edsumar's repertoire, but the leader of the dragons had disappeared from prying eyes as he grew into his new body. Or more fitting would be that his body was growing to fit the ancient dragon's spirit, which was actually five or more people bound into one.

Dragons used magic to do many daily tasks. Communication was a mix of vocal and mind magics, allowing Trinity to talk to someone without knocking them over from a rush of air from her lungs. Flying was also partially mind magics, allowing them to lighten their massive bodies covered with thick scaly hide into the air. The fire breathing was an intuitive link to the elemental magics. Trinity had been working on other types of elemental breathing, as well. She could breathe ice, lightning, and fog. She wasn't sure how useful the last was, but it was really cool to rise out of a fog bank when trying to look impressive. Next, she wanted to try mixing fire and earth magics to make a lava spray. She thought that would be pretty kick ass, too.

She'd heard humans tell tales that all white dragons, like her, sprayed ice. All red dragons sprayed fire, and so on. But that was ridiculous. She was white because of where she came from, the frozen lands in the north. Most dragons were beige, or kinda bronze. A few had other pigment tints to their skins, and a few were like reptilian peacocks, like the crooners and preeners of the continents of South Mirron and Aeifa homelands across the oceans to the south.

"Why is Zykrite delaying?" Aiyana's question drew the dragon's musings back to the present.

"He's being methodical, cautious." Trinity said, lowering her face to the level of the wizardess. "He just wants to make sure nothing goes wrong."

"It feels like purposely trying to slow down the entire process, and it doesn't make sense." Aiyana said.

They were eye level with one another, though a single orb of Trinity's was larger than Aiyana's entire head. And Trinity's head, even with her chin resting on the stone floor, was taller than the aeifain.

"You could be down there right now, telling them this," Trinity said, "because they're all getting ready to leave in the next hour. So, why are you really here? What did you want to talk about?"

Aiyana gazed into one of the dragon's eyes, defiant, then deflated with a sigh.

"Should I release the magic into the world?" Aiyana said in a rush. "I tried to do it with the Tower of Onyx, then when I reconnected the portal network, and now with opening this place where so much power is hidden away. I want to give it to everyone, to level the playing field, and not just have it in the hands of the few."

Trinity considered, then snorted her own sigh, blowing the aeifain's silvery hair back.

"That is a huge discussion, and I have debated it before," Trinity said. "It's a mixed bag and brings good and bad with it. It *does* level the playing field, to use your words, but it also puts a lot of potential power into the hands of the uneducated and ignorant. And many of those people don't want to learn, they just want to have a free ride and an easy way out of their problems."

"So, I shouldn't do it then?" Aiyana asked.

"I didn't say that," Trinity chuckled. "Besides, I think you've already made your decision, and you just want someone to tell you it's the right one. I can't do that for you though, because I'd be misleading you. It's not the wrong decision either, though. It's merely a decision that will change everything."

"Oh, it that all?" the aeifain muttered, her voice dripping with sarcasm.

Deep beneath the Nine Towers of Magic, an ancient figure drew back from a scrying pool, rocking on his heels. The night whispered to him in a voice that would be cold to most but was long familiar and brought comfort of the changes that were coming.

He'd watched Trinity grow from a hatching to a fierce warrior to a clever advisor. The dragon was young, but she was wise for her age. He'd been there when Edsumar had been sacrificed, along with the priests, and their spirits drawn into a dagger that would one day bring the dragons back together in a community. In the future, that dagger, and the dragon, would shatter a land. But as one thing dies, something else is born.

"Unlike me," the withered being said to the air and earthworms.

Both answered him, offering soft caresses and whispers of consolation and sympathy before growing distracted and moving on. The ruins sang around him, and the core of magic, so deep underground, boomed in rhythm with his own heartbeat. They'd aligned recently. Well, it was recent to him, meaning sometime in the past few centuries.

Magic surrounded this place of learning and tragedy. The walls of the buildings and the very dirt on which those same buildings were built had been infused with tragedy and magic. The arcane energy was so concentrated the runoff had poisoned the lands to the south, and the remaining sands tinted blue with the residue of unused magic.

Fate was in play, and the Changing Wheel was spinning once again. Ages and eras would swim past in the current of time, just a glimpse of their silver scales rising above the waters of eternity before disappearing once again.

The Changing Wheel rarely spoke directly to anyone, and when they did, it was even more rare to comprehend the meaning. The ancient concept wasn't a god, not in the way mortals thought of gods. This being wedded Time and birthed Chaos. The latter, in turn, took the name Quixe and befriended the new gods. Those three were older than the figure, who was in turn older than the new gods.

He reminisced how he'd watched Jonath meet, wed, and bed Latress. Watched their twin children grow into godhood in their own right. Seen The Walking God when he first appeared in the land from somewhere, or somewhen, else. Was a guest at the wedding for the Walking God and Promethene and blessed their children upon their birthing. He'd taught Senaria the way of the wood and water and showed Chanian how to tame his Lightning Falcon.

The creature beside the scrying pool smiled, recalling the day Jonath gifted the essence of chaos to The Walking God. The latter released Quixe back into the world, explaining that chaos contained was a danger because it was focused. Chaos left free disrupted nothing specific and was always random.

The Traveller had his fingers in this one, again. The Troll Lord could feel it in his bones. Jack Tucker, which is what the Traveller went by currently, was a meddler. Always thinking he was helping, never realizing that he himself, and his travelling inn, were nothing more than the bee that pollinates the flowers to bloom.

Zykrite was a meddler, also, but blind to the larger picture, even though he was older than the white dragoness. Aiyana was his latest project, and that would not end well. She was a stranger in this land, but also a child of it.

This whole skein was a tangle. The Changing Wheel manipulating the gods, the gods pulling the strings of almost ageless beings, and the powerful heroes fighting blindly, thinking they had a light that allowed them to see, never knowing how many layers of cloth had been put across their eyes. And he, one of the remaining four Troll Lords, observed it all.

The Troll Lord glanced back at the scrying pool and saw Reginald.

"I could bear that man to be my friend," the creature mumbled. "It would be nice to have a friend again. It's been too long."

Shaking his head, he stood, knowing he had to prepare for those who would be coming. He'd either be saved or killed, and one person would claim all his magics. Either way, the world was about to change…again.

"Okay, people, let's get this show on the road," Aiyana said, stepping into the cool, dark chamber with an air of confidence. Glancing around, she took in the small gathering of people and the pile of gear near the carved archway that didn't lead anywhere. "Everything ready, then?"

Reginald smiled and gave a small nod, his hand resting on the hilt of his weapon. Griffon waved frantically, dancing from foot to foot, a huge grin on his face. Rose looked over with a comforting look, her arm linked through Axle's. Zykrite stood impatiently, his arms folded, beside the arch that led to nothing more than a smooth, stone wall.

"The minotaurs returned to their people," Reginald said, "following Kajuun home. The rest of the people of Dargaon's Hole are busy rebuilding the what the trolls tore down. We're all ready here."

Aiyana and the others exchanged goodbyes, then she stepped to the side as she prepared herself to create a permanent portal in the anchor point.

She began the ritual, Zykrite assisting. In a few minutes, that seemed to draw out to an impossible amount of time, the portal burst into life within the archway.

Gathering their packs and other supplies, Aiyana stepped through. She was nervous as the energy of transporting across space and time washed over her, though she knew she'd see the towers in just a few moments. Prepared to undo the magic knots of power that held the hidden school from the eyes of seekers, she went over the knowledge she'd learned in Icon Hall a few months ago.

Stepping out of the swirling vortex, warm, dry air wrapping itself around Aiyana, and was met with pitch black darkness. She could see pretty well in the light of the moon, or even starlight, better than a human. But there was no light here. And it shouldn't be dry and warm. They'd been heading north and east, where the autumn rains would cause it to be humid and chilly.

She heard the others, Reginald and Griffon, step out of the portal behind her.

"Oh, chuz!" Griffon squeaked. "What the hell is that thing reaching for you?"

Chapter 10

A small blue-white globe burst into existence, hovering above Aiyana's palm, as she blinked to adjust her eyes to the light. A figure lurched towards her in a broken stumble, its limbs twisted and wrapped in aged gauze.

Griffon drew his sword and darted forward to put himself between the wizardess and the creature reaching for the aeifain's pale, silky-smooth skin.

Can't let a hottie like her get hurt, the gnome thought, *even if she is an ice queen.*

"You're not my real mummy!" Griffon shouted the words like a battle cry.

He cut downward, the blade slicing through the attacker's dusty forearm, then turned sideways and dragged his blade across the creature's midsection.

Bandages parted, and desiccated organs fell to the ground with empty, little noises that made Griffon think of stale brioche buns hitting the floor.

The gauze-bound monstrosity pressed forward, and Griffon flowed into another stance. Before he could follow through, a sword thrust over his head and tore into the creature's throat, followed by a main gauche piercing the thing's left eye.

Reggie—or Kazzek, as Griffon thought of him— leaned over the gnome, bent at the waist. The swashbuckler jerked the rapier left and right, the hole in the monster's throat widening.

The Key of Aiyana flared to life, the blue crystalline flame atop wavering like an actual flame. The ball of light hovering over the wizardess's hand shot across the room, zipping into the skeletal creature's empty eye socket. A small, silent nova of energy ruptured the skull, and the thing crumpled to dust.

Griffon stood in a side stance, one knee bent, the other stretched out behind him, his sword parallel to the floor at the height of his shoulder. Reggie leaned over him, his back arced, and both arms extended from his striking pose. Aiyana stood behind the protection of both men, rolling her eyes.

Stepping in different directions, they disentangled from one another, collecting themselves.

In the center of the room stood a squared off archway, a flat overhead stone supported by two square, fluted columns. Unfamiliar, small, squat stone gargoyle-like creatures bracketed the bottom and top of each. The rest of the room was a barren, yellowed, stone box of fitted stone with faded hieroglyphs across every surface, including the ceiling, floor, and the sarcophagus behind the portal.

"Is this where we were meant to go?" Griffon asked. "Some mummy's tomb?"

"It wasn't a mummy, but close enough," Aiyana said, moving to inspect the walls. "And no, it isn't where we should have ended up. Something went wrong."

She traced a finger along the hieroglyphs, her lips moving silently.

"Um," Reggie shuffled in place, looking around, "is this the tomb of Verl'zen-luk?"

"What?" Aiyana's head jerked around. "How would you know that? Because you're an archaeologist and can read these sigils?"

"No," Reggie drew the word out, "because I saw a vision of it once. When we were at the ogre's tower a while back, right after we met. I saw into the mind of one of my men as we released his spirit."

"Okay, but it doesn't explain why we ended up here." Aiyana pointed out, turning back to the wall and picking up reading where she'd left off.

"It might," Reggie said, again slowly, "I was kinda wondering how I could get here, and if there was a portal that led here. Sorry about that."

"No," Aiyana said, her words clipped. "It doesn't work that way. You can't just divert an experienced caster from where they were going by wondering. Your will isn't that strong, and you have no casting ability. So that isn't why we're here. Something else happened."

"Like you screwed up?" Griffon suggested, tired of not being in the conversation. The gnome smiled innocently as Aiyana turned to glare at him.

"Maybe," she said, surprising both of the men, "but I don't think that's what happened, either. Something, or someone, redirected us."

"Oh," Griffon said, sheathing his sword, "could it be this Verl'zen-luk guy?"

"He's a god now," Reggie moved to look at the wall opposite from where Aiyana was. "But there'd be no reason for him to bring us here."

The group fell into silence. The only sound was their boots scraping along the thin layer of sand on the floor.

Griffon shoved his thumbs into his wide belt and moved to a wall to look at the etchings. He stared at the little pictures, and they almost seemed to move, just slightly. Like an animated gif that was glitched.

Reaching up, the gnome activated his earring and studied the language with the help of the magical translator.

"I learned a little of this language while I went through the information at Icon Hall," Aiyana said after a few minutes, "but not enough that I can figure it all out. As best as I can make out, this is a forbidden place."

"I can't make it out, either," Reggie said, "but with a few weeks, I could probably make sense of most of it. These carvings seem to indicate that it's dangerous, and nothing should leave. Like it's locked down."

"Ha, ha!" Griffon said in a sing-song voice. "I know something you don't know!"

The other two turned to look at him, confused.

The gnome grinned. He liked this. These two thought they knew it all, but they couldn't figure this place out. But he could.

When he'd go dungeon diving on raids in his video games, he was always the tank, or the one that ran in to hold the mobs'—or monsters'—attention while the others did the damage to take down the enemy. He hated being the healer, and the damage guys, or DPS, were always annoying whiney people who thought they did more than anyone else.

But Griffon had never been the one to figure out the puzzles, clues, or research the dungeon. But here he was, in a real-life VR game, and he—Griffon—was the one who knew what happened and how to get out of it.

His grin was huge as the other two stared at him, waiting for him to share what he knew.

"Spill it, pipsqueak," Aiyana growled.

"I will, and happily," Griffon said, rocking back on his heels in amusement, "right after *someone* shows me what's under their shirt!"

"What?" the aeifain asked, incredulous.

"That's right," Griffon crowed, "show me the goods, and I'll show you the way out!"

"You promise?" Reggie asked, and Aiyana spun to face him.

"W-what?" the aeifain sputtered, her voice rising in pitch.

"Just promise me, you little goblin," Reggie said, not taking his eyes off Griffon, "if you get what you asked for, you tell us what you know."

"Deal!" The gnome was beaming, his eyes sparking with excitement.

"Oh, don't think for a second that I'm going to agree to…" Aiyana trailed off as Reggie moved in between her and Griffon.

The archaeologist unbuttoned his vest and pulled his shirt from his waistband.

"No, no, no," Griffon squeaked, "wait a second, this isn't what I agreed to!"

Reggie lifted his shirt, showing off a runner's build of ropey muscle with a thin trail of hair running down the breastbone.

"Yes, it is," Reggie smirked. "You said *someone* had to show you their goods, what was under their shirt. You never said it had to be her. So, I showed you mine. Now show us yours."

"But I meant her!" Griffon whined. "I didn't want to see some hairy moobs! I wanted to see the lady bits!"

"Whatever." Reggie pulled his shirt down and tucked it in. "I fulfilled my part. Now you do your part."

"Yes," Aiyana said with obvious relief, "you got what you asked for, even if it's not what you wanted. Now, tell us or I will just disintegrate you like I did that undead guardian."

Griffon sulked, jamming his hands against his sides where his pockets would've been if he had real pants.

"Fine," the gnome said, reluctantly, "it says that we can't open the portal back unless we have something else in this place."

"What *something else*, Griffon?" Reggie asked.

"It's like a short pole or stick thingy, with a loop at one end," the gnome said.

"Like a scepter? An ankh?" Aiyana asked.

"I guess," Griffon shrugged.

"Oh heavens, why is this like pulling teeth?" Reginald threw his hands up. "Did they say what it looks like? Where it is? What it does? How do we use it? Anything at all that would be helpful?"

"Did they say how to get out of this room?" Aiyana asked.

Griffon smirked and noticed that the elf chick looked pretty hot with the pale light washing over her. He once again wished for time alone with the internet.

"There's a panel that slides out." Griffon pointed at a wall. "And the stick is about as long as a man's forearm. It's in the map room off the throne room.

It's the key to activating the entire dungeon, or temple, or whatever this place is. And we just bring it back here and it will activate the gateway to the stars. Okay? Anything else you guys wanna know? Maybe my shoe size?"

"Where's the panel?" Aiyana asked.

"Behind the fall of time," Griffon sighed.

"Behind the, what?" Aiyana sputtered. "What's that mean?"

"Wait," Reggie said, holding up and finger and turning towards one of the side walls. "I saw something about that over here."

Aiyana moved to follow the archaeologist, and even the gnome looked interested.

Griffon was disappointed though; he'd hoped it would take them longer to figure it out. But these people had to be experienced gamers and knew how programmers thought.

Reggie traced a hand across the pictographs, his lips moving in a whisper, bungling the translation that was obvious to the gnome.

Griffon could see exactly what panel to push, it was behind the image of an hourglass. He didn't bother to tell the rest of what he had read though, that could be a little surprise for later.

"Here," Reggie called out.

The archaeologist jumped a little when he turned and Aiyana was directly behind, and slightly to one side, of him. That made the woman jump a little.

Reggie laughed, chagrinned, and even the aeifain smiled a little.

"The fall of time," Reggie pointed out an hourglass hieroglyph followed by a door symbol.

He ran his fingers along the edge of that stone, and it was obvious to the gnome that he was looking for a release or a fingerhold. He tapped on the stones surrounding it, then it, listening for any differences in the sound Griffon guessed.

"Push it," the gladiator muttered.

The other two glanced at him, then back at the panel. Reggie put his open palm on it and drew in a breath.

Aiyana put a hand on his shoulder.

"Wait," she said, then looked at Griffon. "Any traps?"

"How would I know?" he asked, shrugging.

The two watched him, studying him, and he felt like they might be able to tell when he's lying.

"Maybe." Under their piercing stares, he amended his word. "Probably. The rest said that hand of the one who reached beyond the sands of time would give it in sacrifice."

"Allow me," Aiyana said.

She gently pushed Reggie aside and stepped into his place. She did something with her hands, then pushed while still an arm's length away from the symbols.

The panel slid into the wall, accompanied by a grinding noise of stone on stone. A guillotine-type blade flashed in the light, dropping halfway into a slit in the bottom of the small opening. Then, with a clicking noise, it retracted upward and back into the ceiling of the cubicle.

"Thanks for that, Aiyana," Reggie said sincerely.

She nodded.

"I'm not fond of people losing hands," she said, "and a one-handed swashbuckler didn't fit into my plans, so you're welcome."

Aiyana leaned her staff towards the hole, looking into the recess. Set into the alcove, the size and shape of a man's head and off to one side, was a small metal lever.

She raised her hand again, without putting it inside the space, curled her fingers like she was gripping something, and pulled towards herself. The lever quivered, then snapped in the direction she pulled. The mini-guillotine snapped down again, repeating its earlier process.

Something clicked in the stone wall, and a door-sized section moved a finger-width into the wall with a loud grinding noise. A popping noise followed, and the whole panel shifted a handsbreadth to one side.

"Heh," Reggie said, "it's a pocket door. Always loved those."

The human leaned forward, gesturing for Aiyana to bring the light closer, and examined the edge of the exit.

"Looking for more traps?" Griffon asked.

"Mhm," Reggie said without looking back.

"There aren't any," the gnome said, "at least not in the door. But this whole place is a trap. They made it to keep the dead in…like they were going to get out."

"One did, a lich," Aiyana licked her lips nervously, "and he became a god."

"Verl'zen-luk?" Reggie gripped the edge of the sliding door and pulled it, so it receded into the pocket built for that purpose.

"Indeed," Aiyana nodded.

"Well," Griffon said, "let's hope we don't wake up the rest of his posse."

The human and the elf turned and looked at the gnome.

"The rest of them?" Aiyana asked.

"Yeah," Griffon nodded, happy to be the center of attention again. "I told you they built this whole place to keep them in. There's a bunch of them, all sleeping or something. The sleep of the dead, I guess. But we can wake them up. Bet they'll have to pee like crazy! All Austin Powers cryo-sleep bladder!"

The gnome laughed, and the sound echoed off the walls, repeating ominously as it traveled down the corridors on the other side of the opening.

"Hush!" Aiyana hissed. "How do we know that won't wake them?"

"Enh, it won't," Griffon said, still giggling. "They have to be woken by powerful magic. Like brought back to life when this place is brought back to life."

The gnome stepped into the hallway, looking left and right in the light of Aiyana's staff.

Reggie and Aiyana exchanged worried glances.

"What're you worried about?" Griffon asked. "Aren't you a mage or something? You can handle them!"

"No, I can't," she said flatly.

"Really?" Reggie said, leaning back in surprise. "But you're like one of the most powerful spellslingers on the continent. Well, at least from what I've seen and heard."

"It's true, I may be," Aiyana said, following the gnome, "but these liches are from a thousand years ago, an age where magi held a lot more power than now. And there wouldn't just be one, from what the gnome says, there'd be…more."

"Thirteen," Griffon said over his shoulder, "well, twelve if one got away and became a god. How do you become a god, anyway?"

"He got out on the Day of Phāz," Aiyana said, as if that answered the question.

"Um," Reggie mumbled, "what's that mean?"

They moved to an intersection, and Griffon inspected the walls, reading the glyphs to choose their direction.

When they started moving, Aiyana answered.

"It happens every four years, an extra day between the end and beginning of calendar years. It's a time when magic is boosted," she continued, "and if legends are true, and this is where Verl'zen-luk came from, it only shows itself on that day. And he became a god by challenging other gods on that day, killing them, and taking their power. It's the same day that the Towers of Onyx first appeared across the land, and a few other things. The Travelling God changed forms because it ripped away part of his power in the fight. Onyx took over ritualistic magics. The Travelling God took over innate magics."

"And what did ol' Verlzie get?" Griffon asked.

"Everything he wanted," she said, "darkness, evil, destruction, power. He took what he wanted, then threw the scraps to others waiting in the wings. He may have been the one that manipulated Onyx into making his move at the same time."

The group fell silent, continuing to make their way towards their goal, Griffon checking each intersection to find the path. The light only lit a few dozen paces ahead, and darkness seemed to follow them from behind, devouring the retreating light. The gladiator was unusually quiet, lost in reflection.

This is so chuzzing much, he thought. *I'm traveling with one of the most powerful mages around, and she's afraid. Here I am, just a little person with a sword. Sure, I'm strong and skilled with my weapons, for a gnome. But that doesn't mean I can go toe-to-toe with an undead that could become a god. Maybe I should tell the others about the rest of the stuff I read on the walls of the portal room.*

It's too late now. He shrugged and led them towards the throne room. *If I say something now, they'd probably be all mad that I didn't say something before. They would've probably just let us die in that first chamber if I'd told them. Besides, I've gone up against gods in games before. They set up the dungeons so you can beat them. You just need to know the secret to that level. And I'm smart enough to beat any game!*

The hallways weren't dusty, per se, but had a layer of sandy grit. Their feet shuffled on it, causing whispers of their movement as they navigated the tomb. Griffon's nose became clogged with grit, and he felt it in his mouth, grinding between his teeth whenever he moved his jaw.

The air was stale, as if it had been far too long since the halls felt a breeze, and low ceilings—just a little taller than Reggie's head—gave the entire place a claustrophobic feel.

The passage ended in a pillared throne room. The light from Aiyana's staff caught thousands of crystal shards and beams of light shot from pillar to pillar, transforming the chamber from a dark hole to a dazzling spectacle.

Chapter 11

Reggie looked around, his heart beating with excitement at the sheer immensity of the throne room. Gold filigree and silver inlays decorated every surface. Swirls of precious metals interwove with gems of every color but were dominated by the light-spreading crystals.

"Magic?" he asked, pointing at the beaming quartz-like mineral throughout the room.

"Probably," Griffon shrugged, looking like he was trying not to be impressed.

It was hard not to be, though, and Reggie didn't hide his amazement. This was the sort of find that every archaeologist dreamed of discovering. The untouched tomb of an ancient person of power.

"Who made this place?" Reggie whispered in admiration. "And if it was a prison, why make it so ornate for the sleeping dead?"

"They made it," Aiyana said, her voice quiet, taking in the décor. "The men imprisoned here. It's in the middle of The Great Desert, but it wasn't always a desert. When they first came here, it was a thriving plain. They sucked it dry, and anything within a week's ride became a sandy waste. When they were locked away by the other mages, it pulled even more of the life from the region, creating what is now known as The Great Desert. We lost any other name for it to history and shrouds of myths."

"Very poetic," Reggie said, looking around in awe, then saw the look on Aiyana's face.

"Not the land dying," he corrected. "The way you put it. That was poetic. Anyhow, what's our next step? I see eight doorways leading out of here, including the one we came through."

Both Aiyana and Reggie looked at Griffon.

"I guess we look into each of the side chambers, and we'll find the map room," the gnome shrugged.

"Yes," Aiyana said, her voice slow, low, and terse, "but are there any traps or guardians?"

"Do I look like a trap-tripping thief?" he asked. "Or some Wikipedia page all about the Tomb of Dead Mages? I don't know, but I guess we can go find out."

Griffon walked into the room like he was taking an afternoon stroll, and he even tried to whistle. Tried was the keyword. It came out as an airy hum more than anything else. And even that trailed off as soon as his mouth dried out, the air sucking all available moisture from any source around.

Reggie followed, gesturing for Aiyana to stay behind him.

"I don't need a nursemaid," she snapped.

Reggie stopped, and so did Griffon, turning to look at the aeifain.

"I know you don't need a nursemaid, Aiyana," Reggie said, his voice placating, "but we need you. And if a trap is sprung, I'd rather myself or the gnome take the brunt of it, rather than yourself. Actually, I'd rather Griffon take it, but beggars can't be choosers."

"Hey," Griffon groused, "you know I'm right here and can hear you, right?"

"Yes, but you're tough," Reggie turned to the kid, "and you've got some, how do you like to say it, mad skills? With your massive sword. Which, I must say, impresses everyone who sees it. I mean, men and women alike stop and stare when you handle your massive weapon."

"Yeah!" Griffon's face lit up. "I know, right! Wait a minute…"

The gnome looked dubious.

"Are you throwing shade?" he asked. "Shining me on? Messing with me?"

"If any of those are bad things," Reggie said with a straight face, "then definitely not. I am completely serious right now."

The gnome visibly preened, and Reggie shot a quick grin at Aiyana, who rolled her eyes.

"Can we get on with this, please?" Aiyana asked.

Griffon turned back to the room, then stopped.

"Oh, wait!" he said, spreading his hands out to his sides. "Hydrate!"

"What?" Reggie asked.

"Streaming games is exhausting," Griffon turned to explain, digging into his pack, and pulling out a waterskin. "We need to drink."

He followed his words with action, squirting a stream of water into his mouth.

The other two exchanged looks and shrugged, each pulling out their own water and drinking.

Reggie uncorked his canteen—something most considered something new he'd picked it up in the Rammen city—and took a few quick gulps from the cloth wrapped metal flask.

"Okay," Griffon nodded and turned back towards the open passages on the right-hand wall, "let's do this thing. Just do it. YOLO."

"Hey," Reggie said.

The gnome turned around to look at him, his eyes brows raised.

"Let me take the lead," Reggie said. "There's no glyphs on the wall, and my experience may do better than your bravado."

"Sure," Griffon shrugged, "why not, old man?"

Reggie moved forward, watching the throne. In his world—the real world in his head—he'd never actually encountered any booby-trapped ruins. People didn't leave things that would kill anyone, except curses. Which he'd never believed in before, but in this world, which was very real to him right now, it was a proven possibility.

"Do you both see that?" Reggie asked, pointing towards the throne.

The others looked, Aiyana cocking her head, and Griffon squinting as Reggie watched their faces.

"Um, no?" the gnome said. "Is it a ghost?"

"Possibly," Reggie replied, which made Griffon do a double take, "but probably not. There are footprints. They're covered by a layer of…whatever, sand, dust, something. But there was a fight here. Maybe a half dozen different people, and lots of scuffs and marks in the old layer, covered by a new layer."

"Hmph," Aiyana grunted, and the men looked at her. She raised one shoulder and tilted her head. "Probably when whoever freed Verl'zen-luk came in here."

Reggie considered, nodded, and moved forward to the wall. He followed the side of the room, looking at each pillar, which matched the ones in the portal room, but on a more massive scale and with ornate decorations embedded in them.

He reached the first chamber, gestured for Aiyana to join him so he had some light, and looked in. It was a smaller room, lined with benches. Wide charcoal braziers sat in each corner; the rigors of time had hardly touched the wooden seating.

"A waiting room for visiting dignitaries," he guessed, "so they could hear everything said without being seen. More of an insult than anything, making them wait without witnessing what was going on."

They moved to the next opening and repeated the process. Reggie gasped when the light from Aiyana's staff lit up the room.

The entryway was in a corner of the new chamber, and the builders lined the walls with relief carvings of the world. One had a full oval showing all the continents. A second showed the continent they were on, Teurone, in detail. It included geographical features and points of interest, and a key to the right to help decipher it. The third wall showed the region—Reggie guessed—the place they now stood had once dominated.

The last wall showed a map of the ley lines crisscrossing the continent, and how they intersected with major cities, roads, natural features, and magical nexuses.

Aiyana pushed past Reggie—causing him to stumble—and beelined for the wall of ley lines.

The wizardess moved past the massive stone table dominating the center of the room and stared at the wall, captivated, her head pivoting left and right, taking it in. She nodded as if listening to someone talking to her, agreeing with them.

"Something of interest?" Reggie said from over her shoulder, making her jump.

"Yes, very," Aiyana nodded, her arms folded with one hand on her chin, and the other pointing where she was looking, her words coming out slowly as she studied the relief. "I can…"

The wizardess trailed off, her attention focusing on the wall.

"Yes," she mumbled, distracted, and nodding again, "you could be right."

Reggie looked around, taking in an ancient source of military and magical strategy. He'd seen bits and pieces of this ancient complex in the memory of the other man who'd died, but not like this. Thomas only saw the entryway to the temple and a single interior room, and Reggie would be able to recognize it when he returned to delve the mysteries of where an evil man had plotted to overthrow the gods.

Here was a map room built for global conquest, or maybe just to set up Verl'zen-luk's rise to celestial power?

Reggie wondered what else lay forgotten in the other rooms off the throne room. It could be anything, from lost gifts of emperors to powerful magical tools to enslave a civilization. Sure, it could be gold and jewels, but those things didn't have the draw that secrets held. He wanted to know how—and more importantly, why—someone did what they did. And someone who wanted to rule the world, and overthrow the gods themselves, that would be the ultimate in sociopathic tendencies, if not outright psychopathic.

The artistry that went into the carvings was astounding, and Reggie wandered down the mental rabbit hole of how they got the information. In his world, men had mapped continents and ocean currents, just imperfectly. But there was a chunky style to the land masses when it wasn't right. These looked right, but maybe they weren't.

"Hey," Griffon said, "I got the thing! It's called the Scepter Key, and it was right here, in the center of the table."

Reggie glanced at the table, thinking it resembled a Zen Garden, covered with a thin layer of sand and small figurines of horses, troops, buildings, and other items of note.

The gnome was standing in the center of the table, pointing down to a place where he'd dug away the sand. An indent in the shape of a scepter lay empty in the middle. The item in the gladiator's hand looked like a thin, elongated ankh, but without the crossbar below the hoop.

Reggie smiled and shook his head, haranguing himself for trying to superimpose the cultures he'd explored into this new and alien one.

The building rumbled, a noise that was heard and felt, sand drifting down from the ceiling. Distant thumps echoed through the chamber, and it made Reggie think of the sound when they opened the door of the portal room.

"We need to go," he said, urgency in his voice, "now. Right now!"

"But I'm not done—" Aiyana said.

Her words were cut off as Reggie grabbed her arm and pulled her towards the doorway.

"Griffon," Reggie barked, "weapon out, and give the scepter to Aiyana. You take the lead, head back to the portal room, defend the wizardess. I'll guard our rear."

"What's going on?" Aiyana asked.

The wizardess planted her feet, put a hand on her hip, and thumped her staff against the floor.

"I think we just opened all the doors of whatever else was put to rest here," Reggie explained, spinning the aeifain towards the door, "and they may come looking for what woke them up."

"Oh, bidj," Aiyana swore, moving to follow the archaeologist's instructions.

"Aiyana," Reggie said as Griffon drew his blade and moved in front of the group, "keep that light going, no matter what, and use your magic over the gnome's head on anything that gets in our way."

She nodded and stepped into the throne room.

"Quickly, Griffon," Reggie urged. "Maybe they'll take time to wake, or maybe they're already filling the halls."

The throne room, scattered with brilliant beams of light, was empty except for them, and they half walked, half ran for the passage that led them here.

They moved through the halls, retracing their steps, taking three turns before something appeared in front of them. From a side passage, three figures lurched in the hallway, coming towards the light.

Griffon let out a guttural war cry, calling upon Torr, and charged the figures. His sword lopped off the head of the lead creature, and a gout of flame from Aiyana took out another. The gnome spun, his blade ripping through the midsection of the third. Coming to a stop, he withdrew the weapon and thrust it into the triangular opening where a nose once had been on the third creature. The sword slid into the thing's skull, piercing whatever was behind the glowing orange eyes. It collapsed onto the grit-covered floor.

Aiyana dropped balls of flame on the animated, desiccated corpses as she strode past them, finishing the job.

Reggie followed, shaking his head sadly at the beings that had lived a thousand years before dying for their final time, wondering what knowledge of history died with them.

A blue, glowing spectral figure in robes rippling in an ethereal wind blocked the next intersection.

Griffon hesitated and the three stopped.

"Will steel hurt that thing?" the gladiator asked.

"I don't think it will," Aiyana growled, "step aside and I shall dispose of this abomination of—"

She didn't finish her sentence; the undead wraith screamed and surged forward.

The sound made Reggie go cold to the bone, like he'd been in a chill artic wind without a coat. He stiffened, locking up, and his sword arm trembling. He couldn't take his eyes from the thing.

Griffon whimpered, the small noise filling Reggie's mind, and his own voice echoed the noise.

A golden light flooded the hall, and the swashbuckler wanted to close his eyes and shut out the warmth and comfort of it, but he couldn't. He mentally reached out for the pain and anguish of this figure in front of him as he heard words of power in Aiyana's voice.

Amber and yellow rays shot through the thing, and its ghostly form shredded like a flag left in strong winds for too long. The undead spirit struggled forward, transparent clawed hands reaching for someone outside of Reggie's range of vision.

A strangled scream came from the man's left, and a magical wave of bright energy washed over the penumbra. It struggled like fish straining against a current, shreds tearing away from it until nothing remained.

Reggie's breath—that he didn't realize he'd been holding—rushed back into his lungs. He collapsed to the ground, Marcid clattering to the stone beside him.

He looked up from his hands and knees and saw Griffon dealing with a similar reaction to the…whatever it was.

Shuffling and moans came from every direction, and the archaeologist realized the worst nightmare researchers of antiquities feared the most: the dead had risen, and they were not happy about it.

"Get up, boys," Aiyana urged, "there could be more, so suck it up, and let's get out of here before they organize."

"What?" Griffon said, pushing back to his feet from where he'd been laying, weeping, on the floor. "You think these things organize? In all the other games, only three or four mobs were ever linked. We always laughed when we'd take out trash mobs, and the other pat—or patrols for you newbies—wouldn't even flinch because they were just a smidge too far away."

"Oh," Reggie said, recovering his magical rapier, and sighing, "I'm pretty sure these things will let all the other crazy things know. This is real, not some game."

"Sure, old man," Griffon teased, "and I won't log out after we do the big boss or have total wipe. A TPK, or total party kill for you old people."

"Shut up," Aiyana said between gritted teeth, "and let's get back to the portal room before we run into more than one of those things."

That was enough to get them moving. The next few encounters were a handful of the first kind of walking dead they'd faced. Griffon took down most of them, with backup from Reggie. Aiyana torched the twitching corpses in passing, making sure they stayed really, truly dead.

They burst into the portal room, the wizardess working the lever to close the door after Griffon pulled it closed.

"Where's this go, gnome?" Aiyana spat, holding up the Scepter Key that she'd picked up when the gnome had dropped it while encountering the wraith.

"There," Griffon pointed at the indent on the column without arguing or a snarky comment, "and that should remove the lockdown, and let you put your magical jammy-whammy on it, and make us a way to where we want to go."

The aeifain took two long strides, slapped the artifact into place, and a deep blue swirl filled the space between the pillars. She raised her hands, twisting them, as if dialing a knob no one else could see.

"In we go," Aiyana said, stepping into the energy vortex.

Griffon whooped and jumped in behind her.

Reggie paused, looking around the room.

"So much here," he said to the empty chamber, "so much lost knowledge, so many beings who knew things no one else knows."

Clawing at the door drew his attention, and he sighed.

"But they don't want to talk about it," he muttered, "and will kill to protect it. But I will return to…"

He paused, his eye on the glyphs on the wall, dancing in the portal's light. He squinted, wondering if what he'd just spotted meant anything, especially if it meant what he thought it meant.

"Disease of the dead?" he said to no one.

With a shake of his head, he stepped backwards into the vortex. The portal took hold of him, and he reached out, snatched the scepter from its resting place, and pulled it to his chest.

The surge of travel, power, and the magical reconstruction of his entire being, burst inside of him. He'd vomited more than once after moving between places, and he wasn't sure if this wouldn't be another time that happened.

A room burst into reality around Reggie, jarring his body and mind like slamming into a lake after leaping from a tall cliff. He collapsed to his knees, losing the remnants of his last meal.

"Oh, man, lightweight!" Griffon chided.

"Hush gnome," Aiyana's voice came from pitch black, and then her staff reignited.

The chamber burst into visibility, and had a familiar feel, but new at the same time.

"We made it," she whispered, "but I don't think we were here first. I feel…something else here."

Chapter 12

Aiyana heard the whisper in her head, louder than it had been before, sounding like an actual voice.

You have made it, child, the voice was clear, almost loud, and Aiyana felt a pleased tone in the feminine sound. *Soon you may be able to release me. Just raise the hidden city, remove the trolls that move across the surface, and find me. Once you've done all that, I shall be able to touch the world again.*

Who are you? She asked the being that had been calling to her for years now. *And why should I trust you? You could be...*

"Sweet," Griffon's very real voice cut through the answer of the voice in Aiyana's head, "look at this place! No sand, that's a great start. Are we in another dungeon? I've never moved from one dungeon to another. Or is this the same one? What're we facing? Elder gods? A cult? Fish men from below the waves?"

"You're a pemtie," Aiyana said without looking at the gnome, instead studying her surroundings. "This is not some pemtie-ass game, you pemtie. This is the real world, and the sooner you realize that, the better. Chuzzing pemtie."

"Wow," Griffon grinned, "she can actually swear. I'm impressed, and more than a little turned on."

Ignoring the gnome, Aiyana felt the weight of the soil above her, and currents of earth ley lines threading all around her. She felt points of power, like artifacts of mind mages set to boost their abilities. Flavors of alien magics trailed across her arcane senses, hinting at points of summoning. Anchors of holy power shone in her mind, chapels to various gods that pulsed with power. Conduits ran through the underground complex, like veins in some mighty behemoth sleeping beneath the world.

"I never knew this was all down here," Aiyana breathed.

"What was that?" Reginald asked, tucking the scepter key into his satchel.

"Where'd you get that?" she asked, pointing at the artifact.

"This?" the archaeologist held up the key. "I grabbed it right as I came through. Thought it would be better if we had it and keep those things from using the portal network to get around the continent."

"Good thinking," Aiyana gave a sharp nod.

"But they can still walk out the front door, right?" Griffon asked, sounding a little concerned.

"I assume so," Reginald grunted, closing his satchel. "I believe we unlocked all the doors when we grabbed the scepter. But they'd have to cross an immense desert to reach anyone. And bodies of that age don't do well in direct sunlight, battered by grinding sandstorms, and oven-like temperatures. They'd likely be nothing more than dust by the time they reached any city or village."

"Like, sentient dust?" Griffon asked. "I mean, would the undead consciousness be inside the little dust cloud? And what would happen if someone breathed them in? Could that spread a disease, or something, like during the 'Rona pandemic?'"

"I guess," the archaeologist shook his head, smiling at the small man's sudden concern. "Why all the worry, chap? It's like you pushed all your chips into the pot, then an ace hits on the river, and you're holding jacks. What has you so worried?"

"It's nothing," Aiyana interrupted, "he's being a pemtie, like he always does. Ignore him."

Griffon stuck out his tongue at the aeifain as she turned away to study the room, and Reginald chucked the gnome on the shoulder with a grin.

"I saw that," the wizardess said with her back to them, "now hush and let me concentrate. There's something going on here, and I need to figure it out."

Nine Towers when built, the voice in her head said, *then four destroyed, and one sat atop their ruins. Which four were destroyed, and why them? And in the place that once had the greatest minds on the planet working on the hidden secrets of magic, why didn't they know Onyx was coming, aided by Verl'zen-luk's mad quest for power?*

Taking in her surroundings, Aiyana let the voice wash over her. It wasn't trying to control her, but instead it was asking questions she wouldn't have thought of, in ways she wouldn't have considered.

Between the various libraries at Icon Hall, Rugber Whitley Estates, Dargaon's Hole, and others, Aiyana thought, interrupting the voice, *I only need a few more things to figure out how to send a message through time. Do you think we can find that here at the Nine Towers of Magic?*

If there is, the voice said, *it will either be the library, the headmaster's private quarters, or the vault of the Division of Protective Evocation Services. Maybe a bit of both? They are the two remaining vestiges of unlooted knowledge within the complex.*

Aiyana looked around. The chamber was longer than tall, and large enough that the ceiling felt low even though it was too high for any of them to reach, even on tippytoes. It stretched into the distance. The portal faded on the wall behind them, and three rows of columns ran the length of the room ahead of them, tables spaced in between each. Brackets for torches—with a hook for oil lamps jutting from it—were on opposite sides of every column, and a quarter of the way around the rounded surface were more hooks, for hats, cloaks, or bags.

Beakers, flasks, tubes, and long-defunct burners littered the tables. A few cloaks and coats hung on hooks, and someone had stacked stools along the wall, one turned upside down on each of the upright ones.

The room was cool, like a cellar, and neither damp nor dry. The furthest corners of the room hid in the murk of shadows where the light from Aiyana's staff couldn't reach. There was an aroma of old herbs, chemicals, old tomes, and musty dank that layered the room, covering every surface and rising with each step. Those spices and seasonings, crushed in ancient mortars with lost pestles, mixed with the alchemical oils and acids long past and coated her throat. It made Aiyana scrape her tongue against her teeth, vainly trying to get the taste out of her mouth.

"Hm," Aiyana mumbled, walking in a wide circle, taking in her surroundings. The slap of leather soles echoed with each footstep, accompanied by her staff hitting the floor.

"Talk it out," Reginald encouraged in a quiet voice. "Hearing it may help, and we may be able to add to your own observations and thoughts."

"They built the Nine Towers of Magic," Aiyana said slowly, "to study magic and further the ability to wield it. But they were destroyed when a new god of magic rose to power, quite suddenly. That was Onyx. He rose on the back of Verl'zen-luk, whose tomb we just escaped from. And we came here, to the one place that Verl'zen-luk's lackey wanted to utterly crush."

"Oh," Griffon drew out the word, "good world lore! Great plot for the dungeon bosses. So, what's it all mean? How's it tie together so it helps us beat the boss?"

Aiyana looked at the gladiator but didn't see him. She looked through him, working at the problem in her mind, trying to shuffle the puzzle pieces together so they fit and make a larger picture.

"Is that why it was abandoned?" Reginald asked.

"What?" Aiyana said, focusing on the archaeologist.

"Did the people leave here because Onyx showed up and tore down the towers?" Reginald clarified. "Most civilizations are abandoned for a few very particular reasons. Natural disaster on a massive scale, including disease, volcanic explosion, and so on. War, and the populace is killed or enslaved, and they leave the land empty or burnt to the ground so they can't rebuild their culture. And the third reason is a mystery."

"That sounds interesting!" Griffon chimed in. "What is it?"

"That's exactly it, Griffon," Reginald said, slipping into his lecture voice, "we don't know. It's a literal mystery. Back on Earth, we've found a dozen or more empires across the world, which were just abandoned. Like everyone woke up one morning, packed a bag, and walked away. Some of them didn't even do that much. We've found whole towns with beds left unmade, food on the table, and personal items still there. It's like they walked away from their entire lives for some reason. No signs of violence, or anything…they we're just…gone."

"Maybe they were abducted by aliens!" the gnome suggested.

"That is something many people consider," Aiyana said. "There's a whole thing with an alien saucer crashing in Roswell, New Mexico, about twenty years ago."

"That's ancient history, girl!" Griffon laughed. "That was like back in the forties."

"I know," she nodded, only half paying attention, "and I'm from the late sixties, so just twenty years ago for me."

"What?" Griffon gaped at the woman.

"And won't happen for about another twenty years from where I came from," Reginald added.

"Weird," the gnome said, his voice full of wonder. "But what else happened to the places that just disappeared, like this one?"

"They didn't just vanish from here," Aiyana said, pointing around the room. "They cleared this place out. They took the supplies they needed and left the rest. They may have joined the new god or had some small warning signs and got out before it happened."

"Good eye," Reginald smiled. "So, what are we looking for? What's our next step here?"

"We're here to release the stored magic of this place," the aeifain said, "which may mean destroying the Tower of Onyx above us somehow."

"That's a tall order," Reginald quipped, causing Aiyana to smile. "And how do we do that?"

"We need to raise the city," Aiyana said, pointing at the far wall. "See the windows? Why would they put windows in something that's underground? This was originally above the ground, and they probably sunk most of the city to hide the power from the invaders."

"And to stop the trolls," Griffon added, and the others looked at him. "They're coming here to use that stored magic to undo what had been done to them a long time ago. Apparently, their race and yours were once the same species?"

Aiyana cocked her head at the gnome.

"Didn't I mention this back at the dragon-cave-place?" Griffon asked. "I learned this from the trolls when I was skillfully stalking them. I was like a shadow among shadows. I couldn't be seen. It was right before I killed like a dozen of the monsters."

The other two just stared, both looking ready to throttle the gnome.

"Anyway, yeah," he continued in a rush, "they said they were trying to combine all trolls and aeifain, so they could use magic again."

"Well, that explains a few things," Reginald grunted. "And should give us access to the full power—"

"Of this fully operational space station?" Griffon interrupted. Seeing the confused looks of the other two, he sighed. "Come on, Star Wars? Death Star? Don't you two know anything?"

"Nineteen sixties," Reginald jabbed a thumb at Aiyana, then himself, "thirty years before her. Remember? We don't know about all your space programs."

"We need to go," Aiyana said, heading for the single door that led out of the room, "I assume this place had a single point of control, just like Icon Hall, and we need to find it to bring the full might of—"

"This fully operational space station?" Griffon interrupted again, following the wizardess. "Can we call this place the Death Star? Please?"

They moved along darkened passages, threading their way through the abandoned ruins. Aiyana reached out with mind magics, seeking nodes of stored energy. Once they reached the foyer of the building, standing in front of the double doors that should've led outside, they stopped.

"Do you think they cleared a tunnel between buildings?" Reginald asked.

Underground network of tunnels, the voice in Aiyana's mind said.

You couldn't have told me that before now? She asked silently.

No, the voice replied, *because the door to the left is a stairwell that leads up to the higher floors, and down to the tunnels. And you should turn on the lights, to use a colloquialism from your world.*

"No," Aiyana echoed the answer from her mind. She pointed at the wide door to one side of the entryway. "We go here. It has stairs that lead to a network of tunnels that connect many of the buildings in the complex."

"They set this up like a university up north." Reginald said, pushing open the door. "Lots of institutes of higher learning would do the same so students could get around during bad weather, especially when snowed in. Amazing that such a primitive culture had similar ideas, as well. It's almost like they were more advanced in some ways than my time."

"They were," Aiyana said, pausing and reaching out with her mind, "and I'll show you."

She found the dormant reservoirs of magic, dull pulses in a dozen different places. She touched them with a flicker of power from the earth's elemental ley lines.

Crystals flared to life, casting muted, amber light along the darkened corridor they'd just left, and inside the stone stairwell beyond the door.

"That's handy," Reginald nodded, holding the door open for Griffon to pass through.

"Sure is," the gnome said, stepping through the door, "but why didn't you do that right after we got here?"

"I only just found the switch." Aiyana shrugged.

The gladiator threw a look back over his shoulder, then shrugged, as well.

"Fair enough," was all he said before heading down the stairs.

They descended in the dull murk of crystal-lit passages that branched out in a half dozen directions. Aiyana studied the words on the walls, choosing their path, and directed Griffon towards their goal.

"Will this place be guarded?" Reginald asked.

"Maybe," Aiyana sighed, "but I don't think so. It looks like they had some warning but didn't have full defenses in place for such an occurrence. My people in Icon Hall set up things so no one could take the city unless they were aeifain. The Tomb of Verl'zen-luk was rigged to stop anyone from coming in or getting out, probably by the same mages that studied here, and who learned from my people. But they never considered having to abandon this place, so hadn't set up guardians or defenses."

"That's good to hear," Reginald breathed a sigh of relief.

"But that doesn't mean there aren't lingering residents," Aiyana said. "Torrents told me that when he'd come here—but he was only above—magical constructs still roamed the grounds. They were mostly docile and avoided them, but something more powerful might be lingering. We should be careful."

As they moved through the abandoned university corridors, noises echoed around them. The thump of something dropped. Sounds of footfalls that weren't theirs, whispered voices, or a giggle in the distance. Sometimes ahead, sometimes behind, sometimes from side passages and stairs they passed.

"What are those?" Griffon asked.

"Shades of the past, perhaps?" Aiyana shrugged. "Perhaps memories of magic, or it could be something more sinister lingering. After facing a wraith a few hours ago, it doesn't seem impossible for a spirit to be still trapped in the halls."

The three fell silent.

Twenty minutes later, Aiyana spoke again.

"Here," she said, pointing at a stairwell, "this will lead us up and into the building we want."

They ascended with caution, watching for signs of anything that might be interested in them.

They stopped on the stairs to eat, and to use the privy room just outside, before continuing. They washed down the meal of dried meats, cheeses, and tough bread with water. Reginald offered a flask of brandy to the others, and Griffon accepted, gulping greedily. Wiping at his grinning mouth, he offered it to Aiyana. She waved it away, passing a hand over the small cup of water she'd poured, transmuting it to wine.

"She's got moves," Griffon giggled, reaching for Reginald's flask again.

The older man took a quick swig, corked it, and tucked it back into his pouch, then stood and readied himself to move on.

The building was decorated more than the learning hall they'd come from. Alcoves with busts of arch-magi—plaques describing their deeds and contributions to the world of magical knowledge—lined the passage. Dilapidated paintings on the walls between the niches showed signs of age and decay. Flaking paint mixed with dried rivulets of color that had run black with moisture from mold.

Some were portraits, others were scenes of moments cut from the fabric of time, and all of them had an incredible clarity. The men and women in the portraits looked like they were suffering the ravages of time that showed in the art. Strips of flesh melted away from their faces or ripped from their bodies. The drooping paint of the scenes made the atmosphere of the moment look like the people and animals were suffering in eternal torture, everything drooping, and faces drawn out to twice their original length.

The light crystals here didn't cast the gloomy amber of the tunnels below. Instead, they were a harsh flickering orange, like the reflection of distant fires on the walls, making the place feel uncomfortably warm.

Aiyana traced the ley lines and found more than one intersected with this building. Earth, air, and fire each had a thin thread coursing through the structure. The hall was lined with power focuses for mind mages, engraved with symbols of the gods on the lintels above doors and passages. The entire building was a conduit for magical energy.

Icon Hall's center of power had been almost opposite in design, built to focus power outward into the surrounding city. This place drew all power here so it could be harnessed.

Cultural differences in how humans and aeifain minds worked? Aiyana thought.

Different purposes, the voice in her head answered. One *was there to serve the populace, the other is to use the populace as a source of energy.*

They left the hallway and emerged into a large circular room. Rows of standing desks circled each stratus of the chamber. Seven circles spiraled down to the center circle of the auditorium.

"A lecture hall," Aiyana said, "I think."

"Reminds me of a surgical theater used to teach new students," Reginald said.

"Or an arena," Griffon added.

"Could be a little of each," Aiyana suggested, "but all the magical energies intersect here."

A small swirl of wind rose on the floor in the center, loose bits of debris fluttering in the whirlwind. It grew stronger, and veins of red sparks burst into existence. Dust and rocks flew up, but not caught in the disturbance, instead it formed a humanoid outline.

"Looks like—" Reginald began but was cut off as the room boomed and shook.

"Uh, oh," Griffon muttered, drawing his sword. "Magic users love to do that, don't they?"

The figure grew more solid, and Aiyana drew in power of her own.

Chapter 13

Griffon looked around, trying to figure out where best to stand for this boss fight. He missed the bright green or red splashes on the floor that told him where the danger zone was in other video games. This was much too real, and it felt like it.

In all the games he'd played, even in VR, he never had to eat, sleep, or take a dump. It showed when you were low on health or how long your special attacks lasted. Here, he didn't even know if he had special attacks.

I'll just have to make a few, he thought, *like when I gutted all those mummy things in the tomb. That could be one!*

The thing in the center of the mini arena solidified; fire, rock, and wind coming together to form a body. It didn't have legs—just a wide column of elements that looked like a dress—but two thick arms formed. There wasn't a head either, just a lump on the top, centered between what could be called shoulders. Within the head-lump, spaced every hand-span, appeared gleams of blue-green fire.

It was huge, probably four times the gnome's height, and twice as tall as Reggie, the Swashbuckler, who stood to one side and looked just as lost as Griffon felt.

It doesn't matter, the gladiator thought. *In the games, you can always hit something with a sword and do damage!*

"By Torr's fiery fury!" Griffon shouted, ducked under a railing, and dropped to the next level.

"Griffon, wait!" Aiyana shouted.

"No way," he called back, rolling off the edge to the next lower floor. "I'm gonna kick some ass!"

He traversed the next five plateaus the same way, landing at the edge of the arena floor.

Looking over his shoulder, he saw Reggie running down the sloped incline, circling the room to get to him. Aiyana was spinning her hands like she was collecting cotton candy out of the huge metal bowl at a carnival. Pink swirls of energy gathered around the woman's forearms as she lifted them upward.

Griffon barked a laugh and turned back to the foe, ready for glory. He launched himself towards the almost completely formed figure, slashing across its middle. It was like striking a wall of air and stone, his weapon stopping without penetrating or having any visible effect.

The monster flicked an arm towards him, not physically touching him, but he felt the blow all the same. A solidified column of air slammed into him, and the gnome flew backwards and up, smashing into the railing. It knocked the breath from his lungs and his sword flew from his hand, skittering across the floor. He fell to the ground, gasping, and his vision swimming.

He looked around, trying to clear his head, and noticed fist-sized crystals set into the wooden railing supports around the bottom level. There were white, blue, red, and brown for twelve in total. He stared at them, feeling like they were important and trying to figure out what it meant.

Maybe they match up with different elements? Griffon mentally murmured, struggling to catch his breath.

Rolling to his feet and scrambling towards his sword, his stomach quivered, and his lungs pulled in air for the first time in almost a minute. Snatching up the blade, he stumbled towards the railing.

He swung his blade at the nearest crystal, a red one, shattering it. The creature behind him moaned, and the sound made the gamer once again miss his daily interludes with the internet.

Griffon took three steps to one side, throwing a glance over his shoulder at the magical construct. It had both arms in the air, thick, mitten-like hands grasping at nothing.

He smashed the next gemstone, a blue one. The thing moaned again. When the gnome turned to look back, the elemental looked smaller. Just a little, but he was sure he was doing something to it.

"Griffon, no!" Aiyana screamed. "I need those to raise the city!"

"So what?" Griffon shouted back. "Die with the crystals intact or live with them broken. Simple choice!"

He moved to the next post and slashed the embedded stone. The white gem burst, sparks of light scattering across his muscular, sweating form.

Then the swashbuckler tackled him, knocking him to the ground. The floor bucked underneath them, lifting the two into the air on a pillar of stone.

"Stop it," the old, young man shouted into the gnome's face, pining his wrists, "she needs those!"

"Suck a bag of d—" Griffon's words cut off as a column of fire from above rushed down to meet the column of earth beneath him.

He shoved the human off with a twist of his hips, and rolled after the man, moments before the two elemental forces crashed into one another. The bottom pillar melted into slag, and a rivulet of molten earth slid towards the two.

Griffon rolled again, lifting Reggie with one hand, and tossed him away from the lava flow—and towards the creature—without thinking.

The man came up on his feet, his rapier shifting and growing thicker, double blades appearing at the top. He hewed into the giant, slicing out the thing's midsection in a gout of dirt and flame.

Aiyana strode between the monster and the human, thrusting her arms toward the elemental being. Pink energies shot from her hands like a wispy geyser. The magical web drifted down over the thing in the center of the chamber, coating, enveloping, and entrapping it in a cocoon of arcane power.

The elemental raised its arms, batting at the air in a vain attempt to toss the webbing away from its form. The thing's movements slowed, and it struggled weakly. A moment later, the construct's hands fell to its side, and the creature stood docilely.

"What the hell were you thinking?" Aiyana shouted, spinning to face the gnome.

"That we had to do something," Griffon shouted back, "and you two were chuzzing useless! You stood there doing nothing while this monster pulled magic in, getting ready to fry us all!"

"You, I, this…" Aiyana sputtered.

The human stepped between the gnome and aeifain, panting, his hands held up.

"Okay, everyone," Reggie said, "take a deep breath, and calm down. What's done is done. Let's see what we can do now that we have the situation in hand."

"You want to see what I can do?" Aiyana snapped and threw her hands above her head.

The elemental mimicked the wizardess, as the power of the guardian answered the command of the woman.

Reggie threw himself at Griffon, and the two crashed to the ground as a tremor rattled the building.

They were moving upward. Not just them, the entire building and, from the increasing vibration of the ground, the entire city.

Light showed through the dirt-stained panes of windows high on the walls, and a dull yellow-white orb appeared beyond one of them. The opacity of the glass shifted, the window cleaning itself as they rushed up—or the ground rushed down.

In less than a minute, the room quieted, and everything grew still.

Griffon pushed the swashbuckler off and climbed to his feet, reaching down to pick up his sword.

"If you ever," the gladiator gasped, "touch me again, I will cut you into little, itty-bitty chunks, and dance on your bloody remains. Do you understand me?"

"Shut up," the swashbuckler spat, "I saved your worthless little life. What the hell did you do?"

"I'm the reason either of you did anything at all!" Griffon screeched.

"No," Aiyana spat the word at the gnome, "you aren't. I was already creating the cage that would harness the power of the elemental. You almost ruined everything! Because of you, we almost weren't able to raise the city. That man…"

Aiyana pointed at Reggie.

"…he saved you from that elemental," she continued, "and from me. Because, so help me, by the Travelling God's boots, I would've ended you if you messed this up!"

"You don't know that!" Griffon shouted, his sword coming up.

The flat of a rapier slapped the weapon to the ground, and the gladiator turned to look at the swashbuckler standing over him, his own blade leveled at Griffon.

"Don't ever," Reggie said, "raise a weapon to Aiyana again. Or I will cut you up into chunks but won't bother dancing on the remains. Do you understand me, little man?"

Griffon's sword was a blur, slicing towards the swashbuckler. Blade met blade, and the human danced backwards, his main gauche flashing into his other hand from nowhere.

The two each took a step back and squared off. Reginald held his rapier parallel to the ground at eye level, his main gauche mirroring the position at waist level. Griffon gripped his two-handed sword at an angle across his body as the warriors circled one another.

"Boys!" Aiyana barked.

The two flicked their eyes towards her, then back to one another, neither willing to give their opponent the advantage.

"Stop this, right now!" the aeifain continued, dropping her hands, her magic dissipating. The elemental melted back into the ground, the crystals around the room going dull and lifeless again. "You're behaving like children. We have an *actual* enemy to worry about and shouldn't be fighting each other!"

Distant shouts broke into the trio's awareness, and they looked up at the windows. Guttural voices echoed through the air, and the ground trembled again. But this time it wasn't because of magic, but thousands of feet running.

"Oh, bidj," Aiyana muttered.

"What is that?" Reggie asked, turning slightly away from the gnome.

Griffon huffed, flipped his sword up, and guided the tip into the scabbard on his back.

"It's the trolls, you pemtie," Griffon said, "and they're coming into the city to reclaim their lost magic. And we're the only ones standing in their way. Good times."

Zykrite studied the broken complex once called the greatest school of magic in the world from a hilltop. The city stretched upward from the churning grass and dark soil, caressed by the breeze for the first time in a millennium. Layers of sediment streamed down from buildings, sluffing off the stone walls and sliding back whence it came.

Ancient maples and oaks broke through the earth, their foliage the brilliant reds, oranges, and gold of autumn, and the aeifain laughed. He wondered if something had preserved the trees exactly as they had been, and the city had been hidden in the autumn, or if the local flora had continued to magically go through the cycle of the seasons even though they were buried.

Of the original Nine Towers of Magic, only five remained, gleaming as they grew from the ground like stone stalks of immense trees. The wizard almost expected branches and leaves to sprout from them, instead of balconies and buttresses. The four broken towers supporting the Tower of Onyx lifted the squat, ebony structure higher into the heavens.

Tiered buildings, taller than any other on the continent of Teurone—barring the Highest Spire in the west—rippled from the dark soil next. Brass and copper dome-topped structures that were as tall as any structure anywhere else in the world followed. Streets appeared; cobblestoned roads lined with brick sidewalks rose from the earth, and magical lights twinkled to life in the shadowed recesses of alleys and cul-de-sacs.

Zykrite felt a yearning for the epoch when wizards ruled the land. Civilization had expanded so much during that period. People had come together under the protection of the powerful and worked with one another to make wonders that would dazzle the people of this era.

The wizards, mages, and priests had done a fine job of preserving the city when they sunk it beneath the soil. For centuries, only the tops of the magical towers had shown, and a few superficial buildings. Mostly administrative and dormitories left on the surface for when the casters returned to claim what they'd buried. Homunculi and constructs had cared for the complex, creating, and tending gardens around the structures. And everyone thought that was all remained of the school's former glory.

Now he, Zykrite, had returned the beacon of arcane arts and knowledge to its former glory. People would thank him in hushed tones of wonder and awe. The wizard tugged on the frill of his cuff, freeing it from his coat sleeve, and pulled his waistcoat down over his belt. Adjusting his torc and rings, he tested the magic in each again, priming the magic within for use.

He thumped his walking stick on the ground. The cane was something he hadn't kept with him in Dargaon's Hole, but he'd carried everywhere else. It had been his greatest creation and was taken from him when the aeifain had imprisoned him for what they considered evil deeds. It held elemental magics, fire and lightning, something most of his people never learned.

But the girl, Aiyana, had learned about them, and much more. She'd lived with the dasism, learning everything she could about the ley lines and all that could be done through them. She'd grown so knowledgeable about portals, how to make them, direct them, and use them, that Zykrite suspected she knew more about them than the ancient builders had known.

He could only access the ley line magic minimally, but he'd attuned his walking stick to them, and his two rings and the torc around his neck each connected with different magics. This was his arsenal in the upcoming battle in a war that had gone on for far too long.

He looked at his assembled army of trolls. There were nearly two thousand of the beasts. The hairy ones from the north stayed separated from the southern ones. But the beasts would work together to get back what they thought was rightfully theirs—magic.

He'd made this plan before being imprisoned in Icon Hall, but it lost all momentum in the millennia they'd locked away him from the world. The trolls hadn't forgotten, though, and his plans had become myths among his primitive cousins. The brutes handed down the legend that told of the day when a man of magic would return to call upon the tribes and unite them. He would then raise them up and cast down their ancestral enemy, the aeifain.

After he'd manipulated Aiyana into freeing him, he'd sought the scattered tribes and reignited the memory of his legend, using the recently reestablished portal network to move across the land to find them.

Zykrite surveyed the culmination of thousands of years of work and planning and smiled. In just a few scant hours, he'd have everything he'd struggled to achieve for a hundred human generations.

He knew wards and traps waited in the city below, at least on the outside. Those were made even more dangerous, with the Tower of Onyx standing like a pitch-black pustule in the center of the metropolis. The trolls thought he wanted the city to release them from their broken half-lives, reuniting his species and theirs, so be one again. He was fine with them fighting for their cause, but it wasn't his cause.

He had no interest in becoming one with a race of pemtie brutes who couldn't touch magic. He aspired to a higher goal, a nobler purpose. With all the magic under his control here and back at Icon Hall, he could raise other casters from the squalor this world had become. He could make Teurone great again.

Finding any others with designs that paralleled his own would be the first step. He'd offer to let them join him and squash them if they didn't. Then he'd search out anyone with magical abilities, and bring them under his guidance, nurturing them to follow his vision to a better future.

He knew he'd have some resistance, but that didn't matter. With this much power, anyone standing against him wouldn't stay standing for long.

He was the ultimate puppet master. He'd influenced the council of this city to imprison his greatest rival, Verl'zen-luk. He'd convinced the aeifain council to build Icon Hall as a repository of all knowledge and create a system where he could access all of it instantly. He'd imprisoned the one person who could have stood against him, a priestess of Promethene, in her own magical sword. The very ivory horns of unicorns she held in such high esteem it was almost worship had become the things that had locked the woman into the ivory blade.

One minor setback had seen him imprisoned, until he caught the mind of this woman from another world, Aiyana, and convinced her to continue his work, ultimately freeing him to pick up the pieces and move forward. Now, she'd raised the last thing he needed to conquer the land, bring it to heel: The Nine Towers of Magic.

He would lead the world into a new age of knowledge, under his direction, and of his making. First by taking this college of magic, then the other points of arcane knowledge and power: Pantages, the Twin Mountains, Silver Keep, the Olde Kingdom, and other nexus of arcane energies. He hoped the wizardess would join him, stand by his side, and help him guide fate to bring about his vision of Utopia. A queen, a wife, or a servant. It didn't matter which she chose to be. All things would bow to his will. One more day, and no one could stop him.

Raising his walking stick, he slammed it down once more, and a peal of thunder echoed across the hilltop and rolled into the city below, signaling his troops.

Every troll raised their voice in anticipation of the joy of battle and killing. They banged their wood and stone weapons on hide and bone shields, stomped their feet, and surged down the hill towards the city. Zykrite guided the troll leaders with slight touches of his mind magic, moving them into the ancient city waiting to be shucked like a shell of an oyster grown to full maturity.

Zykrite could feel the ground tremble at the might of his army and knew that the puppets inside—who'd been working so hard to do his bidding—would tremble, as well.

The Troll Lord sighed. The city was raised, exposing its heart to any who would take it. There was an army of his descendants rushing to do that, and two more from the other branch of the people who'd been created from his own society so long ago.

The trolls and the aeifain had come from the same stock almost ten thousand years ago.

"Or was it longer?" he asked the empty space around him. "Twenty Thousand? No, it couldn't have been that long. But I do no longer recall."

The wind hugged him gently, and the grass whispered condolences and sympathy for his loss. The pale autumn sun lay across him, warming his skin with its love. These things soothed him, calming his eternal anxiety of merely surviving so the world could go on as it was. His emotions could change the course of a river and cause a mountain to crumble into the seas.

He often wondered if it was just the forces of nature in the things he felt, or if the new gods were reaching out to him. Other gods had hunted him and his three brethren. Of the Troll Lords, one was killed, and another was missing. Perhaps slumbering, perhaps dead. Once all four were no longer walking the lands, then magic would die.

Never sure if those who hunted him knew that he considered what would happen if one found him. Would they beg for gifts, or try to take his mantle of responsibility, mistaking it for power?

Invisible to those below, the Troll Lord rose on the wind and moved towards the tower he'd chosen. There he'd wait for the others to find him, like some child's game of hide and seek.

Looking across the complex and the countryside, he could see each figure below. He saw the northern and southern trolls, segregated from one another by their own choice, and the aeifain who led them.

The promises given were possible. He could join the two races and make them one again, but they'd never be like him, or the other survivors of his people. To be like that took thousands of years of culture and growth. They may be the same in body, but not in mind and society. Their minds could never gain all the things that had been lost.

He sighed, his foot touching the stone of the balcony. He'd meddled too much over the ages, though it wasn't as often as others did. But it was enough that he was now a creature haunted by myth and hunted by legend.

It would end soon, once someone came to the tower and did whatever it was they wanted to do. He was too tired to care anymore.

Glancing into the streets below him, he saw the trolls breaking down doors and smashing windows, hunting him. He saw the three people of the other world standing on a building not far away, looking around with awe.

That made him smile a little. It was good to know there was still wonder in the land. He hoped they'd win. Maybe that amazement could give birth to hope. Maybe it wouldn't hurt to meddle again, just this once, and give things just a little nudge.

Chapter 14

"This is as tall as a twenty-story building!" Reggie said, leaning over the stone railing, looking at the street far below. "How did they get the engineering skill to build this when most other places can hardly build a three-story building?"

"Magic," Aiyana was scanning the sky in the distance. "And I know that sounds like a cheap cop-out of an answer, but it's true. In our world, men studied—"

"People." Griffon interjected, looking over his equipment that he'd spread out on the balcony.

"What?" Aiyana asked, raising an eyebrow, and looking at the gnome.

"No," Griffon corrected, "not people here. 'In our world *people* studied'. You can't just say men anymore. Keep it gender neutral. It's not the patriarchy's world anymore."

"Well," Reggie drew out the word, "that's a good thing."

"But it's wrong," Aiyana said. "Men studied all the things. Women may have helped and influenced, but even up to my time—and apparently past—we couldn't choose what the world studied. We could only go along with it and try to branch out in directions we were interested in."

"No, you're not understanding," Griffon sighed, "this isn't about women's rights. This is about gender identity. Keeping things neutral when it comes to…never mind. Let's just get ready to rumble."

"I agree," Aiyana turned back to studying the approaching horde, "but at least women are equals in your time in our world."

"Oh, they're not," Griffon said absently, arranging some rope and net. "They're still treated like bidj."

"But…" Reggie said, holding up a finger and wrinkling his brow.

"Guys," Griffon looked up from his squat, holding one hand up, "I'll explain it all later when we're not about to be massacred."

"If it's supposed to be gender neutral," Aiyana tilted her head, "why do you keep calling us 'guys'?"

"OMG!" Griffon spelled out the acronym in frustration. "Because I'm a horrible person, okay dude? I don't care about your pemtie feelings, alright man? Can we focus on dying now, guys?"

"I get it," Reggie said. "It's the same, but different."

The other two turned to look at him. Reggie was staring at the other buildings, some of them another half-dozen to a dozen stories tall.

"They did the same thing, but took a different path," Reggie explained.

He raised a hand to trace the cornerstones of a distant building a few blocks away, using his finger as a guide to his eyeline.

"They achieved buildings as tall as the Flatiron Building in New York," he continued, "I mean, nothing as grand as the Woolworth Building, which is sixty stories tall, but twenty-two stories are nothing to sneeze at. And instead of electrical lights, they have the crystals powered by ley lines, which appear to be a much cleaner source of energy than electric."

"Electric is clean," Griffon said. "I just flip a switch, and it works. Never any mess."

"Electric is filthy," Aiyana said absently. "It uses coal and oil, both of which the world has a limited supply, and pollutes the air, land, and water."

"No, it doesn't…" Griffon held up his hands again. "Stop, all of us need to stop. I get that it's pretty, and we all want the world to be a better place. But these topics will be here tomorrow, we may not be. So, let's focus, people, get your game face on. We need to figure out how to run or fight so we can survive."

"Or die while doing the most damage to the enemy," Reggie muttered.

Aiyana looked at the archaeologist. She tilted her head while giving a one shoulder shrug and dropping the corners of her mouth.

"No, let's not do that," Griffon said. "I appreciate this is a video game, but I haven't seen one person respawn, or a mob do it, for that matter. So, I'm not sure if there are respawns here, or even save points. So, I don't want to risk it. I'll play it their way. Oh, and by the by, do either of you have any healing pots?"

Reggie grinned at Aiyana, and she smirked back at him. Reggie looked at the gnome. Griffon was laying out all his gear, organizing it and arranging it obsessively.

So, that's how the kid handles stress or fear, Reggie thought. *He over analyzes and micromanages. And if that is his pressure mechanism, that means that is closer to his real self. Which means most of what we've seen of him is a façade.*

He may have a chance to be a decent human being after all. Of course, that is, if we live through this.

Turning to study Aiyana, her collected composure immediately struck him. She didn't seem confident or arrogant, but neither did she look afraid. She watched the approaching army, her arms folded underneath her breasts, and scanned the edge of the newly risen city, looking for something.

Reggie had seen leaders fear what was coming. He'd seen leaders remain calm in the face of impossible odds. He'd even seen the same leader do both on the same day and during the same battle. It was a normal process, and a good leader used the right tactic on the battlefield, and the right tactic off the battlefield. Sometimes troops needed to see you cool and calm, other times they needed to see your raw emotion. The former made them admire you, the latter made them relate to you. And too much of either could ruin their faith in you.

Aiyana had been driven since the first moment Reggie met her. She pushed herself, and those around her, and expected results. But she was different now, and the swashbuckler had seen this in other leaders as well. It was the posture of accepting the inevitable.

Aiyana watched the smudge and rumble of the mass of the approaching army growing closer, and their fate with it. She looked down into the streets, observing the breaking tide of the leading troll warriors. She didn't even flinch. Others who saw this sort of reaction called it stoic and were in awe of someone who could stand on the brink and not break. But what it really was, was acceptance. That simple.

Something about that last thought caught his attention, and Reggie focused on that.

"Hey, I had a thought." Reggie held up a finger to stop Griffon, who had his mouth open with some forthcoming annoying comment. "Let me just talk this through with minimal interruption. Bear with me on this. Something isn't right here."

"One," he continued, talking slowly, "someone sent an army to capture the city. Two, they didn't send them in to do it until we raised the city, but they had an army ready and waiting for the moment it was done. Three…"

Reggie hesitated, his eyebrows coming together as he put his next thought into words.

"Three, why send an army to kill three people? Four, what are they really getting out of this?"

The man trailed off, staring at the growing cloud of dust of the approaching force.

"Horrible," Aiyana said, staring at him with the side of her mouth quirking upward. "You started good, stating facts. Ended horribly, with questions. No consistency. If I tried that in my courses, I'd've got a failing mark. I thought you were a professor, but that was shameful whether you are or aren't."

Reggie nodded in concession to Aiyana's point.

"I think a better question would be, how do we stop an army, or get away from it?" Griffon interjected, attaching his length of rope to his belt next to a few pitons.

"I think if we address the points that I made and the questions I asked," Reggie suggested, "our conclusions will answer your question. Let's start with the last one, shall we? What are the people who orchestrated this getting out of doing it?"

Reggie clasped his hands behind his back and began pacing. Griffon opened his mouth to say something, but Aiyana laid a gentle hand on his shoulder and shook her head when he looked at her.

"They didn't do this to kill us," Reggie continued. "They could've done that anytime, anywhere. This isn't about us. We're just a tool, a pawn in their game. So, what do they get out of it? A magical city that houses great secrets, maybe?"

He stopped his pacing and turned to look at the others, as if searching their faces for clues. Neither appeared to have an epiphany that they cared to share, so Reggie started pacing again.

"I don't know!" the archaeologist threw up his hands. "I absolutely and completely have no clue! I think we have an entire city though, and if we can't fight the trolls because of their numbers and their resistance to magics, then we hide. It's that simple."

Aiyana pressed her lips together, thought for a moment, then gave a curt nod.

Griffon scooped up his pack and bedroll, slinging it over a shoulder.

"About time," Griffon muttered, "let's do something. The damn trolls will be here faster than Door Dash, but we're the meal. And, for the record, a twenty-two-story tall building is nothing. The Burj Khalifa is over one hundred and sixty stories tall."

They moved to a door, pulled it open, and stepped into a stairwell. Griffon led the way. Reggie took up the rear, with Aiyana in the middle, in their usual order.

"Where should we go, Aiyana?" Reggie asked. "I'd say you have the best idea of what here may be defensible, or at least keep us hidden from prying eyes."

"Aren't you forgetting something?" Griffon looked back at them over his shoulder. Seeing their blank expressions, he continued walking down the stairs, adding, "Don't you think we should try to stop the trolls from combining their species and Aiyana's to make them into one again? I don't even know what that would look like. Will the next generation born be like the original race, and the two divided types just die off naturally? Or maybe, would it be like the skeksis and mystics in The Dark Crystal when they get sucked back into one another? Or, ew, even worse, every troll and aeifain get sucked together making some horrible combination, like a mutant monster thing. Oh! It could be like Jeff Goldblum in the remake of The Fly!"

"They refilmed The Fly?" Aiyana asked. "I saw that picture with Vincent Price. It was horrifying."

"People!" Reggie said. "Can we talk about all this after we stop it from happening? Where do we go, Aiyana, to hide? Or is there an armory?"

"Whoa!" Griffon shouted, stumbling in his excitement. "Is there? Can you find a room full of magic armor, swords, healing potions, flying boots, fireball wands, and all that stuff? I wanna go there! Maybe they have a directory somewhere? Like they do at malls, so you can find all the stores with the cool things and avoid the boring ones with scented candles and hair bungees."

"Actually," Reggie cocked his head, "is there a place like that here? Wait, they have entire stores with just candles, and they're scented?"

"Yeah," Griffon said grimly, "weird, right?"

"Come on, boys, focus," Aiyana said. "No directory, and I don't know of an armory. But if they had one, then it would probably be located in the Division of Protective Evocation Services."

"Hold on," Griffon stopped, and turned around to look at Aiyana. "The Division of Protective Evocation Services? So, the acronym for it would be DOPES?"

The gnome burst out into a high-pitched laugh.

"Yeah," he said, "let's go there! Sounds dope to me! Is its address 420 Derp Derp Way?"

The gnome continued down the stairs, giggling, and Reggie and Aiyana exchanged glances and shrugs about the gladiator's reaction.

"If we do find an armory," Reggie said, "can we get him some different armor? I'm tired of watching his tiny, pimply butt cheeks try to eat his leather underwear."

"I know, me too!" Aiyana agreed. "And the way his nipples get all angry and red and puffy when the straps of his harness rub on them. It's freaky-deaky!"

Reggie fell into his own thoughts as they moved through the underground tunnels towards the armory.

We won't be able to use these tunnels once the invaders get settled in. It would be too easy to get cornered. Once that happens, we'll have to move the through the streets at night. Or day. I remember being told trolls have issues seeing in the daylight.

I can't shake the thought that an entire army can't be coming here just to kill us. There's more. There has to be. Something else that I haven't seen yet. There has to be an ulterior motive. Maybe it's to transform the trolls back to their original race, but I've had seen too many leaders who manipulated others to do what they thought was right and for one purpose, when, in fact, it was neither.

A magical city had to have a lot of stored weapons and power. It would be like an enemy force taking over an abandoned military base.

When they arrived at The Division of Protective Evocation Services—or DOPES—building, they came up through the basement. There'd been wards, but Aiyana took care of them using the control she'd gained in the magical arena-theater-lecture hall with the elemental.

That had been like a key to the city, Reggie thought, *realizing it to rise, but also to open almost any door in the complex at Aiyana's whim.*

Deep in the bowels of the city, below the DOPES public offices, below the level that held cells for offenders of the law, below the subbasement that held long forgotten paperwork (where Aiyana spent a few minutes looking through rolls of parchment) and crates of discarded evidence, was another subbasement. At the far end of that room was a carved stone door.

On each side was a statue of a woman in a toga. Each woman held a long sword at waist height. The one on the left held the weapon face downward, and the point touched the stone at her feet. The one on the right held it upright, and the tip touched the rock ceiling. Both statues may have once been a polished marble white, but now were almost featureless as moisture and mold had deformed, decayed, and decimated their delicate characteristics.

The door between the women was equally marred, but they could vaguely see the etchings and carvings of gods and elements underneath, along with a series of knobs and spoked handles that reminded Reggie of bank vaults or a gangster's safe back home.

Knobs, dials, and spokes spun, and the massive stone door swung open at a wave of Aiyana's hand. Inside, illumination flooded the room, causing polished steel to gleam, burnished leather to shine, and a rainbow of colors to burst forth from prisms and potions, the light reflecting and refracting from bottles and crystals throughout the chamber.

It was a room as long as the one they'd first arrived in, but not as wide, with just a single row of columns supporting the ceiling. Along the left wall were shelves from floor to ceiling, evenly interspersed with large, open-faced, vertical, cubby holes that held hooks for clothing. Above and below the larger opening was a smaller cubby. It reminded Reggie of the days in his youth when he played field hockey in the summer and ice hockey in the winter.

The shelves held all sorts of knick-knacks of various shapes and sizes, as well as books, rings, bracelets, and wands, each on a stand of its own. The longer openings had swords and other weapons within.

Open faced wardrobes lined the space between the pillars. Inside, some of these were full sets of armor, while others held various greaves, bracers, or breastplates of leather or steel. Boots, shoes, and slippers lined the floor level shelves underneath the upper cabinets.

On the right-hand wall were large, wide tables and more shelves. The tables were mostly cleared, but the shelves above held a plethora of poultices, pastes, and potions. Each row was neatly labeled and organized.

It was a veritable smorgasbord to Reggie's eyes, but he was no wizard.

"Aiyana," he said, turning slightly towards the woman, "can you tell if any of this is magical, and maybe their uses? Even if it isn't, it looks like it's quality stuff and may be an upgrade to—"

"Whoa!" Aiyana said, stumbling back and raising her hands in front of her eyes. "The entire room is enchanted. Every item, every piece of furniture, every wall, and even the floor and ceiling have magic coming off them. It's like seeing heat rising from the blacktop, but if that heat had color, sound, and sensation attached to it. It's a bit overwhelming—"

"Woo!" Griffon shoved past the two and ran into the room. "I can finally get armor that isn't exploring my backdoor gnome bolt hole!"

The gladiator ran back and forth from the shelves to the wardrobes, grabbing things and jamming them into his pouches or backpack, tucking them into his belt or harness, or just wedging them under his armpit.

"Think any of that stuff could be protected or warded?" Reggie asked, leaning against the open vault doorway.

"A bag!" the gnome said, looking around the room. "I need a magical pouch or backpack that holds a bazillion things, like I have in the games!"

"It could be," Aiyana said with a smile, "and probably has a few cursed items in here, too. Hard to say, but it's possible."

"A new sword!" Griffon crowed, his voice mimicking a game show announcer. "No, three new swords, in a variety of styles and sizes!"

"Care to wager if the gnome ends up exploding, transforming, or some other sort of life-lesson while he's just grabbing stuff?"

"Growth potion? Strength potion? Invisibility potion?" Griffon gasped, uncorking bottles, and drinking them down like they were a line of whiskey shots. "I don't mind if I do!"

"That's a sucker bet," Aiyana said. "At minimum, he's getting an upset tummy because of mixing alchemical blends. If they're even any good after sitting for a thousand plus years."

The gnome's body started stretching and thickening, his muscles swelling from the effect of the potions. The straps of his leather armor began popping, snapping off his body as it grew. His leather G-string ripped free right as he faded from view as the invisibility potion did its magical mission.

"Whew," Reggie puffed, "that was a close one. We almost got to see his little gnomish *dirk*."

"His 'gnirk'?" Aiyana pronounced the 'g', giggling.

"More like a claymore," Griffon's voice hadn't changed with his growth spurt, still coming out high and squeaky, "a huge two-handed sword, that's massive and hard to hold on to, and can rip someone in half."

"You should *see* a doctor about that," Reggie said, grinning.

"Must be terrifying to the ladies," Aiyana added, "just one more reason it has to be *so hard* for you to get a date."

An hour later, after the puns and potions had run their course, they stood ready. They'd each picked out items to bring with them to help in the upcoming battle.

"I got new armor, which is a relief because the witches had magically stuck the old stuff to me, so I couldn't take it off." Griffon jammed a thumb at his new gleaming brass cuirass, codpiece, greaves, and bracers that covered his chest, groin, legs, and arms, respectively, leather spanning the space in-between. "I guess the other magics countered it. I found a belt that makes me stronger, boots that let me leap, three new swords that can target magic, trolls, and undead. One sword per thing, they can't all do all that. I also picked up potions: healing, invisibility, smoke form, speed, and a few others. I got a ring that makes it so I never get too hot or cold, and protects me from elemental things. I got a bracelet that allows me to never get exhausted or need sleep. Another ring that makes it so I don't ever need to eat or drink. I also got a magic backpack and filled it with little statues of different animals that I can bring to life, and I can ride them, or they'll fight for me, and stuff like that! Oh, I just put a bunch of junk in there!"

The gnome ran out of breath and looked at the other two.

"What'd you guys get?" he asked.

"I got a bracelet that makes me harder to hit with a weapon," Reggie pointed out each item in turn, "a ring that makes me notice more things, and a pair of glasses that shows me things like illusions, kinds of magic, or if someone is disguised."

"Oh!" Griffon stood on his tippytoes, reaching for the rose-colored lenses perched on the bridge of Reggie's nose, "I want some of them!"

"Then get your own," Reggie slapped the gnome's hand away, and it was like hitting a slab of stone.

"I picked up these chain mail shoulder pads," Aiyana tapped the indicated items, "which will deflect weapons, and then this scaled skirt that will keep my clothes clean and repaired. They both fit nicely over my current dress and fill in a niche I hadn't had covered before."

"That's all you guys got? I mean, Aiyana, didn't you spent most of your time going through some old books and mumbling to yourself?" Griffon asked, his tone somewhere between confused and disgusted.

"Well," Reggie said thoughtfully, "I'll admit, I did get a bit greedy, but I also picked up this pouch that can hold as much as my satchel. Very handy."

"We should go," Aiyana interrupted. "We have an army of trolls to defeat."

Chapter 15

Aiyana felt the itch of impatience. Far above the well-looted, hidden chamber was a horde of monsters ravaging the city, seeking a way to activate the magic that would change them back to something that hadn't existed for…how long?

Definitely more than a thousand years, Aiyana thought. *Six thousand? Ten thousand?*

It doesn't matter, the voice in the aeifain's head answered. *The only thing that matters now is stopping them. If not for the trolls' sakes, then for the sake of aeifains across the globe. I think you've wasted enough time with your friends. It is now that you must find the collective, the Chamber of Power, that place where the greedy and selfish wizards and mages stored the power of magic, stockpiling it for their own purposes.*

And what about the trolls? Aiyana asked the presence. *Should I just kill them all?*

I'm sorry to tell you this, child, the voice said, emotion staining its tone, *but it doesn't matter how many lives end here. Including your own. If the Adversary gets what they've sought for millennium, then more lives than you can imagine will end because you failed. I chose you because you're driven. You're angry about injustice, and that's why I was drawn to you. You're seeking answers and change, and that's why I was able to speak with you.*

The voice sounded urgent and frustrated, and it made Aiyana wonder aloud.

"Are you the same voice I heard when I was seeking Icon Hall?" Aiyana's question made Reginald turn and look at her.

He watched her, considering.

No, the voice answered, *the Adversary had your mind before I got to it. They were drawing you to their own goals and blocking me from speaking with you. Now that they've been returned to their mortal form and exist in the world, they cannot enter your mind.*

"Are you well?" Reginald put a gentle hand on Aiyana's arm.

"What?" She turned to look at him, walking a step behind her. "Oh, yes. I'm fine. No problem here."

"Voices?" Reginald's single word was a question, but he went on like it wasn't. "I suppose that might not be an issue in some cases, but you've heard more than one, and it may not be the same one. Glad to hear it isn't a problem."

Aiyana didn't meet his eyes, instead watching the gnome's back as he led the way with her, directing him where to go and which turns to take.

Reggie cared for her, like a kindly uncle. He meant well, and he was a wise man without an agenda to control or manipulate her. That was odd. Most people who tried to help her wanted something.

That wasn't completely true. She'd had teachers and professors help her, guide her, encourage her in her studies. Few others, though.

Her parents pushed her to find a man, marry, and have children. Men approached her, attracted by the conquest, or her family's money, and wanting to bed her. As much as she yearned to be the pretty one, she knew better than to think she was.

In this body, she *was* the pretty one, and she quickly tired of others coveting her, or being envious. Looks like either way, people made her feel…inadequate or like she was a trophy, a prize to be won.

But Reginald didn't come across as either. Neither did Nathan. Nathan had always supported her. She loved him for that.

That thought surprised her. Did she *love* Nathan, or was she *in love* with him?

"Which way?" Griffon asked, his new sword casting a pool of light around him, spilling into the light from the magical crystals embedded into the wall niches and the light from Aiyana's staff.

She drew in a deep breath, forcefully pushing her thoughts and doubts away. She had to do this, because if she didn't, she would fail.

Clearing her mind, she pulled her shoulders back. Doubts and fears would not help her do what needed to be done. An unfettered mind would have room to face the challenges ahead.

And she had her…friends. Reginald was there, immovable in his confidence. Griffon, though a little bidj, always jumped at the next thing, not letting his mind cloud moving forward to face whatever came next.

The sound of feet on stone echoed through the hallway. Trolls, and lots of them, but it was just a fraction of the impossible odds they faced. They turned a corner and saw a dozen of the monsters crowded together, blocking the path to what would ultimately save more than their lives. It would change the world.

They stood in the way of her succeeding, resistant to her magic, fierce warriors, and driven by a greater purpose. She knew they could be defeated. Farmers had beaten the invading beasts, so she could do it.

More trolls filled the passage behind them, covering their retreat. Roaring battle cries, the creatures rushed them.

"Griffon!" the wizardess shouted. "Forward, take them out! We must get to the Chamber of Power!"

The title of the place they sought slid into her head, followed by the thought, *How cheesy is that name?*

"Reginald," she called to the swashbuckler, "cover our asses, crippling is as good as killing. Just make sure they can't follow us!"

Griffon raised his gleaming blade and cut into sinew and muscle. The magically enhanced weapon sliced through the enemy's primitive armor, flesh, and bone, along with the stone behind the beast.

Spinning, he led his next attack with an upward thrust through the throat of a second troll, jerked it out, and stabbed a third in the chest.

Reginald turned, walking backwards, his own weapons striking as fast as a serpent. One troll took a rapier to the eye, and the main gauche knocked a stone axe to the side, exposing the creature's midsection. The rapier cut back and forth three times, in a "z" pattern, and the monster collapsed under the sign of Zorro.

Within moments, the hall was littered with bodies of trolls, and the trio moved forward, stepping over the writhing forms.

"Won't they just heal and come up on our flank?" Griffon asked.

"They heal quickly," Aiyana agreed, "but not quick enough to matter in this battle. If we get to our goal, we should be able to lock them out and shut down the source of power of this place, ripping it from their grasp."

Griffon pulled a potion from his belt and gulped it down and his wounds closed, healing. The gnome pulled out two more potions and drank them. His skin writhed and changed, becoming a deep grey, matching the stone floor. His muscles rippled and his physique transformed into something from a body-building contest.

Enhanced by his magical items, Reginald moved with unnatural speed and grace, on the lookout for hidden pitfalls or enemies.

Aiyana was tired. Tired of fighting, and tired of feeling helpless. She was one—if not the—most powerful spellslingers in existence, but felt like she couldn't help because of the enemies' ability to avoid magical attacks.

But they can't avoid a ceiling collapsing, she thought, *or the claws of a summoned creature pulled from another plane of reality.*

She called upon the elements, reaching out to all five powers, and a creature rose from the stone passage. It was a mix of earth and fire, steam rising from its limbs, with a small whirlwind encasing its form. As a non-sentient elemental, but not sentient, it was a puppet of her abilities and only reacted to her.

Aiyana found her concentration cut in half. Part was to control her movements, the other to command the summoned being. The thing solidified and slid along the passage at the wizardess's command.

They emerged into a chamber with eight passageways—including the one they'd entered through—leading away at the compass points.

The aeifain could feel her goal, the Chamber of Power, pulsing like a heartbeat to the north, only a short way away.

Trolls poured through every doorway, filling the room as the three companions reached the center. They turned, so they were back-to-back, and rotated slowly to see the enemy.

Shouts filled the room, and the trolls charged, weapons raised for a killing blow. More poured in, crowding the room, the three heroes becoming the invaders that needed to be destroyed.

Wheezy saw the gnome, the little bastard who'd cut his tendon and made him limp for days. It had healed, it always healed, but it was an inconvenience that made Wheezy made him look weak and lose face in the tribe. Grunter had even beaten him in his sleep to show that he was stronger than Wheezy.

But that wasn't the way to do it, and when Wheezy had healed, he had beaten Grunter into a quivering, blubbering lump in front of the others. That was after they'd raided the human cavern, and the troll had limped behind everyone trying to keep up.

And it was all because of that scrawny gnome. The annoying elf woman was second to the gnome, and the human with the blades should just die because it was the right thing to do.

Grunter rushed past Wheezy, charging the wee warrior, axe raised above his head. The tiny terror took the blow to his shoulder, and shrugged it off, his own two-handed blade sliding into the troll's gullet.

Gurgling blood, Grunter backed away, his face contorted in confusion and surprise.

The gnome leapt across the space between them without effort, and Wheezy heard the troll-slaying sword whisper Grunter's name as it sunk into his chest. The sword drank hungrily as his life force ebbed.

Then Wheezy was there, stabbing at the gnome a half dozen times, knocking him—and the deadly weapon—away.

Wheezy smiled down at Grunter, but it wasn't a 'happy to see you' smile. It was an 'I'm going to take you out' smile. Wheezy thrust his spear into Grunter's chest.

The last thing the warrior saw was his best friend standing over him, twisting the shaft of his handmade spear. Grunter's final thought wheezed from between his lips.

"Good for you, brother," Grunter whispered and slipped into darkness.

Wheezy whirled, looking for the gnome. He'd ended his friend's life and would gain honor among his tribe for his action.

Poor Grunter wouldn't have to live with the embarrassment anymore. He'd died well. No screaming or crying, just a proud, defiant look on his face, and murmuring encouraging words to Wheezy.

The bastard gnome cut down three more trolls, laughing in mad glee, and jumped across the immense chamber to the other side. The wee warrior landed in a clump of Wheezy's tribesmen, laying about him with his pemtie, shiny sword, cutting them down.

Wheezy had always been the low man on the tribal totem pole because of his breathing problems. He didn't breathe right, gasping and struggling for air whenever he exerted himself or in damp air.

But here, in these tunnels, there was only dry air, and he could catch his breath without a problem. He'd be the hero, but only if he was smart. He backed away from the fight and called out commands. To his amazement, the other trolls listened.

This is how leaders do it, he thought. *They fight when they need to, but tell others how to do it when they don't. The other trolls admire that and do what they're told.*

Wheezy called out warnings and moved further away. Not all the way to the edge of the room, but enough that he wouldn't be attacked. There were others to face the blades of the human and gnome, and the raw power of that weird elemental.

The One of Legend had spoken of these three, and his tribe laughed at the idea that the lesser races may be of some danger to them. Wheezy listened instead of mocking. That was the advantage that Wheezy had, knowing that you could die no matter how much strength you had.

The woman wizard's magic had little, though some, effect on the tribesmen, but her elemental was breaking the rush of trolls without effort. There were six warriors atop the monstrosity, but it just took the beating and kept coming.

The flow of warriors into the room slowed as well. The tribe may be plentiful and have many, many warriors in the city, but only a few dozen down here.

Wheezy considered how to stop these monsters from keeping them from reaching their goal. He looked at the fitted stone in the walls and ceiling, and an idea came to him.

He jabbed his spear up into the mortar between two fitted stones and wiggled it. Dust drifted down and one stone fell, exploding on the floor.

"Bring the roof down on them!" Wheezy yelled to his people. "Tear out the stones. The dirt will fall and bury them!"

The gnome's head whipped to look at him. It was impossible that the little bastard could understand him. The lesser races weren't smart enough to make out the complicated language of his people. But this one seemed to comprehend.

The gnome jumped at a group of three trolls following his order—stabbing and tearing at the stone ceiling—and cut into their legs. Wheezy's brothers fell to their knees, taking thrusts and cuts to their chests and throats in reward.

"The weak must die!" Wheezy shouted, backing towards the exit. "Destroy them! Those near them, jump on them with your bodies, brothers! Those far from them bring down the roof. Let the earth do our bidding and kill these monsters so we may once again be whole!"

Wheezy retreated into the hall he'd come out of, stabbing at the mortar above. The ceiling came down, dust billowing around him, and he turned and ran, confident that none of his tribe would live to know he'd fled.

"They're bringing the ceiling down!" Griffon screamed, his sword slicing through another troll.

Aiyana looked up, the heartbeat of power so close, but so far. She saw the fitted stones coming loose and tumbling to the floor. Dark dirt tumbled after, slowly at first, then faster.

"Into the center!" Aiyana shouted, hoping that Reginald and Griffon would obey for once instead of arguing.

She called her elemental to her, commanding it to form a dome overhead and protect her and the others from the collapsing cave in of the chamber.

Falling to her knees, Aiyana threw her hands over her head, trying to protect herself from thousands of kilos of earth coming down on her head. It was foolish, but what else could she do at a moment's notice?

She felt an arm go around her and someone bend over top of her, protecting her from a mountain of stone falling on top of her and crushing her.

Reggie? She thought. *How pemtie is that man that he thinks he can protect me from the inevitable?*

Didn't you ask that once before? About another man, in another place, in another time? The voice in her head asked.

The light from the Key of Aiyana revealed Griffon sliding underneath Aiyana, using her as a shield from the collapsing room.

Reaching out with her mind, ignoring the screams around her—her own blended with that of her friends and the trolls—and bonded her summoned minion to the element of earth crushing downward. She formed a bubble, shoring it up with the surrounding bricks.

The sounds of clacking stone flying together to form shallow walls mixed with the grinding of detritus. The noises died away to a dull shifting noise of sifting sand and settling rock.

Letting out a breath, Aiyana collapsed, feeling the literal weight of the world on top of her.

"Hey," Griffon complained, "do you mind?"

She reached up, and felt Reginald's stomach above her head, as the man tried to single-handedly hold the world away from her.

"You can stop now, Reggie," she said, dropping her hand.

The man fell into a crouch beside her, looking exhausted but smiling.

"What?" she spat. "What could you possibly be smiling at in the last moments of our collective lives?"

"You called me Reggie," he grinned.

"Reggie wedgie," Griffon giggled.

The swashbuckler joined in the giggling. It was infectious. In moments, all three were laughing uproariously, and more than a little manic.

It died down to gasping breaths and ragged sobs.

"We're gonna die," emotion broke Griffon's words, "and without a save point. I don't even think we could make the dead run back to our bodies down here. And if we could, we still couldn't get out."

"Doesn't matter," Aiyana said, "even if this was a game, and what you thought was true, there'd be no air, and you'd just die again."

"Don't say that," Reginald smiled, wiping dirt-stained track of tears from his cheeks, "as long as we're alive, there's hope."

"You're a pemtie." Aiyana said bluntly, the light of her staff flickering. "We're under ten thousand tons of earth, and the trolls will reach the Chamber of Power soon. Once they do, it'll all be over."

"At least," Griffon panted, his breath coming in quick gasps, "it might suck you through the dirt and join with a troll, letting you live a long and happy life as some sort of a mutant hybrid of elf and troll."

"You're a pemtie, too," Aiyana said, less force to her words than a moment before. "And it's aeifain, not elf."

"Calling an aeifain an elf is insulting," Reginald explained to the confused gnome. "Not to mention that she might be forced into a joint body with something she considers a monster."

"We're the monsters to them," Griffon muttered.

"What was that?" Reginald asked.

"Playing these games since I was a kid," the gnome began, "I've thought how it was for the NPCs and mobs. Wouldn't we be the monsters to them? I mean, we run in, killing them, and steal all their treasure. Isn't that the bad guy? Aren't we the invaders? I know we have quests and missions, but maybe they have them, too? Protect their home from us or something?"

The group fell silent, listening to the creak of settling stone around them.

"That's very insightful," Reginald said quietly.

"For a pemtie," Aiyana added, and the three chuckled again, but with no humor.

"So," Reginald said after a moment, "how do we get out of this?"

The air grew thick, and Aiyana shook her head, causing her to wobble on her feet.

"I don't know," she muttered.

"In the Egyptian pyramids," Reginald said, taking on his lecturing tone, "they discovered air shafts. Cut at a perfect angle from the surface to the hidden chambers within. They let air flow get to the most hidden rooms within the tombs. Can you make those using your elemental powers?"

Portals: Book 5 – Towers & Trolls

Chapter 16

Reggie looked at Aiyana, trying to smile encouragingly. He felt the pressure of the depth, but he'd felt that before in his other adventures as an archaeologist.

But not like this.

The dome of dirt and detritus was barely two paces across and only tall enough for the gnome and aeifain to stand up. Reggie had to hunch slightly. The light from the wizardess's staff flickered against the irregular surface of the stones and earth, and the smell was old and dusty. It wasn't like freshly tilled soil that had a rich aroma of rain, sunshine, and living things. The sound of shifting rock and falling pebbles surrounded them.

He'd never been trapped under tons of stone in an ancient structure. There'd always been a path out, usually the same way he'd come in.

"We can't give up," Reggie said. "Let's talk this out. First thing is to get us air. Aiyana, can you make shafts about as thick as three fingers to the surface? Make them in twos, but aim to get at least four of them."

The aeifain looked exhausted and broken, staring at him with sunken eyes. But she nodded and closed her eyes, looking haunted and close to breaking into tears.

Dirt drifted down, and the light of the Key of Aiyana fluttered and dimmed. Reggie looked up, squinting, and saw thin holes forming above them.

He'd been in dangerous situations with students before, and he knew the importance of keeping them on a task to distract them.

Looking at the gnome, he wracked his brain, trying to figure out something to keep the younger man busy. The gladiator might be a forty-seven-year-old man here, but his mind was half that age, and entitled. He needed a task to help stave off panic.

"Griffon," Reggie said, and the gladiator didn't appear to hear him, lost in his own head. "Griffon!"

The harsh whisper caused the gnome to look up at him, a hopeless expression on his face.

"You got a bunch of magical things from the armory, right?" Reggie asked.

Griffon stared at him blankly for a moment, then nodded. Opening his magical bag, he began setting items out in front of him.

"Anything we can use to get out of here," Reggie went on, "or to help us in any way? Take an inventory and see what you've got."

"I have a voice in my head," Aiyana said quietly, "and it's been talking to me since before you arrived on this world. I think it was whoever was doing this at first, but now it's their enemy. So, I guess it's our friend. Or someone else trying to manipulate us. Considering the last voice helped me open Icon Hall, I don't know if I should trust the new voice."

Griffon paused in his sorting of trinkets on the dirt floor, looking up at the woman.

"This is so much more than any other game I've played," the gnome said. "It's never this real or in depth. I don't think I like this game. It's too much."

"That's life. Don't let it pwn you," Reggie said to the gladiator, setting a hand on the man's shoulder. "Go on, Aiyana. What's the voice telling you?"

Great, Reggie thought, *one is hearing voices, and the other is ready to give up when things are at their worst. But then again, so am I. I'm barely holding it together.*

"She says," Aiyana said, her words coming out haltingly, "that I could draw on the power of the city. I can act as a conduit for that energy since I've taken the key from the elemental in the place we went to. Do you think that's true? Or am I being manipulated again?"

Reggie mulled it over, and his mind turned to his time at the poker table. Many masters of the game won by manipulating others. But was this just a game? It wasn't to him; it was his life, and the life of the two people trapped with him in a dome of dirt barely large enough for him to stretch out in, and not enough for him to stand up to his full height.

"This place was a school, right?" Reggie asked, trying to keep the others distracted.

Aiyana nodded.

"And it had nine towers, one for each school of magic, right?" he asked.

Aiyana nodded again.

"But you said that when the Tower of Onyx crashed into the city—" he went on, only to be cut off by the aeifain.

"It didn't fall from the sky," she said. "It rooted and grew here. Sucking the magical power from the other towers."

"Which ones?" Reggie leaned forward, intense.

"Um," Aiyana thought about the question, her words coming out slow and considered, like she was getting the information from somewhere else. "Necromancy, enchantment, transmutation, and divination. Those four towers were crushed and absorbed into the roots of the Tower of Onyx. It left protection, conjuration—which is sometimes called alteration—illusion, and evocation (also a crossover with invocation), and psionics."

Her words were coming faster.

"The holy magics," she said, "the ones that were the realm of the gods didn't seem to be affected. This is why necromancy became a blend of the five current magics. Psionics bled over into enchantment and illusion. The ley lines absorbed evocation and invocation, being a mostly untapped force before…"

She trailed off, then continued.

"When Verl'zen-luk broke the pantheons of gods, killing some and stealing powers from others, passing it to Onyx and other new gods, it reformed how magic worked. And the Tower of Onyx settled over the Nine Towers of Magic, using Raven Stealer as an anchor."

Both men stared at her.

"Who's Raven Stealer?" Griffon asked, hovering over his collection of magical trinkets. "They sound creepy. Why would anyone steal a raven? Weirdo."

"Besides the voice I've been hearing, I'm not sure," she said.

Aiyana shook her head and sat back on her heels, running fingers through her hair, leaving a dark streak along one side.

"She says she is, was, a priestess of Promethene," the aeifain said, her head cocked, listening to something the others couldn't hear. "The adversary imprisoned her in a sword made of the horns of unicorns, which is the holiest of animals for that goddess."

"Sound and light," Reggie added, "Promethene's domain is the sun and song, communication and giving life to all things. She is a goddess of everyone, and her clergy is always female and often are the ones who run orphanages."

"Yeah, that's her," Aiyana agreed.

"So," Reggie drew out the single word, "if we get to this weapon, can we chuz up the plan of whoever has been messing with us?"

"Um, yeah?" Aiyana shrugged. "I think so, or more precisely, she thinks so."

"Why's she called Raven Stealer instead of Brittany or something like that?" Griffon asked. "Didn't she have a real name?"

The wizardess tilted her head again, listening.

"She lost her identity when imprisoned," the woman said, "and used as a tool against the god of chaos, Quixe, for a long time. Their symbol is three ravens and is one of Promethene's allies. But Raven Stealer was used to create a rift between the gods."

"Let's stick to what we need to do," Reggie suggested, bringing them back on track. "We get to the sword, and since it's the anchor for the Tower of Onyx, what would happen?"

"It would cause problems at minimum," Aiyana smiled, "but first we need to get out of here."

Reggie drew in a deep breath, then pointed at the shafts the elementalist had been making.

"Looks like you've given us a fighting chance," he said, "and since we can breathe and won't be dying of asphyxiation in the near future, we can plan for the rest. If—when—we make it out of here, can you use your magic to drop a building on the trolls, or flip a road over them? Would that hurt them?"

"I think so," Aiyana nodded.

"And with your power over earth," he continued, "can you make a tunnel heading straight for this Raven Stealer?"

The aeifain considered, then nodded again.

"Yes," she said, "I think I can do that, but I need to eat first. I'm pretty exhausted, and barely keeping the world from falling on our heads. You're asking a lot of me."

"Okay," the swashbuckler said. "We eat, drink, and rest a little. Then we go."

"I don't think we have time to rest," Aiyana sighed. "The longer we wait, the closer the 'Adversary' gets to their goal of harnessing the magic of the towers."

In less than an hour, Reggie stood behind Aiyana as she redistributed the earth and rock around them, creating a tunnel leading towards the artifact they sought. Moving the dirt from in front of them to behind them, she created a constantly shifting arched tunnel. They took a few steps forward, and she moved the earth to where they'd been a moment before.

It didn't feel like they were making progress, and the aeifain showed the psychological strain of being underground. Her race was one of the open air, sun, and forests.

Griffon was doing better, being of a species that lived underground most of the time, coming to the surface for trade and foraging. But even the gnome showed signs of stress. Wide-eyed and sweating, the gladiator didn't even complain or keep up his constant flow of inane complaints and bragging.

Reggie had been underground often enough that he knew the feeling, but he'd always been able to walk out the way he came in and into the open air. This was very different, and his nerves were frazzled. He tried to keep calm and stay encouraging,

Time passed slowly, and the weight of endless earth above them made Reggie hunch, even though Aiyana kept the ceiling high enough for him to stand up straight.

When they broke through a wall to one of the underground tunnels, they all sighed with relief.

"It's in front of us," Aiyana pointed at the wall across from them, "do we try to find it in the maze of rooms, or do we keep pushing forward like we've been doing?"

Reggie didn't want to go back into the box of enclosed dirt they'd been trapped in for what seemed like forever, but trolls might be in these halls hunting them, and he said as much.

"We might run into trolls if we try to find it through the halls," he said, "and there's a good chance that the room the sword is in is secluded and not connected to the main passages. Can you keep doing this?"

"Well, I can," the aeifain sighed, rubbing at the dirt on her forehead, "and it'll be easier since I can fill this hall with the dirt and create a larger opening for us to move through. But it'll also be harder to move that much more dirt. So, it's win-win, or lose-lose, depending on how I hold up."

Her clothes were still spotless because of the magical scaled wrap around her waist, but that didn't appear to extend to her body.

"Why don't you just throw the entire city into the air?" Griffon muttered. "I mean, kill a bunch of trolls, topple the buildings, and kick some ass! That'll mess with this chuzzing pemtie!"

"Griffon," Aiyana said, and her voice was patient and commiserating for once, "I feel the same way. But I want to save as much of this place as I can, so I can release the magic to the world. I want others to be able to access it when we're done."

"Wouldn't my way do the same thing?" Griffon asked.

Aiyana considered, smiled, then shook her head.

"Yes," she said, "I think it would. But it would make it much harder to find this holy relic that can help us end this for good."

Reaching up, Reggie took a glowing crystal of light from the niche on the wall where it had rested for more time than he cared to consider.

Looking at the light source, Aiyana nodded her thanks and released her own light on top of her staff. She turned to focus on the far wall and held her arms out in front of her and pulled her hands apart from one another.

The side across the hall ripped open, the fitted stones shifting to form a half wall on each side of them. Dirt slid and tumbled, shifting to the other side of the alternative route, and moving behind them to fill the alcove that the wizardess had left open when they'd broken through.

Looking at Aiyana, Reggie saw she was exhausted. He and the gnome only had to walk along beside her, but she had to control the elements themselves. People didn't realize that magic had its own cost. Though it may not take the same toll as using a pick and shovel, you did pay a price for the power.

The tunnel formed slower than before, sluggishly rolling past them to pack itself into a wall on each side of the passage they left.

Reggie worried the woman would drain herself before they faced the trolls and whoever was controlling them. If that happened, then it would be up to him and Griffon to face down thousands of trolls and someone powerful enough to have brought them all to this place.

It didn't look good for them. But they pushed on, each step back into the gloom of the personal shaft thrusting through the underground a challenge, mentally, physically, and for Aiyana, spiritually.

Reggie didn't know how long it took. Time passed oddly when in the bowels of the earth, but eventually another wall of stone crumbled in front of them.

Reggie had an expectation of the hidden chamber and guessed the others did as well. He was disappointed though, and turning to look at the others, he saw they were also underwhelmed.

Instead of a grand cathedral with ornate architecture and scrollwork marking a powerful artifact of magic, this was a dank tomb. There weren't any features to make the chamber stand out. Nothing.

It was an enclosed space with a floor of loose-fitting cobblestones without mortar. The walls were plain and squared off, and there was barely room for the three to crowd into it.

In the center of the floor was a dusty blade, unceremoniously tossed down and left to be forgotten. There wasn't even an altar or stand for the mythical weapon. This wasn't much more than a charnel pit for someone who hadn't even had a name.

But the blade drew their attention; a subtle, pure white glow rising from it. The light layer of the dust of ages wasn't enough to hide the beauty and craftsmanship of the weapon. The hilt was a thick spiraled ivory, as were the cross guards, and the long, white blade was similar material.

"She's so loud," Aiyana said, stumbling backwards, one hand touching her temple, "and joyous at our arrival. She's singing!" Aiyana gasped, stumbling to one side, grabbing Reggie's wrist for support. Continued in a whisper, she said, "As a reward, she's helping me with the knowledge I've collected, organizing the secrets I've been researching. She is the key to the schools of magic."

"I get to use it!" Griffon exclaimed, leaping forward to snatch it from the floor.

The gnome's hand wrapped around the handle, and he lifted the blade from the floor. The weapon flared, the dim glow radiating outward until it filled the room with a blinding light. The light went out, leaving only the comparatively dim glow of the crystal Reggie held.

"She's gone silent," Aiyana said breathily.

"Oh, wow," Griffon said, "she talking to me now! She sounds hot! I mean, all sweet and smoky, this is so sexy!"

"I don't know if you're the right person to wield such a blade," Reggie said, stepping forward with his hand out to take the weapon.

Griffon jerked it away from the swashbuckler.

"You both already have really cool magical weapons," the gladiator said. "It's my turn to have one. And she agrees…sorta."

Reggie and Aiyana exchanged a look.

"Sorta?" Reggie asked.

"She says I have to always speak the truth," Griffon said, his hand sliding along the length of the blade, wiping away the dust, "and that the Adversary has tapped into the source of power of the city, and that…"

He trailed off, his eyes moving down to look at his chest.

"He's sucking off the city!" Griffon exclaimed, giggling.

The magical glasses Reggie wore showed the immense magical power emanating from the blade. As he took in the sight, it faded, and he knew that his magical glasses were failing. He felt his coordination shift, returning to normal as his other magical items lost their magic.

"Aw, bidj!" Griffon whined, his backpack regurgitating the mass of items stored in it. "That bastard de-magicked my stuff! I hate this guy!"

"Yep," Aiyana said, drawing her lips into a tight line, "I can feel the chain mail and scale armor I picked up growing heavier, becoming normal."

"Chuz! Bidj!" Griffon swore, stomping in a small circle, figures, bottles, and trinkets crashing to the floor around him and shattering. "I just got these!

Worst game ever! What kind of bidj is this? Let you get all this cool stuff, then take it…"

The gnome trailed off as the crystal Reggie held winked out and the group stood in the renewed glow of Raven Stealer.

Aiyana's staff burst to life, blue, flickering flames overlapping the white glow of the artifact in Griffon's hands.

"It looks like time has run out," Aiyana said. "This jerk is draining the magic, and there's only one reason he'd do that. To get all the power for himself. It's do or die time. We either slink off with our tails between our legs and let him do whatever he wants to do. Or…we go face him and kick some ass."

"He took away all my cool bidj," Griffon said. "I say we go beat him to a pulp with my awesome new amazing unicorn sword!"

Reggie looked back and forth between the two, wondering how kids did it nowadays. He was beat down and whipped. But the only other option was to roll over and die. Giving up wouldn't solve anything, though neither might fighting.

But one was a much better option than the other.

Reggie sighed and patted Marcid on his hip.

"I've got my awesome magical weapon," he said, blinking the exhaustion and grit from his eyes. "You have yours, Griffon, and Aiyana made her own. Alright then, let's go take down the bad man."

Chapter 17

You are a heathen and a brute, the voice inside Griffon's head said, *but I think that deep inside of you, there may be something good. Of course, I've been wrong before.*

"Yeah," Griffon said, "and you said, 'deep inside you', that's hot!"

Aiyana and Kazzek (he still refused to call the swashbuckler Reggie or Reginald, and thought of him as Kazzek von Twinkletoes), looked over at him. The three were rising towards the surface of the complex above them in a makeshift elevator Aiyana had constructed on the fly.

The aeifain leaned heavily on her staff, her eyes vague and unfocused. Griffon was ready to go, though, shuffling impatiently from one foot to the other.

"You know," Kazzek said, "you can speak to the sword in your head, so we aren't forced to listen to your side of it, which appears to be mostly juvenile commentary."

"She says she likes it," Griffon smiled.

I said no such thing! Raven Stealer shouted inside Griffon's mind.

"Do you want me to tell him that?" the gladiator smirked.

You know, the sword said, *I can hear your thoughts, and I know you are terrified right now. You doubt the reality around you and just want to wake up in your own bed, tangled in the blankets, even if you've peed yourself as you used to do.*

"Shut up!" Griffon shouted. "You don't know what I did!"

Aiyana turned her head and covered her mouth, hiding her face.

Griffon glowered at the only other people he'd trusted beyond the minotaurs Tory, Tower, and Fred. The two beside him looked out for him and protected him. Sure, the old man was annoying, and the elf chick was bossy and moody, but no one was perfect.

This game, like no other he'd ever experienced, was confusing to him. He'd never been able to log out at all, never even seen a hint of it on his GUI or HUD, and wondered for a moment if this was all real.

Shaking his head, he dismissed the thought.

So, you're deluded and confused, the voice said. *Great, the perfect person to wield one of the most powerful tools of vengeance ever created by the gods. You do you realize I was made by the gods, don't you?*

She went silent for a moment, waiting for her wielder to reply. When he didn't, she went on.

He thinks he imprisoned me in this form, she said into the gnome's mind, *but he merely killed me. Promethene herself put me here. And she's brought me out more than once to fight the battle of good versus evil, but always put me back here once I was lost. I hope you will be the last to carry me, and that I may be free of this task after we slay Zykrite.*

"Zykrite?" Griffon blurted out. "*He's* the Adversary?"

"What?" Aiyana and Reggie said as one, the rock elevator stuttering in its ascent.

"She just said the guy doing all this is Zykrite," the gnome said. "Isn't that the other elf dude from that dragon cave?"

Aiyana nodded, her mouth drawing into a tight line.

Yes, the sword said, and it felt smug. *He is the one who slew me and attempted to bind my spirit to that of a dead unicorn. The goddess brought the others, sacrificing them, so I have the abilities of her holiest of holies and would be a beacon of hope, backed by their purity and grace.*

"What?" Griffon jerked a shrug at the others. "This sword is crazy, and arrogant, and thinks she's super important."

"Then you two are a matched pair, I would think," Reggie chided.

The old man was annoying and always thought that he knew best. But Griffon knew he was pretty awesome also and would totally rock the world of this guy and his trolls.

Will you now? Raven Stealer asked. *But without my help and powers, you wouldn't stand a chance.*

"Powers? What powers?" Griffon asked, glaring at the sword, shaking it.

The blade fell silent, and the elevator slowed.

"Are you okay?" Griffon asked the wizardess.

The aeifain had already looked tired. Her hair was matted with sweat, and her whole body shook. Her eyes were sunken pits, and she moved like she could fall over and pass out at any moment. But now she clutched her staff like she was in a rushing river and holding onto a branch to keep from being washed away.

"The magic is being pulled away from the city," she said, her voice coming in short bursts between shivers, "and that includes stored magics from below, and the ley lines moving through the air, earth, and rivers. That's sucking away some of my own abilities at the same."

"What about that thing?" Griffon pointed at the wizardess's staff. "Isn't that supposed to be like the most powerful magic item on this continent? Except for my sword, of course."

The gnome patted the ivory blade in his hand.

"My staff hasn't been affected," she replied, "but I think that's because its creation wasn't tied to this place."

"Same for Marcid," Reggie patted the rapier on his hip, "but my glasses and the other jewelry I picked up in the armory no longer seem to work."

The gnome looked up and saw the turf above him opening like twin doors, folding back so the rising platform rested even with the landscape.

Trolls rushed around them, attacking small demonic looking beasts and animals in some sort of insane rage.

"What are those?" Reggie asked, pointing at one of the knee-high beings that Griffon thought were demons.

"Homunculi," Aiyana answered, sounding tired, "magical constructs created by mages or wizards to assist in tasks. No one has used them in decades. But they and familiars were once commonplace. The former being created, the latter being animals bonded to a spellslinger who cast a very specific ritual."

"Heads up, incoming." Using Raven Stealer, Griffon pointed at a group of trolls who'd broken away from the others and moved towards them. "Boy, they always looked like someone pissed in their Wheaties!"

"They still have Wheaties in your time?" Reggie asked, drawing his rapier and main gauche.

"Yes, Kazzek," Griffon sighed, "you can still buy old people cereal in my time."

"Make this quick, boys," Aiyana panted, "we need to get going. I have a date with an arrogant aeifain, and I need you two to cover my back while I take care of him."

"I'll get their aggro," Griffon shouted over his shoulder, "you guys DPS!"

The gnome was already moving, the ivory blade in his hands whistling through the air. The first troll went down, both of its legs severed clean through. Toppling sideways, the giant landed on top of its dismembered limbs with a scream.

Griffon didn't stop, already engaging the next pair. Thrusting into the belly of another, he pulled the sword sideways and tore out the creature's midsection. Following through with the cut, he angled it up to decapitate the next troll.

That took care of the first group, but the gladiator saw another contingent heading towards him. He wondered if he could get behind them and cut them down. With the disadvantage of height, he needed something to...

He blinked from a sudden bright light and the blaring of trumpets. He was behind them, their exposed legs in front of him.

Strike now, Raven Stealer said in his mind. *Take them down!*

Without a thought, the blade cut through the air and flesh. The first two trolls went face down in the dirt before the third realized what had happened. The giant warrior spun, his axe coming down. Griffon raised his blade, and the wooden handle of the enemy's weapon sheared off just below the head of the axe. His follow through cut into the throat of the marauder and the creature slid down the blade, his mouth opening wide as it drew closer to the gnome.

From out of nowhere, a bugle sounded a charge accompanied by a flash of light. Griffon blinked again, and was behind another group of trolls, further away from Reggie and Aiyana.

You're welcome, Raven Stealer said, *now slay these things. If we keep this up, we'll take out the whole slew of them single-handedly. Then, you'll be the hero of the battle. Bet that'll get you laid lickity-split. If you're into licking such things.*

"So, you teleport?" Griffon gasped. "And how do you know all the slang? It's the game's programming, isn't it?"

The trolls turned at the sound of his voice, surprised to see a tiny package of death behind them.

Duh, the sword said in his head, and Griffon took out the first troll. *I teleport. It's a unicorn thing, you wouldn't understand. As for knowing your silly and simple colloquialisms, I'm in your head. Not much to do in here besides riffle through the information. And you don't even have anything passworded!*

Griffon whooped, a clarion call to battle for dozens of bloodthirsty trolls around him. He popped in and out, teleporting across the streets to slay without effort.

Raven Stealer crowed with him, and even sang battle tunes out loud, flashes of light accompanying each effect. She seemed to have a great time after being locked away in a deep, dark basement with no way out or anyone to wield her.

The armor the gnome wore, though no longer magical, protected him better than the quasi-fetish outfit he'd worn previously. It was coated in a sheen of blood from arterial sprays in short order, but his grip on Raven Stealer never slipped or faltered.

When he got hit—which wasn't often because he actually had a level of skill—the sword's magic healed him of the worst of it, leaving only scratches and bruises. Each time it performed that magical stunt, there was the sound of harps and a gentle, golden glow around the wound.

"Can you take care of those little cuts, too, Raven?" he asked, cutting down his latest target. "They sting, and my arms are sore, so do something about that too, okay?"

Nope, the sword replied, *if I heal all the little things, then I can't heal the big problems. Besides, you'd just get lazy and stop trying to stay alive if I took care of everything. So, looks like you just need to suck it up, buttercup, and deal with it. Okay?*

"OMG," the gnome spelled out the letters, "you're just like a healer in a boss fight!"

You're welcome, she said, *so quit with the QQ, and kick some troll ass already!*

Griffon whooped, spewed out a maniacal laugh, then threw himself into the fray again. He thought of those old-time farmers who didn't have power tools and had to use sickles and scythe, like they were Death himself, but of plants and crops. He hewed into the enemy, cutting them down in steady swings, leaving the ground littered with hundreds of bodies!

Then the beasts routed, fleeing in all directions to escape his wrath. Griffon felt powerful, he felt mighty, and he knew that they'd spread his name in terrified whispers to all the troll babies at night when tucking them into their little troll baby beds.

Hammocks? he thought, *Piles of hay? What do trolls sleep on, anyway?*

Depends if they're northern or southern trolls, but you can count on furs and pelts in general, Raven Stealer said. *And in case you didn't realize it, that little laugh thing you did? It's really annoying. It felt so fake and forced. When a kid laughs at an adult joke, it was like that. I don't think you're there yet. Maybe consider shelving that one for a while and practice it when alone. And by alone, I mean when I'm not around, okay?*

"Whatever," the gnome said. "You're just jealous that I have legs and you don't."

Hurtful! The sword replied. *But why would I be jealous of your knobby-kneed, spindly little pins that you call legs? Though, I must admit, they got you pretty far away from Reginald and Aiyana.*

Turning back to see if the others were following him, Griffon saw only a dozen or so dead trolls, rather than the hundreds he'd felt should be there. What he didn't see were his friends.

He spun in a circle, confused about where he'd started and what path he'd taken to get here. Between his nimble footwork, tremendous speed, incredible skill—and some small help from the teleportation supplied by Raven Stealer—he'd gotten quite turned around in his directions.

"Oh well," Griffon shrugged, "if the party can't keep up with the tank, that's their problem. I got my own pocket healer, and that's good enough for me."

You know, the blade said, *that isn't limitless. I do have to rest, recharge, and reset after doing it a few times. It's like the batteries in your world, those things you use for your beloved*

Purple Power controller for the games you play? I need time to recover my power.

"I think you meant, 'a game like the one I'm playing right now.'" Griffon crowed triumphantly. "I knew it! This is a game! I *am* in a video game!"

No, you're not, Raven Stealer sighed. *What would make you say that right now?*

"Because you know about game controllers!" The gnome grinned at his bloodied blade and poked at it with his free hand. "If this was real, you wouldn't know about those things! Only a video game company would put an Easter egg into the game about knowing it's in a game. Great way to break the fourth wall! Very meta!"

Or... the sword drew out the word in the gnome's head. *I'm in your head and can read your mind. Maybe that, instead? If you need more help to figure out if it's real or not, ask why the trolls don't disappear after they die? Why aren't more respawning? But a better question would be, where did all the trolls go?*

"What?" Griffon scrunched up his face and leaned away from the sword. "They all ran away because they fear me. They chose to live this day to fight another day, and stuff like that."

Griffon scanned the surrounding area. The dead and wounded trolls were still scattered around the street, the living ones dragging themselves away. On a nearby rooftop, a single troll stood, taking in the lay of the land, and looked like he was considering what comes next.

Walls of ancient buildings rose all around him, off white, each embellished with adornments that ranged from statues to scrollwork, from columns to relief carvings. Every rooftop had parapets, crenellations, domes, or some other architectural topping. The roads were brick with mortar that had been leveled out so smoothly that it was almost magical.

But there were no healthy troll warriors in sight anywhere, and that concerned Griffon.

You didn't kill them all, Raven Stealer said. *There were thousands in the city, and dozens here. Now, there are none. And these creatures came to achieve the dream of their people, to better themselves and rise from the squalor of their fate. Do you think they'd just keep throwing themselves at a gnome with an incredibly powerful—not to mention stunningly beautiful—sword to die?*

"Yeah," he drew out the word, "I guess I smell what you're cooking."

No one says that anymore, the sword chided. *Are you picking up what the Rock is laying down?*

"This has to be a video game!" Griffon stomped. "No other way you could know all these references."

Like so many other things in your life, the sword said, *it might just be all in your head. Oh, and you might want to step to one side.*

"Wha—" Griffon said, then he took an arrow to the knee.

With a shout, the gnome crumbled to the side, dropping the sword and clutching his leg. The wooden shaft had gone in from the back, and a stone arrowhead and a hand span of the shaft had come through the front, tearing away the flesh and exposing the plate of the kneecap.

Seeing his own muscle and bone, the gnome's eyes went wide, and he screamed. It was loud and shrill and went on for long moments before a stone to the side of his noggin shut him up. The world spun as he crashed onto the cobblestones.

He heard the slap of troll feet, and a moment later they came into view, huge leering faces leaning down into his vision.

One creature stepped on the gnome's shattered knee, twisting its foot to make the sinew tear further.

Griffon screamed again and his vision swam to a narrow tunnel, staring at Raven Stealer laying on the cobblestones, out of reach.

Portals: Book 5 – Towers & Trolls

Chapter 18

Reggie watched the gnome run into the trolls, lifting his own blades to join the wee warrior. The gladiator was impressive to watch, wielding the ivory blade like a meter-long scalpel. He took down the first set, then another, then disappeared from sight and reappeared a few blocks further into the city.

"Well," Reggie said, raising an eyebrow, "that's interesting. The little jerk can teleport now. Guess it's that sword. I'll have to do some research on it. I wonder if this place has any records about it. Of course, I'd love to spend a year or two here, looking through the city and learning about it, as well. But that can wait until we've taken care of the trolls and Zykrite—"

"I've found the bastard," Aiyana said from behind the swashbuckler, "and he's alone."

Turning to look at the wizardess, his forehead wrinkling in confusion, wondering if she meant the gnome. Reggie saw her staring to the southwest. Her eyes focused on something only she could see, like she was looking through the buildings.

She might be, Reggie thought. *Who knows what her powers can do? It's not like Merlin from King Arthur or Gandalf from that new book that just came out, where a wizard has only certain spells they can do.*

Aiyana could draw upon her mind magics to temporarily improve her physical body or influence the minds of others. She could call on the elements and shape the power of the ley lines for a wide variety of uses. Her staff bridged her lack of natural ability to include alchemy, holy magics, and conjuration, though she rarely drew upon them.

Most people could only access one sort of magic, and usually only one aspect of that magic. Many elementalists could only tap one sort of ley line, for example, fire, and limited to doing small things like lighting a fire or warming themselves or the surrounding room. Mind mages usually could only influence their own bodies to strengthen themselves, faster, or heighten their senses. A few could create psionic weapons, cast illusions, charm others, or even heal themselves or others.

Aiyana was the one in a million who could do most of those things and use multiple types of magic in a wide variety of ways. So, she could, in fact, be looking through the buildings, or tied into the vision of a bird like Captain Farrell, or just seeing the magical spectrum and zeroing on the largest output of energy in the area.

"Great," Reggie said to the wizardess, "let's go get him, but you're exhausted and in no shape to take him on alone. Griffon has run off to who knows where, so we should stick together…"

As he was speaking, Aiyana opened a portal and stepped through, the iris of the aperture snapping closed behind her.

"Great," he sighed, looking around, "then there was one. And he's talking to himself."

Looking down at his magical blade, he smiled.

"Hey Marcid," the swashbuckler said to the weapon, "is it too late to be eccentric and talk to you? I know you can't answer, as apparently Raven Stealer can, but I'm pretty sure you have some sort of sentience."

Reggie looked up and down the street. The only signs of life were dead or dying trolls. The wind whistled down the stone canyon of buildings, an eerie counterpoint to the moaning of the injured.

"Where should we go now?" he asked his sword. "I mean, we can hunt trolls, or try to follow Aiyana to Zykrite. It's annoying that those two get to blink in and out of existence and move across time and space from one place to another, but I have to walk everywhere. It would be swell to be able to fly. Yeah, that'd be good. Got any flying powers, Marcid? That would be handy right now."

The man walked as he talked, and the mention of flying made him think of Captain Farrell again. He missed talking to the raven but was glad the bird had remained in the Traveller's Inn after his wing injury. The bird might never fly again, but he'd have a good life there.

"I guess we could go up to a rooftop," he went on, "that would give me a better view of the city and allow me a better chance of finding one of my missing people, the headstrong aeifain or the impetuous gnome."

He sighed again and scanned the buildings, searching for the best candidate that would fit his purpose. A very tall one, not too far from the one they'd climbed earlier, caught his eye. It had a domed cupula on top that gleamed in the late afternoon sun.

"That one, Marcid," he said, using the sword to point at it, "it calls to me, and I think it'll do."

The metal leaves of his swept hilt writhed and curled tight around his hand.

"Oh, don't worry, my metallic friend," he smiled at the sword, moving towards the building, "I'm not putting you away right yet. There's too many uglies out here that would like a bite of a handsome, debonair, and charming swashbuckler, such as myself…"

He stopped talking and pulled open the door to the towering structure he'd chosen.

"Ugh," he said, stepping inside, his voice echoing off marble and granite walls, "I can't do it. I can't talk about myself like that. I don't see how Griffon does it. It just feels cheap. You know what I mean, Marcid?"

The hilt of the metal vines moved again as Reggie put his foot on the first step of the wide staircase that would lead him to the roof. The sword loosened its grip, so the man had more maneuverability of his wrist and hand during the climb.

"And that, my friend," Reggie said, craning his neck to see how many stairs were above him, "is why I think you have some sort of sentience and intelligence. You do things like this. I know it may seem like a small thing, but the little movements at the right time help me so much more than I ever can say. Thank you."

He continued to talk as he climbed the steps. Talking to himself was an old habit, something he did only when alone and either under stress or trying to figure something out. He'd do this when exploring lost temples, poring over forgotten texts, or sometimes when pacing his study with a pipe and a brandy.

"Flying would be good," he prattled on, his voice echoing off the walls, "or even just gliding. Not the taking of a bird shape, though. No, not that. Not after what Captain Farrell went through when that arrow went through his wing. I don't want to imagine what that felt like."

He only spoke every few flights of stairs, most of his monologue internal.

"I would like a pipe right now, though. Been too long since I've had one of those. It's been nothing but running all day. First to that place in the desert…"

He trailed off, stopping in the middle of a flight of stairs, still staring up. His eyes and mind were far away from the wall in front of him, though. They were back in that tomb. The same one he'd seen through the eyes of his dying man, Thomas, he'd now visited. And he felt he should go back and visit again.

They'd released something, and not just the creatures wandering the halls. The writing on the wall has spoken of the disease of the dead, literally. If that was what he suspected it was, he would be responsible for releasing it upon the world. He would be the one that has to go back and fix what he'd caused.

Shaking his head, he continued upward.

"After that," he went on, "we came here. Fought an elemental mutant hybrid, raised a long-dead city from the bowels of the earth, caught the attention of a mad wizard and his army of trolls, found a bunch of cool magical trinkets, had them drained of magic, found a magic talking sword, and then came up to fight the aforementioned host and madman. Then we all ran, willy-nilly, in opposite directions. And now, I'm climbing the stairs of the tallest building to get a good view, to find my friends, and then run down all these stairs to help them—and that's only *if* they are still in the same place I spot them."

Reggie stopped again, turned, and sat on the steps. He put his forearms on his knees, sword dangling in his hand.

"This is a mess," he let out a long sigh. "No planning, and that's how people die. I should've kept them together. Not that I can control either of them. Both of them are utterly bull-headed."

He laughed, the sound echoing off the walls in the stairwell. Marcid squeezed his hand.

"Udderly," he coughed between laughs, "bull-headed. Aiyana would've had a beef with that one since it's so cheesy."

Another laugh echoed down from above. It was deep and throaty, and cut off suddenly.

"That wasn't Aiyana or Griffon," Reggie whispered, standing, turning, and looking up all in one motion, Marcid held at the ready. "Someone else is in this building."

He started upward again, falling silent as he climbed. Within a few minutes, he'd reached the topflight of stairs and squinted into the late afternoon sunlight spilling through the opening at the top.

Something moved. Just a shuffle of a boot or a foot on the stone floor at the top of the stairs.

He stood poised, waiting to hear more, and debating whether or not he should call up.

Whoever was up there had been listening to him and had understood him. The laugh hadn't been cruel; it had been a reaction to his puns. He didn't feel threatened by a laugh like that. But one did not rush around a blind corner when in a magical city when under siege by thousands of monsters and a wizard of dubious moral convictions.

"It seems I have a choice," he said loud enough for whoever was up there to hear him, "but I think all of them include me going up there. I only hope I don't need to wield my weapon when I do."

"That will be your choice," a slow, deep voice answered.

"Who are you?" Reggie called up.

The sound of leaves skittering across the landing and a bird chirping was the only answer.

Putting one foot on the next step, Reggie drew his main gauche and moved upward. He stopped a few steps from the top, at the edge of the shadow and the beam of light, teetering on the edge of the two.

The birdsong warbled on. With a smack and a crunch, it cut off suddenly.

Reggie bounded up the last few remaining steps and burst onto the balcony, sword and dagger at the ready.

An enormous man sat crouched on the stone, chewing noisily, a few feathers sticking from his wide, thin lips. He wasn't a pretty man, the layers of dirt and travel-worn clothes saw to that, but neither was he repulsive. Besides maybe the chewing on a bird.

He had a runner's physique, thin and muscled, covered by breeches that barely reached his knees in his crouched position, and a billowing poet's shirt that was stained and sported a half dozen patches. He had tucked a small hunting knife into a wide leather belt, and a walking stick lay beside him.

His eyes were wide and angled, his hair as dark as iron, and his skin mildly tinted with color under the dirt. He smiled at Reggie, almost eye to eye even though he wasn't standing.

"Did you just," Reggie hesitated, "the bird, did you…"

"One must eat," the behemoth said in his basso rumble, "and the nearest inn is much too far away. Though I rarely patronize those."

"I can see why," the human said, looking the man up and down. "I want to ask more about you, but don't want to appear rude."

"I know," the stranger said, swallowing the last bit of the bird, "most do. Well, the ones that do not run away in a fright. Do ask, and I shall forgive the rudeness."

Reggie nodded slowly.

"Are you human?" the swashbuckler asked, gesturing the length of the figure's body with the tip of Marcid.

"My people once were," the being nodded, "but they created changes to improve the human condition. I am no longer human."

"What are you then?" Reggie asked.

"I am called a Troll Lord, or sometimes The Troll Lord, because most do not realize there is more than one of my kind remaining in the world."

"You're a troll then?" Reggie took a step back, half in the shadows, half in the light.

"No," the Troll Lord shook his head, and seemed melancholy, "though they are the descendants of my people who no longer exist, as are the aeifain."

"But you just said you're not the only one left." The swashbuckler stepped further into the shade and jabbed his sword towards the being in punctuation.

"You can put that beautiful weapon away," the Troll Lord gestured at Marcid. "I give my solemn oath to not attack or harm you in any way."

"What if I were to attack you? Would you harm me then?" Reggie was all the way in the shadows now.

"No," the stranger said, "it is not my way. I would let you do as you will, without harming you. It is a promise."

"That's hard to believe," Reggie said.

"It may be," the Troll Lord shrugged, "or it may not be. Believe as you will, because belief is a choice that becomes a habit. But I am going to stand now, whether or not you believe me about my promise."

The figure rose from his crouch to his full height. He was at least one and a half times the height of the human. He turned away from the swashbuckler, rolled his shoulders, stretched, and clasped his hands behind his back and looked out across the city.

From the shadows, Reggie studied the figure, noting that his rapier could easily pierce a vital organ before the alleged Troll Lord even knew he moved.

If he was looking at the source of the trolls, wouldn't it be best to eliminate the creature from the world before it could do any more harm?

His mind argued with itself, wondering if the aeifain were a blight on the land. Or were trolls? They were part of the ecosystem now, and nature had a way of balancing things. It was natural disasters, or the thinking races, that unbalanced the system.

"Beautiful, isn't it?" the Troll Lord asked. "Can you feel its pulse? The people who created this place designed a system that worked with the world around it, while still making something for the various races.

They tied the entire complex into the ley lines, and now it has a heartbeat."

Reggie wished for magic of his own again, this time something that could help him determine if this being was good or evil.

Things rarely come in such black and white terms, the archaeologist side of him thought. *Even the trolls are just trying to survive and grow past their current position in the world. Are the humans, aeifain, dasism, rokairn, gnomes, torck, or other races any different?*

It's like sitting at the poker table, the gambler side of him pointed out, *they deal you cards, but you can up the ante and bet heavily. You can bluff to make others fear you, or to make them complacent so they make a mistake. So, what is this new player in the game doing? What's your gut tell you about this opponent?*

"It had been slumbering for a long time," the Troll Lord continued, still facing away from the human, "but I feel it has risen from hibernation, and now will either flourish or die as it wakes. Like so many things, this is a delicate time. And this place has an illness."

The figure pointed at the massive black Tower of Onyx, which stood on four other broken towers, using them as legs to raise it higher.

Reggie decided, and stepped from the shadows and into the light, sheathing his weapons. He stepped up beside the giant man, but not too close.

"You're connected to his place, aren't you?" Reggie asked.

The Troll Lord looked down at him and smiled a sad smile.

"Only as I am connected to any other place of magic," the giant said, "our heartbeats beat together. We are joined in some ways, but all are individual."

"I'm not sure that makes sense," Reggie said, looking up and meeting the Troll Lord's eyes.

"It's an ecosystem," Reggie jumped a little as this magical being used the words that had been in his own head a few moments before, "and one thing affects the other. Imagine a forest, or even just a single yard. Bees pollinate, the plant eaters spread seeds through their waste, and the predators make sure no single population overwhelms the system."

"I can follow all that," Reggie nodded.

"But remove one thing," the Troll Lord continued, "and the entire system must adjust or fail. If the plants die, the bees can't do their job, and the grazing animals starve, which makes the predators starve in response to the events. Remove the herbivores and the same thing happens. Remove the predators, and the herbivores grow too numerous and overgraze, causing the same issue."

"Right," Reggie agreed, "but how does that apply here?"

"I am like the bees when it comes to magic," the Troll Lord explained. "I pollinate areas with magic."

"You control the magic?" Reggie asked.

"No," the Troll Lord laughed, the same sound that had drawn Reggie towards the light at the top of the steps. "I merely help keep it alive by spreading it around, supporting the ecosystem at the most basic level.

"The ley lines are the winds that spread the seeds," the creature continued. "Casters are grazers who use the magic, as well as spreading it. But then we have the predators, which are part of the cycle, until they over hunt. That is what is threatening here today."

"How do we stop that?" Reggie asked.

"The world sends in an apex predator, to clear out the smaller ones," the Troll Lord sighed, "or call it nature, or the gods. Whoever decides to meddle that day. It's all in the cycle of the Changing Wheel. And in this case, your friend Aiyana is the apex predator, sent in to kill or chase away those who would unbalance the system in place."

"What happens if she can't?" Reggie asked. "What if she loses, or is killed? What happens then?"

"The entire system collapses," the Troll Lord shrugged, "and something new rises in its place. It is the way of things. Never ending, ever changing."

Reggie thought about this, looking across the city. He could see tiny figures rushing through the streets, searching for the thing that would feed their need for whatever it was they sought. He couldn't see them well and didn't see any magical lines or anything else.

"Let me help," the Troll Lord said, reaching for Reggie's face.

The human jerked away, nervous.

"It's okay," the Troll Lord laughed. "I hold to my promise of not doing any harm. I merely want to pollinate. May I fulfill a small part of my purpose?"

Reggie nodded, still hesitant.

The Troll Lord touched a single, kielbasa-sized finger to the earpiece of the useless glasses that Reggie still wore, and the world Reggie saw changed.

Where he'd seen sky and buildings above, and roads and specks of figures below, billowed into an array of colors and lines.

Bright white arcs of energy swirled high above the earth, following the curve of the wind now visible to the swashbuckler. A deep ruby color pulsed below the ground—following the tectonic plate under the city—and mixed with threads of the blue of underground rivers and streams. The entire earth shimmered with energy in a deep green. There was a fifth color, more of an ethereal shimmer, and it connected all the beings running around in the streets.

Each living creature below was touched by this, and Reginald's sight zoomed in to see hundreds of trolls milling about in the streets. The form of Griffon, facing down a small army on his own, came into focus a dozen blocks away. On a hilltop outside of the Nine Towers of Magic was a brilliant light in the magical spectrum, showing where Aiyana and Zykrite had begun their own battle.

A similar energy came from the remaining six towers of magic, and that power was being drawn into the Tower of Onyx and burst upward in a single bright torrent. Zykrite had connected to that source and was using its power for his own purposes.

"Are you the thing they seek?" Reggie asked quietly.

"Perhaps," the Troll Lord answered. "I would be one way to get to it, but there are other ways."

"How can we stop it?" Reggie asked.

"Destroying the cancer that limits this place would be a good start."

"The Tower of Onyx." The archaeologist's words weren't a question.

"Yes," the Troll Lord agreed. "That would be a helpful start."

"Should I go help?" Reggie leaned out over the stone railing of the balcony, looking for a way down.

"You can," the mystical giant said quietly. "It is your choice. Or you may slay me. I am another source of power. Or you may do nothing. But remember, you do have another place you need to be once this is resolved."

"The tomb…" the archaeologist whispered, "you know about that?"

"Yes, you are tied to it." The Troll Lord nodded. "It is an imbalance that happened long ago, meant to contain the problem since it could not be destroyed. You will have the chance to be the fulcrum point to bring balance. But it looks like Jack Tucker's meddling is also aimed at correcting that."

"Why am I not surprised that you know Jack?" Reggie laughed. "Everyone who is anyone knows Jack."

"He travels in many circles, literally and metaphorically," the Troll Lord nodded.

"What's your name, anyway?" Reggie asked.

The Troll Lord shrugged.

"I can't run around calling you 'The Troll Lord', can I now?"

"Why can you not?" The Troll Lord asked. Before the human could answer, the mystic spoke again. "You have a choice to make, Reginald Betancourt, sometimes called Kazzek Tel Virian. Will you stay here? And if you do, slay me or protect me when others come to finish their task? Go below to fight? Or something else?"

Reggie looked up at the being beside him, considering.

A loud crack of thunder came from outside of the city, in the direction of roiling clouds and dust. The sound wave traveled outward in a circle, and buildings quaked in its path.

"Uh, oh," Reggie said, holding on to the railing as the structure rattled under his feet, "I feel like I should go help."

Portals: Book 5 – Towers & Trolls

Chapter 19

Griffon looked past the trolls reaching for him to where Raven Stealer lay in the street. Three trolls gathered around the blade, bending over to get a closer look.

"Heal me!" Griffon shouted at the sword, causing the trolls to jerk back in surprise.

I cannot, she said, *unless you are touching me. I can activate no ability of mine without contact. I am sorry. You were an amusing wielder in the short time you carried me.*

"That's not fair!" Griffon whined. "I've played the game, did all the things, and now they're just going to kill me because you're two steps away from me?"

Of course, Raven Stealer agreed, *it is the way of life. You must do for yourself before anyone can truly help you. To lie wallowing and crying in the dirt is not a way to win this game. You are choosing to die just by giving up and taking no action. The quickest way to fail is to not try.*

"Chuz you!" Griffon screamed at the weapon. "You don't know me! You don't know how much I try!"

I can plainly see how much you are not trying right now, she said simply.

A troll rumbled a laugh and reached for the gnome, the creature's hand almost the size of the gladiator's chest. Other trolls gathered around, and the beast wrapped his hand around Griffon and lifted him up to inspect.

Griffon screamed, his injured leg swinging around uselessly below him and almost blacked out from the pain in his limb and the lump on his head.

The trolls laughed again.

"I hate trolls!" Griffon spat through gritted teeth as two of the monsters grabbed his one good leg and an arm in their massive hands and began pulling.

The gladiator guessed they didn't grab his injured leg because none of them wanted the smaller portion of him, a delicious and tender snack. He knew he'd make a sumptuous meal but wasn't really in the mood to be eaten right now. He was too mad to let someone chew on him.

Then you should really do something about them, Raven Stealer advised, *and soon. Preferably before they rip your limbs off and nibble on them like juicy fried chicken legs.*

Griffon screamed again, the ball joints of his captured arm and leg creaking in protest. His free hand slapped around, landing on the small dagger he kept in his girdle. The weapon came free without him thinking about drawing it, and he flipped it around on his palm, so it pointed down.

Red-faced with spittle foaming on his lips, he twisted his body. Slashing at the troll holding his opposite arm, he cut through the beast's tough hide and into the muscle and sinew below.

The monster let go of him, and the other trolls laughed uproariously at the one who jerked back with a cry of surprise.

The gnome stabbed down into the wrist of the one holding his midsection and that one let go with a shout.

He fell, only to be stopped by the troll holding his one good leg. Dangling upside down, the world spinning around him, he saw an enormous fist coming at his face.

His nose popped and his head exploded in pain. The world went grey, and the gnome went wild.

Screaming, he twisted and slashed, his vision blurring as blood poured from his nose and into his eyes. He felt his blade meet flesh one, twice, and then cut through empty air as he fell, the ground rushing up to meet his head.

Arena training kicking in. Twisting, he hit the ground with a shoulder, rolled onto his back, the air rushing out of him, and his vision dimming.

He slapped his empty hand down to steady himself and help stop the spinning. It landed on something firm and cylindrical, and his fingers curled around the ribbed horn of the pommel of Raven Stealer.

Pain exploded in his injured knee as it snapped back into place, the kneecap sliding to where it belonged, and the flesh knitting closed, all in a few seconds.

"Ow!" the gnome screeched. "That hurt!"

Everything that truly teaches you to endure pain in life, hurts, Raven Stealer said innocently. *Perhaps you should quit whining about being healed and prepare to receive the troll's attentions?*

Griffon grunted, not wanting to give the sword any sign she may be right. His vision was clearing, except for the blood, and he could hear trolls closing in fast.

The gnome bounded to his feet, favoring his good leg in case the other wasn't fully healed.

The dozen trolls charged in from different directions, spears and hand axes leading.

Griffon trained to fight mobs of mobs in the arena—his mind mixing the terminology of his two worlds—and he pulled into a crouch to make a smaller target. Spinning and sweeping Raven Stealer in an arc, heads of spears and axes joined a couple of hands in the air as they separated from their owners.

"Throw your hands in the air," the gnome said in a sing-song voice, "like you just don't care!"

Then the gladiator was on his feet, wiping at the coagulating liquid in his eyes, and spitting blood from his mouth.

"How about fixing my nose?" Griffon growled at his sword.

No, I don't think so, Raven Stealer said. *It'll be a friendly reminder for you, keep you from being a pemtie again so soon. Besides, chicks dig scars, and that is going to be a whopper!*

The gnome ignored his sword's words and thrust, stabbing an attacker in the throat. He ripped the blade sideways, cutting across the midsection of another enemy, wet splatters of the monster's bowels on the street following its scream.

The other trolls stepped back, regrouping, and the gladiator took a defensive stance, as well, with his weapon sideways across his chest.

Taking stock of his surroundings, Griffon began counting the enemies and noting their positions. Within a single city block, there must've been thirty or more, not counting the dead ones he'd just slain.

On a balcony three stories above the street stood a single, skinny troll. It watched him and spun a small vertical drum in one hand. Other trolls reached down to touch matching drums that hung from their belts, reacting to something they felt there.

The gnome had seen that sort of drum before as a kid back on Earth. They called them monkey or pellet drums. It was a small, palm sized, double-headed drum atop a stick. Two beads on short strings hung from the sides, and when you twisted or spun the drum in the palms of both hands, it caused the beads to hit opposite sides of the instrument and make a double throp, throp, throp noise.

"Holy bidj, RS," Griffon said to his sword, "they made troll walkie-talkies. Trollie-talkies. TT's. They made titties!"

Ugh, Raven Stealer groaned in his mind, *always straight to the juvenile humor. And don't call me RS. My name is Raven Stealer. I feel a shortened version somehow lessens my stature.*

"What?" The gnome drew out the word in mock surprise, spinning to see the trolls checking their drums all around him, and wondering what message they were getting. "Bewbs are never humorous. I take ta-tas very serious, and only treat them with the utmost respect! I like to take them to nice places. Dinner, movie, maybe to the beach, or out on a...*motorboat!*"

He shouted the last word and shook his head back and forth to make a mbrbm, mbrbm, mbrbm noise.

Sling stones and arrows pelted the ground around the gnome, and he threw himself between buildings for cover.

"Everyone's a critic," Griffon mumbled.

I would've thrown something at you also, if I could do so, Raven Stealer thought haughtily. *You are a dirty little monkey and need discipline.*

"Oh, mommy," Griffon moaned suggestively, "do you want to spank this bad boy?"

More pops and snaps of projectiles hitting the ground around the gladiator made him cut off his teasing.

"It's like they know when I'm talking smack!" Griffon said. "Are you telling them?"

The gnome held the sword in front of him, joggling it with the accusation.

No, but it is a fine idea, she sighed. *But they are, after all, trolls. And that means they may just share your childish sense of humor.*

"Oh, so true," Griffon giggled. "Trolls are infamous for fart and dick jokes!"

Can we quit this now? The sword suggested. *It grows tiresome. We are being surrounded, and my teleportation range is limited, especially when surrounded by beings who dampen magical…*

The sword went silent, and the alley exploded into activity as spears, slingstones, and arrows rained down around the gladiator.

Griffon ducked down, threw his free arm over his head, and bolted for the mouth of the alley, screaming the whole time.

Three trolls poured in from the street, blocking his escape, and the gnome breathed a sigh of relief.

"Thank Parsay! You finally got here!" Griffon slid to a halt in front of the enemy, turning his back to them and looking up at the archers above them. "Those bastards up there were going to shoot me! But I don't think they'll try that when you're right here and could be hit by—"

Arrows flew at him again.

The gnome squeaked, dropped into a ball, and rolled backwards, slashing at ankles and calves of the troll blockade as he passed.

This was all standard theatrics for arena work once you've gone past the simplicities of mere fighting. When you had a following, and the crowd came to see you specifically, you had to give them something more. Make it a show, create the spectacle that took your name from favored to legendary.

It also confused your foe if they'd never dealt with it before. And it worked this time, as well.

The deadly missiles followed the gnome's retreat, sinking into anything between him and them, namely, the other trolls.

Hoarse shouts went up from the trio of trolls, and the sound doubled, then doubled again, becoming a thunderous roar that shook the buildings that held the attackers that had just shot their own people.

"What fresh hell is this?" Griffon shouted as he gained his feet.

Don't panic, gnome, Raven Stealer said, her voice returning to his head. *That is me using the blessing of Promethene to amplify their voices. You should be mostly safe now that you're no longer in the alley.*

"Where'd you go?" Griffon surveyed the street.

He saw an organized phalanx of trolls to his left and right, archers and slingers on parapets, and the single troll with the mini drum that he'd seen before. They boxed him in.

We were surrounded by, and in close proximity to, beings who dampen magic, the sword explained, *and that blocked my abilities. I don't suggest you allow it to happen again.*

"Well, it's about to," the gnome sighed, "unless I can figure out some kind of hack to get us out of this."

Raven Stealer didn't answer, and Griffon tightened his lips into a line. Both formations started towards him, and the trolls overhead drew back arms holding short spears, fingers gripping bowstrings, or began twirling their slings in slow, tight circles.

"I'm alone in the middle of the street without cover," Griffon narrated, "looking around for an answer. Even the powerful magical artifact that chose me over all the others has fallen silent because of the foul magical interference of the approaching horrors. I know I'm all alone, and no one will come to my rescue.

"But I have skills, and am a tactical genius," he went on, crouching, and holding his sword across his body in a blocking stance, "I can, I will, no, I *must* defeat this terrible troupe of troll-ish terrors today."

The ground troops charged with a ragged shout, weapons raised high and ready to come down on the small man.

"Usually," Griffon said, running towards a rushing line of enemies, "being small is a disadvantage in a sword fight, because you lack reach."

He slid into the mass of monsters, one foot leading and smashing into the ankle of a troll. The creatures folded their formation around him.

"But," he continued, rolling between two sets of legs and cutting the Achilles tendon of both with a single motion, "when in close combat, this becomes the advantage of being inside a larger combatant's reach."

He jammed the tip of his unicorn horn pommel into the foot of another troll, splitting the long bones and causing it to tear open down to the toes. The beast howled and bounced backwards on his one good foot.

Thrusting the blade up, he pierced the eye of the troll, leaning into the huddled chaos of the broken formation.

"And to beat a mob of mobs," Griffon leapt to his feet, and swept his blade along the ribs of three more trolls, "you don't have to kill them all, not in real life, you only need to make them all less eager to come at you than their companions are."

The gnome stood in the center of a ring of retreating trolls, grinning, and covered with gore. He'd made a bunch of guys that were three times his height back off. It was like a basketball team being afraid of a preschooler.

Griffon wanted to imagine he looked terrifying, but knew it was hard to do so when you were his size. He wondered if he looked more like an angry chihuahua. Then he thought of the Chucky movies, and how many people were scared of dolls, and that brightened his mood.

The creatures backed away, their magic-dampening circle receding, and Raven Stealer began speaking again.

Get down, she urged, *and raise me above your head!*

Doing as instructed, a shimmering dome sparkled into existence around him. Axes, arrows, and other thrown and fired weapons bounced off the shield.

"That was awesome!" Griffon giggled. "You're the full package! Teleporting, protection, healing, and that sound thing you did! I can't be beat!

This will continue long after I run out of energy to do these things, Raven Stealer said. *We need to end this, and soon, or you will be overwhelmed and die. For real, no save points, no respawn. Just dead.*

"I got this," the gnome bragged, "got enough for one more teleport?"

Maybe, she hesitated, *yes, I think so. You're small and I should have enough to get you to where I see in your mind. I may need to leave behind some extra weight, though.*

"Fine, whatever," the gladiator smiled, "I've got a picture of where I want to go in my head. Teleport me when I say so."

He rose to a kneeling position, like a track star ready to launch out of the starter blocks. He laid the sword flat on the ground, his hand still gripping it, lifted his butt a bit, and nodded.

"Go!" he shouted.

Blinking out of existence under the dome, spears and stones clattered to the cobblestones in the spot he was a moment before.

Griffon appeared, three stories up, behind the thin troll with the drum. The same troll he'd first met in the jungle, and the same troll that he'd seen kill the other troll in the tunnels a little while ago, and then commanded the other trolls to bring down the ceiling of the room, burying him and the others alive.

"Wheezy," he said in a sing-song voice, "I got something for you!"

Rising, he charged the two paces forward to the surprised enemy, who'd spun towards the noise.

The tip of Raven Stealer jabbed into the creature's abdomen, angled upward, and continued sliding into the monster's core. It moved up and through the chest cavity and burst out of the troll's back.

Griffon was standing on his tippytoes to complete the execution of his super awesome epic move, smiling up at the one being who'd been making his life a living hell since they'd first crossed paths.

The troll tottered backwards, dropping the little drum to grip the blade embedded in his stomach and heart with both hands.

A sneer crossed Wheezy's face as his backmost foot found open air, having run out of balcony to stand on. The beast tipped backwards, still holding onto the weapon.

If he takes me with him, the sword said in Griffon's mind, *he may use me to heal himself. Especially if Zykrite told him anything about the target they were looking for. Me.*

The weight of the troll leaning over the side of the building dragged the gnome forward. Struggling to stop himself, Griffon looked around for anything to slow his progress.

Gritting his teeth, the gladiator braced his heels on the small ledge at the edge of the landing and pulled. The troll's descent stopped, his own heels on the outer wall, and the monster spat a thick glob of bloody phlegm at Griffon, hitting the gnome's cheek.

Griffon winced, but didn't let go. If he let go, he'd lose Raven Stealer, but kill the troll. If he didn't let go, he'd either go over the side with the troll, or pull the troll back up.

He shook his head, smiled, and let go, dropping to his belly on the ledge.

The troll released the sword and snatched at the gladiator, his clawed fingers swiping uselessly over the gnome's head.

Griffon latched onto the sword again, shifting his grip to the cross guard of twisted ivory.

The troll, now falling backwards, realized his mistake and grabbed the blade again to stop himself. His long fingers slid along the edge of the weapon as it glided out of his gut, the digits separating and falling away like elongated breakfast sausages.

The troll's fall paused, his own fingers bouncing off his surprised face. Then he plummeted to the road.

Landing with a wet thump, the trolls below looked over from where they'd been inspecting the discarded armor that their quarry had been wearing a few moments before.

Griffon wiggled backwards, dragging Raven Stealer onto the balcony with him.

He stood, propped the pommel of the weapon against his shoulder, and wiped his blood-spattered hands down his bare chest.

"Hold on," he said with a surprised squeak. "W-where's my armor? Where's my clothes?"

I told you I needed to remove extra weight to get you up here, Raven Stealer explained in a calm voice. *The good news is that you may not even need to empty your bowels in the near future.*

"You teleported the bidj out of me?" the gnome exclaimed.

No, the sword laughed silently. *That isn't possible and would just be silly. But I think you may have messed yourself when you were about to fall off the building.*

"I'm a walking fart and dick joke now?" Griffon cried.

A loud crack of thunder came from outside of the city, in the direction of roiling clouds and dust. The sound wave traveled outward in a circle, and buildings quaked in its path.

"Aiyana?" Griffon breathed, staring towards the explosion.

Portals: Book 5 – Towers & Trolls

Chapter 20

Reaching across the ether, Aiyana drew in scraps of energy, calling a portal to her. Already exhausted, Reginald being distracting by blathering on about his research, and the magic in the area being drawn to her enemy, the task felt impossible. The dimensional doorway ripped reality, tearing a slice of air into a thrumming rift to beyond. She stepped through.

The sound of Reginald's voice, the wind, and the rumble of the enemy in the city cut off in a heartbeat. She felt the refreshing surge of energy of the place in between here and there, then and now, wrap around her. It was nothing and everything and was her private hideaway where she sometimes came to recover and refresh herself. It was silent, but the hum of the universe vibrated around her. She drew it in.

She knew she was taking a risk by doing this, and that's why she hadn't done it before. The entire area's tapestry of magic was in flux. Everything dampened or amplified, and most of it seemed to be under the influence of one man: Zykrite.

He was the reason she used elemental magic to move under the city instead of a portal. She couldn't guarantee the safety of herself or her friends. The energy between realities and times made most people queasy at best, and often violently ill. It messed with the mind. In the blink of an eye, she moved from place to place and ripped a person apart atom by atom, reassembling them when she pulled them out of the other side. With the whole skein of magic being topsy-turvy around here, the others could have been torn apart.

But it was different for the Aiyana. Her people were known for their affinity for mind magic, but she'd been doubly gifted. She was a walker of the ways, like Jack Tucker, and, perhaps, the Travelling God.

Aiyana was not to be denied travelling between places like this. It was her birthright; it was her destiny. Bringing the others with her would've probably killed them. They just weren't attuned to it like she was. Pulling on the energy between realms, she felt her mind and body refresh.

The phlogiston around her form—she was never sure if she had a physical body here, or if it was only her mind—pulsed with the magical disturbance of the world above.

Is it above? Aiyana wondered. *It may be beside, or below. It might even be all around. It's hard to map the essence of everything as an overlay to the real world.*

She thought of an overhead projector, where you put down a transparent sheet with pictures or words on it and used light to project it onto a wall. The real world was like the image on the wall, and the transparent sheet on the machine was the core of the source of all things, and she was travelling through the light in between the projector and the wall it projected upon.

Aiming her consciousness to the center of a ripple of magic, she sought the source. It ebbed and flowed, like a tide, and the destination looked too dangerous to emerge at. She'd have to come out before she reached Zykrite and walk the rest of the way.

A tear in time and space appeared in the middle of the street, and the wizardess stepped from the swirl of blue and white energy.

Tall trees in the full splendor of their autumn colors lined the avenue. Reds and golds stood in swaying sprays of branches and limbs, the smell of the world readying for its winter nap washing over Aiyana. Leaves skittered and rolled across the streets, gathering in corners and alleys for whispered huddles.

The sun was close to the horizon and bathed her face and the buildings in its amber glow. Brass domes and cupolas became bright, shining golds that matched the changing leaves. Ivory facades of buildings tinted with yellows, giving them a look of precious metals long forgotten.

Watching the surrounding movement, searching for the invaders of this forgotten school of arcane lore, Aiyana gathered energies to her open palms. Trolls might be resistant to magics—even exude an aura of anti-magic around them—but there were things she could do.

She strode past the last of the buildings and stepped onto the grass beyond the grounds. Angry growls and the slap of running feet came from behind her.

Turning to face the noise, she scattered moisture in a circle in front of her, creating a thin sheet of liquid prisms that intensified the sun's rays. A blinding glare bathed the oncoming trolls, causing them to slow and hold their arms up to block the intense light.

Calling upon the winds and water, she sheeted the ground with ice around the beasts, then pulled on the element of earth. Shards of stone were caught by the wind and hurled at the creatures, their anti-magical aura cutting off the thrust of the arcane power less than an arm's length from them. It wasn't enough. The inertia of the daggers of rock carried them forward, and dozens of the hand-long splinters embedded themselves into the thick hide of the trolls.

They turned and fled, seeking easier prey.

"That's what I thought," Aiyana muttered, turning back towards her final destination.

Within a few minutes, she saw a lone figure atop a hill, Zykrite.

Aiyana stopped, considering her approach. He'd have felt her magic and probably had seen her. She could try having the ground swallow him, but didn't think it would work since he had time to prepare.

Realizing she didn't know what magical abilities he possessed, she tried to remember their conversations for any clues. He'd be adept at aeifain mind magics, but what else?

The ice on the floor of the Grand Cavern! That had to be him, which meant he had some elemental ability. The way he'd inserted himself into the good graces of the people of Dargaon's Hole hinted at some ability to influence emotions of others and charm them into trusting him.

Stretching out her magical senses, she scanned him. She saw the gleam of power on his neck, the walking stick, and each of his hands. Then everything went blank. She saw the expected water and air elemental signature on his hands, and the enchantment of his torc around his throat, but didn't have a chance to divine what his cane held in the way of magic.

The man was holding up a hand and waggling a finger back and forth in a 'naughty-naughty' gesture, admonishing her for looking for his strengths and maybe figuring out his weaknesses. He gestured for her to come forward.

Zykrite's outfit was like the one he'd worn when she'd last seen him. Well-cut with sharp lines, knee boots polished to a shine, with deep blue trousers tucked into them. His waistcoat was a dark burgundy, with a cream-colored shirt underneath, and he wore a capelet of gold material that glowed in the sunlight.

Threads of arcane power wafted past Aiyana towards the man, and she turned to look at the city. The Tower of Onyx was pulling the energy from the broken towers on which it sat, ropes of ethereal power still tied to the remaining standing towers. All of it guttered into the sky, like a flame on a giant Bunsen burner, then bent towards Zykrite.

He was siphoning all the power of the Nine Towers of Magic to himself!

"Come to me, child," Zykrite called to her, his voice clear and understandable even though she wasn't near him, "let us discuss the possibilities of what is happening here today."

"Show off," she muttered.

The man laughed, nodding.

"Perhaps a bit," he agreed.

Walking forward, knowing that if he wanted to strike her down, it didn't matter if she was close or not. She debated how she could beat someone who controlled that much power. She had her staff, but it couldn't compare to the immensity of the amount of magic he was drawing from.

An idea occurred to her, but it was crazy and would kill her if it went wrong. Hell, it could kill her even if everything went right. She wracked her brain, trying to come up with something that would stop him without risking leaving nothing more than a smoking crater where one of the greatest magical institutes now stood. She mentally combed through all her experiences and research, including what she'd learned here at the Nine Towers of Magic. At least she had an idea, though, and she went to work on it.

"A Deadman's switch?" Zykrite asked as she came close enough to have a conversation without using magic.

Aiyana slumped a little, chewing on her lip and looking up at him.

He stood on the hilltop, gazing down at her like he was a king studying a subject that had done something wrong, annoyed but amused.

"Aiyana," Zykrite said, "you've worked hard to achieve everything you've accomplished. You deserve admiration and accolades for that, rewarded even. What you have attained couldn't have been done by many living, and only a handful of those who no longer walk the lands. It is truly glorious."

Turning, he gestured to the rest of the world to the south, from east to west.

"You have conquered warlords to keep magic from falling into the wrong hands," the wizard continued, "and opened the old ways. You've created new passages, safe for anyone to use. You created an artifact that can tap into all five magics and wield them safely. These things are feats that no one has done for thousands of years. It is nothing short of miraculous that someone so untrained and inexperienced could do these things. You've laid the groundwork for the Second Age of Magi, and I commend you."

"Funny how you can be completely demeaning while complementing me," Aiyana spat.

"Don't be so human," Zykrite laughed. "I spoke truth and won't apologize if that hurt your feelings. The aeifain in you should recognize such as high praise, and not whine because of honesty."

"You can tell yourself whatever you like," Aiyana said, "but you're still an arrogant asshole who belittles others to make yourself feel superior."

The wizard laughed again.

"That's the youth in you speaking," Zykrite smiled, "but I do have an offer for you. Are you willing to listen before acting rashly?"

Aiyana glared at him for a long moment before giving a curt nod.

"Good!" Zykrite tucked his walking stick under one arm and gave a single clap, then began pacing. "I want to continue your work. Opening the portal network, opening up magic to everyone. And so on. But as the dragon told you, it can be chaos if everyone can use the arcane energies, so I—in my greater experience and wisdom—would prefer to test and qualify those who seek the knowledge of the magics."

"I think you mean you want to control who has it," Aiyana said, crossing her arms, tucking her staff against her body, her fingers twitching. Her lips twitched like she was speaking, but no sound came out.

"It may appear that way," the male aeifain nodded, still pacing, "but I'll just be a gatekeeper to stop anyone from using it wrong."

Aiyana grimaced. "I've dealt with 'gatekeepers' of knowledge all my life. People who decided who was deserving and doled out portions for those who did as they were told."

"But," Zykrite continued, as if she hadn't spoken, "I want someone there with me, to act as a check and balance. Someone who understands my vision and who would nurture my plan. I'd like that to be you. I need someone to rule at my side. Aiyana, I think you can be that person. You have talents, gifts, and a vision of your own. You have spoken of the greed and short-sighted nature of humans, and I agree with that. I want to help you create the world you've been carefully constructing with all your hard work."

Aiyana listened, tempted. The idea of having someone of Zykrite's power, knowledge, and experience would be invaluable.

"I want to challenge the gods themselves," he went on, "take away the stolen power from Onyx, given to him by the deceit of Verl'zen-luk, and return it to the people. I want to shatter all the Towers of Onyx, not just the one here. I want to break his control over the energies we should be able to use freely, without having to bow to his will and whim. That sounds good and fair, doesn't it?"

"And you would take his place?" Aiyana asked. "You would dole out all the magic instead, deciding who was worthy. If I waited until someone told me I was worthy, I would never have reached the point where I am today. I don't think your plan is any different from what is happening now. It's just a different master holding the leash to the hounds."

"You are refusing my offer, then?" Zykrite asked, turning to face her.

She didn't answer. She stood there, staff against her body, glaring at him.

"I understand," he said, "and have no need for you to answer. You may perish, as the rest shall."

The wizard raised his walking stick, pointing it at Aiyana, and shouted a word of power.

The air shimmered around him, and no sound came out. Aiyana tied off the weave of alchemy around her that dampened any noise with a wiggle of her finger, and then raised her staff, gesturing.

She'd placed a bubble of silence around him, but not herself. Chanting, she moved the Key of Aiyana in a summoning ritual, calling upon the protectors of the lands. Dragons.

Most people thought of the intelligent reptiles as mindless beasts that devoured knights, princesses, and villagers alike. But Aiyana knew differently, and in her studies in Icon Hall, had discovered a few remained, and most were in hiding.

She combined her portalling magic with the conjuration magic and pulled them from across the continent to where she stood.

A dozen colossal forms, all schooled in the use of magics, appeared across the sky and earth. Reaching out with her mind magic, amplified by the staff she'd created, she flooded them with her own memory of the conversation that had just taken place.

The giant beasts raised their long necks to the sky and roared, gouts of flame shooting into the pre-dusk sun.

Reaching out again, she asked for the blessing of the gods. Jonath for protection. Parsay for luck. Latress for wind and weather in their favor. Torr for skill in combat and to be swift in action. Tarra to help heal the land around her. Promethene to light the way and let her voice be heard. And the Walking God to guide her path.

Lightning blasted Aiyana, throwing her down the hill, and a ball of fire enveloped her as she tumbled. The magics she'd invoked wrapped her in a gentle blanket of protection, but she still felt the intense heat of the attack and her clothes and hair smoldered.

Then, a dragon stood over Aiyana, her white neck curled in a protective arc around the wizardess, a curl at the edges of the creature's jaw—the closest thing a dragon can get to a smile.

Aiyana used her staff to rise to her feet, looking up the hill. The pale dragon, Trinity, assisted by moving her neck closer.

Zykrite stood imperiously above the land, guiding lightning and fire from his walking stick towards the newly arrived dragons. The noble beasts swirled and dodged in the air, doing their best to avoid the attacks.

"It is time, my friend," Trinity said. "Rise up and face down this bastard that attacked my home and my people, and we will take care of the trolls in the town."

"You can't get them if they go into the buildings," Aiyana wheezed, holding her chest, "I have a second wave planned. I was communicating with more than just you and Edsumar when distracting this scumbag. I'm about to import a few more people. Then I will end this monster."

With Trinity protecting her, Aiyana drew on the power of the Key of Aiyana, reinforced with the magic she drew from Zykrite's connection to her.

She found the bastard had been tracking her, a subtle link attached to her aura so he could influence, guide, and follow her. She reversed the flow as she approached the wizard and pulled a stream of arcane energy from Zykrite. Now she turned it up and poured it into her staff.

A flash beside the town pulled in a platoon of rokairn. A second burst of light portalled in the dasism and torck people who'd been waiting for the call to battle. Hundreds of allies flooded into the city, weapons ready to face down trolls wherever they found them.

"Go," Aiyana waved dismissively at Trinity, "and take your friends with you. I'll face down this madman."

"You know," Trinity cocked her head, "you may die, or even destroy the city with all of us in it."

"Yes, to the former," Aiyana nodded, "but no to the latter. I've got this. You can go and make sure that the pemties I traveled with are okay. Get them somewhere they'll be happy."

The dragon nodded once, unwrapped herself from around the wizardess, and opened her wings to take to the sky.

"Oh," the aeifain said, making Trinity hesitate, "and tell them I said goodbye."

Aiyana turned back to the aeifain wizard atop the hill, the dragons wheeling and flying out of range of his elemental attacks.

"Zykrite." She spoke in a normal voice, but the sound echoed throughout the valleys surrounding the hill the wizard had chosen to die on. "Time to pay for the ancient crimes against the aeifain, for which you were mercifully imprisoned in days of yore. Now, you shall face the new justice of our people, and not the soft coddling to which you are accustomed. Prepare yourself for the retribution of the arcane."

"You are a fool, Aiyana," Zykrite shouted back down the hill, his voice no longer amplified.

The wizardess smiled and raised her staff.

"Deadman's switch, remember?" Aiyana said. "I will kill us both, if necessary, and the world will figure out the rest."

A portal opened, then another, and another, until four magical gateways surrounded her. She pulled on the arcane of every plane she could reach. On the physical, ethereal, astral, and through the phlogiston, she rerouted the magical power from Zykrite, flooding it into the Key of Aiyana, and thus pouring it into her.

The wizardess glowed with pure radiant power— a small sun in her own right—and Zykrite threw a hand across his eyes.

"Thief!" he screeched. "You cannot summon so many things, call upon the gods, then stand alone and do this, expecting to live."

"I don't care if I live or die," Aiyana said calmly, at peace with herself and the world, "but just so you know, I am not standing alone. I never released the ties to the others. Each being I summoned is receiving their own portion of this power to protect and guide them. We are united. You are the only one who stands alone."

With that, she thrust her staff forward, releasing a torrent of raw arcane power at the man.

A loud crack of thunder came from the hilltop, sending up billows of dust and making the clouds above roil. A sound wave traveled outward in a circle, and the ground shook around the hill, and the buildings of the complex quaked in its path.

Portals: Book 5 – Towers & Trolls

Chapter 21

Reggie leaned against the wide stone railing of the rooftop terrace, surveying the city. The clouds to the southwest were churning up and out, pushed by the force of whatever was happening on the hilltop with Aiyana and Zykrite. A dark crater stood where the knoll had been moments before, and dragons approached the city, wheeling between jagged bolts of lightning.

The man knew he could reach out with the magical vision of his newly enhanced spectacles, but he didn't really want to see. He wanted to know, but not that way. He had to go there, see for himself, and be able to help, if help could be given.

Gazing across the city with a critical eye, Reggie judged his best path to get to the destruction. Small groups of large trolls skulked around, wandering aimlessly, but still dangerous. Dragons flew low over buildings, the sheer size of the beasts causing the swashbuckler to shiver in awe. Groups of other people were entering the city from the southwest, running ahead of the billowing wave of dust and detritus.

"You can go," the Troll Lord said to the human. "I will join you soon, and the people may make their choice if I survive or if I perish."

Reggie looked back at the creature, who stood slumped, a sad smile on his face.

"Look…" Reggie hesitated, searching for the name that was never given, "you sure you can't remember any name you ever had? Can I just give you one? It'll make it easier to do what I need to do over the next twenty-four hours."

The larger man shook his head, then shrugged in answer to the questions.

"My people, when they bestowed this honor and curse upon me, gave me the title of Lord of Magic," he said, "but throughout history people have shortened it to Troll Lord. Quite a different ring to it, don't you think?"

"How about Alexander?" Reggie asked. "It's a name of many prominent men from my world's history. Not everyone agreed with them or loved them, but the tales carry them in high regard."

"Got anything less…" the Troll Lord considered, "remembered?"

"If it is less remembered, then I am not likely to recall it, am I now?" Reggie smiled. "But perhaps, Able?"

"Oh, I like the shorter name," the lord of magic interrupted, "but, perhaps, not an adjective?"

"Okay," Reggie laughed, looking over his shoulder into the distance, "let me see, how about…Albert, or Al for short? There's lots of Alberts, but none of them are too famous, though many of them made huge contributions to science, history, and music."

"Music?" the Troll Lord perked up. "I've always liked music. You can call me Al."

"Great," Reggie was already turning away, distracted, "now to get where I need to be…"

"I've given you the tool you need," Al said, making a small shooing motion with his hand. "Fly and do what you need to do. I shall join you soon."

"Fly?" Reggie put a leg up on the rail and looked back over his shoulder. "You mean, I can really just jump off and…"

The archaeologist made a swooping gesture with his free hand.

Al nodded and waved encouragingly towards the distance.

"How do I know you aren't trying to kill me?" Reggie asked, looking down the side of the building at the drop.

"Because I could've twisted off your head any time I wanted to do so," Al muttered.

Putting a hand on the small of the man's back, the Troll Lord pushed Reggie over the side.

The man lost the last few words, plummeting off the side of the twenty-story tower, a scream ripping from his throat. Throwing his arms out to catch at something, anything, to slow his fall, his cloak whipped around his wrist and ankles, puffing out behind him with an audible pop.

Reggie threw desperate glances behind him, trying to see what had just happened.

"Holy bidj!" the man swore, a rare thing for him. "It's like flying squirrels, or sugar gliders in Australia, or Draco lizards in Asia!"

Twisting his body, Reggie pulled up, riding the current of the incoming wave of dust. He angled, and the cloak pulled him to one side, correcting the angle. He rose on the warm air and glided towards the broken hilltop where he'd last seen Aiyana.

In moments, he'd passed out of the complex and was over grasslands, browning in the autumn season. He flew over a compact figure, running out of the city instead of into it. Focusing on the movement, his spectacles zoomed in, showing Griffon.

"Good for him," Reggie muttered. "Looks like he cares."

His mumbled thought turned to coughing as he took in a breath of the dust cloud, and he added a scarf to his shopping list if he was going to continue to fly in the future.

At the edge of the crater, he circled once, swooped up, and dropped onto the broken turf. He landed with one knee bent, the other in the dirt accompanied by his fist, head bowed. He held his free hand out for balance.

"Cool superhero, landing, brah!" Griffon panted, catching up.

The gnome did a double take.

"Wait, what?" Griffon's words were more of a protest than a question. "Why do you have working magic items? Mine were all drained. That's not fair!"

"I know a guy…" was all Reggie said, standing and surveying the destruction.

The archaeologist had seen ruin and devastation before, and this was only a hilltop, nothing important in the big picture. But it was the last known place of the woman he'd been protecting; someone he'd failed because he couldn't keep up with her.

The gambler in him knew she had chosen this risk and left him behind on purpose. Maybe because he had a different hand to play, maybe because she couldn't handle what was at stake, his life.

"Think she made it?" Griffon broke the man's reverie. "It's a pretty big mess, but she's a tough chick. I think she made it."

"You're an insensitive—" Reggie said.

"Yeah," Griffon nodded, interrupting, "I know. It's part of my charm. I think we should save your crying until we know if she's dead or alive, don't you? I mean, really dude, she's like one of the most powerful mages who ever lived. She made it. Care to make a bet?"

Something inside of Reggie clicked, and he smiled.

He was here for adventure. When he first arrived in this world, he decided to go big instead of going home. But he was going to be here, do things, and enjoy this ride for as long as it lasted.

"Fine," he said, "what would you wager?"

"If she's alive," Griffon said, his hands on his hips, staring into the settling gloom, "you give me a magic item."

"And if she's dead? What then?" Reggie asked.

"I don't know," Griffon shrugged, "what do you want?"

"You don't speak for thirty days," Reggie said, and the gnome opened his mouth to say something, "and if you win, I will get you a magic item, but not one of my own. I know a guy…"

"Um," Griffon squinted up at the human, "fine. Fist bump on it?"

The gnome held up a fist, and Reggie grasped the offered hand and shook it up and down.

"Close enough," Griffon sighed.

The two stepped over the rim of the crater to look for their friend.

Something huge and pale loomed in the murky air, threads of the setting sun radiating out from the form. A small, burgundy form limped in front of the behemoth, leaning on a staff.

Trinity the dragon emerged from the settling cloud, Aiyana hobbling in front of her.

"Aiyana!" Reggie shouted and ran forward.

The aeifain held up a hand to stop the man from embracing her.

"Don't touch me, unless you're going to help me walk," she said.

Reggie moved to the side of the woman without the staff and tucked himself under her arm, his main gauche bumping their hips.

"She did well," Trinity rumbled from above the three, "didn't even kill the man."

"Why not?" Griffon asked. "That's what you do in a boss fight. Kill the bastard."

"Thought about it," the wizardess said, "wanted to, but didn't."

"What did you do to him, then?" Griffon asked.

"Sent him 'in-between'," she said, "to a place where he can't escape. In time, his knowledge and power will dissipate into the space between worlds."

"So," Griffon cocked his head, considering, "it's like a metaphysical Sarlacc pit, where he'd slowly devoured over ten-thousand years?"

"Sure," she shrugged, "something like that."

"We still have something to do here, though," Reggie said and helped lower Aiyana to the grass outside of the crater. "We need to take down the Tower of Onyx, release the control and magic he stole from the Nine Towers of Magic. Otherwise, everything else we did is for nothing."

"Do you think I don't know that?" Aiyana said.

Reggie thought she was trying to be short with him, but her words came out more as an exhausted sigh.

"That is the reason we were originally coming here, wasn't it?" she asked. "I'm just not sure how we take away a god's favorite toy."

"You did it before, right?" He pulled out his waterskin and passed it to the aeifain. "After you first got here?"

"Yes. No. Sort of," she said, taking the skin and drinking deeply from it.

When she was done, she handed it back, wiped her mouth with the back of her hand, and stared at the black monolith in the distance.

"I stopped him from getting a new toy," she continued, "but didn't take away something he already had control over. I have no idea how to do that."

"I think I do," Reggie said, following her gaze, "and you've already laid the groundwork for it."

The wizardess blinked at the swashbuckler.

"Well?" she said impatiently. "Are you going to tell us, or make this dumb gnome guess? Because I'm too tired to bother."

"With these glasses," Reggie tapped his spectacles, "I saw you tied the power flows to the people you brought here, including to the dragons. I apparently also met a being to whom all magic is tied. Someone called the Troll Lord, though he now goes by the name Al."

"You've met a Troll Lord?" Trinity asked, her head joining the small circle of friends. "One of the Lords of Magic? What is he like? What did he say?"

"Hold on, great one," Reggie held up a hand, and Trinity snuffled a reply, though the man wasn't sure if it was at the title or making her wait.

"He says he's ready to die," the archaeologist continued, "if that's what people want. Said it would end magic in the world once he and the other remaining Lords of Magic are dead."

"Chuz that!" Griffon interjected. "I think magic is cool, and anyone who wants to end it is a pemtie."

"I agree," Reggie nodded, "but with him here…who all did you bring here, Aiyana?"

"Oh, everyone," the aeifain sighed, "rokairn, dasism, humans, torck. When Zykrite was babbling about his big plan, I sent out mental messages through mini-portals, so it went back a week. I told them to arm themselves and be prepared to…"

"You sent messages back through time?" Reggie asked.

"She did." Trinity nodded her massive head. "I received mine before she summoned me to Dargaon's Hole."

"Wow!" Griffon's voice was awestruck. "That's badass. I knew you were powerful, but I didn't know you could do that."

"The gods helped," Aiyana said quietly, "and I don't think I could travel through time, just send a single message. As you know, I've been searching for a way to do it. The final bit of information was in those papers under the DOPES building. But, let's not get sidetracked. I think we know someone who can travel like that, the one person who brought us all here, Jack Tucker. I actually sent him the first message, and it may have been him that made sure the rest of the messages got through."

"Wow," Reggie agreed, "with an ability like that…"

"No." Aiyana cut him off. "I can't do anything. Not again. That is too powerful to keep lying around. I won't use it again or share how to do it with anyone else. It was my staff that allowed me to perform this, and the Key of Aiyana is too much power for anyone to possess. It needs to be destroyed when this is over."

The group fell silent for a long moment.

"Alright," Reggie finally said, nodding, "I agree. We will remove it from the table. The stakes are too high when gambling with that sort of ability. It can shift the balance of the game too easily."

"Aw," Griffon whined, "but can't we just use it a little—"

"No." Reggie and Aiyana said at the same time.

"Okay, fine, whatever," the gnome said, eyeing the artifact with a calculating look.

"Anyhow," Reggie continued, "we build the bond you created with everyone, syphoning the magic from the Tower of Onyx, weakening it…"

The man went on with his idea, the others expanding on it in as he explained, until they had a plan of action.

Chapter 22

The morning light gleamed on the towers and buildings of the magical complex. It rained in the night, and the area felt renewed, cleansed.

Everyone gathered at the base of the four towers that held the Tower of Onyx, milling about in the shadow of the structures.

Small groups of the different races mingled, assembled for the event that would forever change the world. Rokairn chatted with dasism and torck, making allies and tentative trade agreements their governments would hammer out later. Humans mingled with others, offering to trade knowledge for goods.

Dragons perched on terraces or soared through the morning sky, lending an air of gravitas and wonder to the scene. The giant reptiles would contribute their formidable magics to the task of tearing down an icon of a god's power.

Last night, the gathered people hunted down the remaining trolls with the help of the dragons. Today, the Tower of Onyx would shatter, or it would break all those who came together in the effort.

"It's a good start," Aiyana said, still sounding tired, "and it'll bring about what I wanted, but to everyone. The different races will provide their own balance."

"Do you think Onyx will interfere?" Reginald asked, a worried look on his face.

"The dragons say he can't," Aiyana shook her head. "Gods can influence people, manipulate them, but can't come down and directly interfere. It's all part of the agreement that the Walking God put into place after he put all the gods to sleep, then revived them a hundred years later."

"That's…" Reggie shook his head, unable to come up with anything to summarize the immensity of his thoughts.

"Indeed, well said," Aiyana agreed. "The gods didn't want anything like what had happened here millennia ago to happen again."

"I killed dozens of trolls," Griffon chimed in, repeating something he'd said a dozen times in the past twelve hours.

"Yes," Reggie smiled at the gnome, "so you've said."

"I really did this time," the gnome whined, "not that I didn't take down a half dozen before…"

"We know," Reggie patted the smaller man's shoulder, "and we believe you, mostly."

"Where is this guy you told us about?" Aiyana said before the gnome could reply.

"Um," the human looked around, "he should be here any time now."

The throng behind the three went quiet, then parted. A figure towered over the gathered races, moving forward with a stately presence, the clumps of people murmuring after he'd passed.

The Troll Lord didn't lumber like a troll, neither did he walk with the grace of the aeifain. He moved with the gravity of age, but had an aura of power around him that Reginald hadn't noticed the previous day.

"I have come as you bid, Reginald," the being said, then added, "my friend."

"Everyone," Reggie said, taking a deep breath, "this is Al, one of the remaining Lords of Magic. And I believe him being here can help us remove the cancer of the Tower of Onyx from this ancient institution. Al, this is…everyone."

"Oh, you're fancy, aren't you?" Griffon said.

The gathering murmured, unsure of how to react.

"Great Master," Trinity bowed her head low to Al, her chin scraping the cobblestones, "it is an honor to be in your presence."

The crowd followed the dragon's example, some bowing, others taking a knee.

"Reginald," the Troll Lord rumbled, "make them stop doing that. I am just a man."

"Yeah, just a man," Aiyana said, "that has been around for thousands of years, saw the birth of two races from your own people, and now holds the essence of magic in the very fiber of your being."

"I bet he still poops, though," Griffon shrugged.

The dragon whipped her head towards the gnome, her jaw hanging open, and the gnome took a step back.

Reggie could see the gnome was trying to appear unimpressed, and that the dragon was aghast from Griffon's comment.

Al laughed.

Reaching out a hand larger than the gnome's chest, the Troll Lord patted the small man's head.

"It is true," Al whispered to the gnome, then raised his voice, so the gathered peoples could hear him. "I am no different from you. And I am here so all of you may pass judgement and decide my fate. If you put me to death, then magic may weaken or even pass from the land. It would change the world and release you from the bonds that tie you down in many ways."

"Well," Reggie said, rubbing his chin, "about that. We've already discussed it. It seems that we all like having magic, and won't be, um, ending your time here. Sorry about that, but it looks like you still must carry this burden."

The Troll Lord gave a small smile—it looked a bit sad to Reginald—then Al nodded.

"But," Reggie continued, "we do have a task for you. Or perhaps I should say we would ask a favor of you, a boon."

"You want to untie the bonds of the black tower," Al rumbled, "and free yourselves from its power. Open up the river of magic for all."

"Yes," Aiyana nodded, stepping forward and looking at the enormous man with her brow wrinkled. "How did you know that? Have you felt something in the flow of energy of this place?"

"No," the Lord rumbled another laugh, "I heard you from where I stood atop a building. I may be old, but my senses are still working fine."

"He heard us?" Griffon repeated, his voice trailing upward. "From on top of a building? I mean, he's got some gigundous ears, but to hear us from way up there? That's awesome!"

"Will you lead us in this, oh Great One?" Trinity asked, her voice full of wonder.

"Great One? Oh, Rykul the Great Bear would tease me about this, wouldn't they?" Al smiled, winking at Reggie. "But yes, I will assist in this task. I will not consider it a boon or favor, just the will of the beings who should be able to choose their own fate and what bonds hold them."

Someone clapped, a single sound. Then it came again, repeating, picking up speed until it was full applause. No one else joined in, and all eyes turned to Griffon.

"What are you doing?" Aiyana hissed at the gnome.

Holding his hands apart, the gladiator looked back and forth between the Troll Lord, the wizardess, and the crowd.

"A slow clap?" Griffon said, but it came out as a question. "You know, they did it all the time in those old movies from the eighties? Everyone is supposed to join in until everyone is clapping and stomping and cheering?"

"No," Reggie said quietly, placing a hand on the gnome's forearm. "No one does that. It sounds horrible and awkward. Let's just move on."

The surrounding group nodded and murmured their agreement.

Reginald turned to look up at the towers, activating his magical spectacles. He saw the threads of energy coursing out of the four broken towers and pouring into the black tower that sat atop them. The energies from the remaining five towers also bent to join the ebony monstrosity.

"How do we do this?" Reggie asked no one in particular. "Do we all just focus our wills on the towers?"

"No," Al rumbled, "we need one person to do the task, but everyone else should lend their strength of will and belief to that being. Aiyana, I believe with your knowledge, and the power of the Key of Aiyana, you should be best suited to the task. Will you do it?"

All eyes turned to the aeifain. She looked around with wide eyes.

Reggie thought this was the only time he'd seen her look nervous, afraid even.

She nodded, and a few cheers broke out, though the audible sigh of relief from the gathering overpowered the smattering of applause and voices.

Reggie grabbed Griffon's arm and shook his head and to stop the gnome from starting another slow clap, uttering a single word, "Don't."

"Yes," Aiyana dropped her head, her voice quiet, then repeated the word louder. "Yes, I will do this."

She raised her head and looked around, shedding her anxiety, her decision made.

"Rokairn," she raised her voice, and all heard, though she didn't shout, "please, move to the base of the broken towers. Be ready to use your gifts to keep them strong, heal them and support them."

The mountain folk moved towards their places.

"Dasism," the wizardess continued, "prepare to call upon the elements to draw away the magic of the towers from the black tower, redirect the power back into themselves, as it should be."

The people of the elements nodded and moved into small groups, preparing themselves.

"Torck," Aiyana said, "you are one with nature. Once the black tower breaks, use your magics to revitalize the land around to help growth."

The rammen smiled and raised their fists into the air as one.

"Humans," the aeifain felt awkward using that term, "you are quick and fast to act. Support the others in their endeavors, shoring up their tasks as they need."

The men and women of Dargaon's Hole, Seawall City, Durgan's Keep, and other cities cheered and ran to find places among the others.

"Dragons," the wizardess paused, taking in a deep breath, and released it, "once we kick the bonds off the tower, you break it by any means necessary."

The beasts on the ground launched themselves into the sky to join their airborne brethren, roaring.

"Until the moment when the black tower's bonds are broken," she continued, "everyone focus your magical energies on me. I'll use my staff to shatter the bindings it has on the other towers."

Aiyana looked around, and Reggie admired her confidence, but not for the first time. This woman was a wonder. She never gave up or flagged in her dedication to what she wanted to accomplish. He'd seen her doubt herself, seen her beat down, but never seen her give up.

"Everyone," Aiyana shouted this time, "let it begin!"

Aiyana's hands shook, and she drew in a deep breath. The crowd moved to their assigned places, ready to do their part, but she still felt like all eyes were on her.

Pulling in the energy with each deep breath she took, she gathered it to herself. She felt the touch of every single person around her: man, woman, dragon, rokairn, dasism, torck, human, and Troll Lord.

It was more power than she'd ever handled, and it threatened to carry her away, or burn her out.

Focusing on her staff, she poured the arcane magics into the artifact, letting it build. Too much and she would destroy it, not enough and it wouldn't break the damned black tower of a god who had stolen his place in the hierarchy of gods.

This is what she'd been working for since she'd arrived in this land almost five years previous. She'd fought warlords and maniacs, beaten every challenge she'd faced, but this was more than all those things. She had to believe that everything she'd done up to this point was to prepare her for this moment.

She thought of Nathan, the rokairn priest of Jonath, who'd taken her under his wing. He'd advised her, even when she didn't want to hear it, supporting her in any way he could. He built furniture for her magical tent. Fought off any foe, whether real or in her own fears. He'd been her rock, which was appropriate since he was a priest of the god of the earth.

He'd always looked out for the people around him, whether they were his friends or strangers that needed protection.

Aiyana wondered if he'd died when he went back to the world they'd both come from. His time, the nineties, was thirty years past her own, but she wondered if she'd ever see him again.

Drawing her mind back to the present, she poured more energy into the staff, then aimed it at the base of the Tower of Onyx. The gesture wasn't necessary. Her mind would guide the arcane torrent she was about to unleash, but she felt it would look good to everyone around her.

Threads of spirit, earth, air, water, and fire wound around her. The minds of the surrounding casters joined with hers, and her awareness expanded to see the world from hundreds of different perspectives. Each one was frightened, but hopeful.

Then the Troll Lord's mind touched hers. It felt old, gentle, and patient. It calmed her, and her shaking hands steadied.

Opening up the staff, she released the stream of magic at the black tower. Everything slowed in her mind, and the rush of power glowed as it slowly reached for the one thing that had held it as a prisoner for so long.

When the torrent touched the base of the tower, the world in her head exploded. Dark things burst outward, not physically, but shards of obsidian flying in the space between waking and dreaming. It was the intention of the gods and the hold the being had over magic in this world, shattered.

Aiyana pulled more power from the people around her and thrust it at the stout obelisk that had trapped generations of ambitions, hopes, and dreams. The torrent turned to an enormous fist in her mind, pounding the structure, then opening to tear chunks of the magical webbing that bound it to the land.

She felt it crack—a thin line in reality—and she called out to everyone around her.

"Now!" The wizardess's voice was a shriek of pain and anger, her single word taking on the emotion of everything she'd struggled with her entire life.

Falling to her knees, her forehead hitting the cobblestones, she continued to pound the structure with the remaining energy she'd collected.

Then she was empty. So empty. Her mind and soul were a void, and she was floating in nothingness.

She felt strong arms wrap around her, lifting her up, and a gruff but gentle voice calling to her, telling her to come back.

Other touches and voices joined the first, and she relaxed, releasing the last of the energy she'd been directing.

Her body was like a sack of sand and her eyelids like lead weights. Her hand opened and the staff that kept her attached to the fight slid from her fingers.

Griffon heard the single word from the wizardess and launched himself forward, drawing Raven Stealer in one swift motion.

Really? The sword said in his head. *And what exactly do you think you're going to do? Hack a vast tower down, single-handedly?*

"Aw, shut up, already!" the gnome sniped. "I just saw the most powerful woman in the world collapse trying to save it! I'll be damned if I'm just going to stand here and do nothing."

People looked at the small man talking to himself as he ran by.

He'd seen Reggie run to help Aiyana and knew she wouldn't want him there. Hell, the old man wouldn't want him there. No one wanted Griffon anywhere near them. They didn't believe he was worth a squirt of bird bidj, and he couldn't disagree with them.

You're horrible at being worthless, you know that, right? Raven Stealer said. *You keep rushing in to help people, you constantly say pemtie things to make them laugh or distract them from their problems, and you look great in a leather harness and thong.*

Looking up at the looming Tower of Onyx, Griffon shook his head. The dragons were taking turns circling the structure, diving in to scorch it with dragonfire or tear at it with their claws.

Mages—or wizards, or whatever they were—cast ice and lightning at the cracking walls, chunks tumbling away from the sides and towards the people.

Griffon followed the trajectory of a massive hunk of black glass and saw it would fall into a small group of rokairn at the base. In the blink of an eye, he'd teleported into their center.

"Get down!" he yelled, the words coming out in the language of the people he thought of as dwarves.

The bearded men and women gaped at him, looked up and saw the rock spinning towards them, then followed his order. They crouched down with their hands over their heads.

The gladiator raised his blade over his head, scrunched his shoulders down, and closed his eyes. The glittering dome of protection burst into life just as the rock hit, shattering into small pieces.

See there? Raven Stealer asked. *You just selfishly saved a bunch of lives. And you saved fifteen percent on car insurance by switching to GEICO.*

"Ha, ha," Griffon grumbled, "hilarious."

A few of the rokairn muttered relieved laughs, and others patted the gnome, thanking him for the help.

Stalking off, Griffon looked around, still wondering how to help.

"Why don't you pemties get away from the damned collapsing tower?" he shouted over his shoulder at the group.

The rokairn exchanged looks, said a few words to each other, and moved away. They shouted thanks and gruff agreement with him.

They like how you speak to them, the sword said, *bluntly. That's how their people talk. If you want to hurt people's feelings by calling them names, try the dasism. They're a bit more sensitive.*

"Shut up," Griffon growled, jogging towards the next group.

No, the sword said saucily, *you shut up.*

Griffon grinned and picked up his pace, readying himself to troll the next group of pemties that didn't have enough sense to get out of the way of falling rocks.

He spent the next few hours dodging rocks and rescuing people, using his sword to heal those not smart enough, or quick enough, to get out of the path of debris.

When the black tower finally lay in a heap of stone and rubble around the base of the four fractured towers of magic, he stared in wonder at their beauty.

They weren't broken off where the Tower of Onyx had sat atop them. They were whole, but cracked. The tops were in full splintered glory in the afternoon sun, standing taller than any other structures in the complex. They were only matched by the five intact towers that hadn't had a god drop a rock obelisk on their heads.

The gnome sheathed his sword, dusted his hands off, and headed in the direction he'd last seen his friends.

Portals: Book 5 – Towers & Trolls

Epilogue

Winter set in over the Nine Towers of Magic. A light layer of snow dusted the newly reestablished community. The trees, once gold and russet, were now bare with mounds of snow held in exposed fingers of branches. Rokairn greeted dasism, and torck waved to humans as they passed in the street, preparing for the season's holidays.

Life had returned to the lost institute, and classes would start in the spring, still a few months away. The council argued over minutia, and everything was going as well as could be expected, considering the plethora of different tribes, people, and cultures.

More laughter was heard in the streets than harsh words, and merchants came in steadily, ready to build a new life in a place that had been little more than a myth a few months before. Barbarians came in from the north, bringing furs to trade, and some settled in. Their trades and businesses were in demand. Knowing how to make a wagon wheel, a barrel, mend a pot, or make a saddle was welcomed.

Aiyana and Reginald were local heroes, and everyone accepted Griffon. The rokairn women often brought him baked mushrooms or newly tapped barrel-aged beers. They often found the gnome frequenting the rokairn establishments and insulting them. The bearded folk found their smaller cousin charming and kind.

"Rokairn are weird," Reginald said, watching an exchange between the gnome and a stout rokairn in a leather apron.

"Shush," Aiyana reprimanded the man with no strength behind it, "my best friend was a rokairn. Is, he *is* a rokairn."

"You miss him, don't you?" Reginald asked, his expression softening.

"Pemtie thing to ask," Aiyana said, turning her head into the chill, artic wind. "It's going to be cold tonight, and they say it's going to drop more snow."

"Oscar Wilde said, 'Conversation about the weather is the last refuge of the unimaginative.' Or something like that," Reginald commented.

"Oh, shut up or I'll bite you," Aiyana laughed. "I'm trying to change the subject, and you know it."

"Yes," the man nodded, "I know it."

"I think things are going well here," Griffon said, joining the other two. "By spring, this should feel like a real town."

"Not a lot of those around," Aiyana sighed. "It'll be good to have one more refuge in the storm of this land."

"Is that what I think it is?" Reginald pointed at a sign swinging in the cold air.

Both of the others looked where the man pointed.

The wooden sign was an oval with cut corners, the words 'The Traveller's Inn' burned into the grain. It hung in front of a wide, thick door of dark wood banded with iron, and golden light cascaded from opaque windows in an oblong rhombus onto the snow.

The door opened, and a man of average height and indeterminate age stepped onto the porch. He wore beige breeches tucked into worn knee boots, with a dark brown leather vest hanging open over a white shirt.

He waved at the group, smiling.

"Hasn't that always been there?" Griffon asked, pulling off a bite of goat jerky.

Reginald and Aiyana exchanged looks and smiled.

"He's new to this, remember?" Aiyana said.

"New to what?" Griffon asked, sounding a trifle miffed. "An inn? I've been to inns before. Even pubs and bars. I just prefer to drink alone, like George Thorogood. Because I'm bad to the bone. And I…"

The gnome trailed off as his two companions walked away from him, heading for the man on the porch.

"Took you long enough," Aiyana said, brushing past him to enter the establishment.

"Good to see you, too, Aiyana," the man replied.

"Hello, Jack," Reginald said with a smile, "glad you could make it. Can I assume tonight will be eventful?"

"That's, as always, strictly up to you," the man said.

"Mhm," Reginald said, his tone humorous, "I'm sure it is."

Griffon stood at the bottom of the two steps that led up to the porch, squinting at the plain man waiting at the door.

"Care to join us, Griffon?" Jack asked.

"You seem familiar," Griffon muttered, feeling off balance. "Who are you?"

"Come inside," Jack laughed, "we can discuss it somewhere warm, with stew and ales. Sound good?"

The gnome's belly rumbled, and he shivered in the cold. He still insisted on not using a cloak, feeling that the ladies liked it when he showed his muscles in a sleeveless shirt.

Grunting in a non-committal way, the gladiator took cautious steps up to the porch. He kept his eyes on Jack, sidling sideways past the man.

It was a standard inn but done in a more modern style than the glorious architecture of the surrounding buildings. Poorly fitted stone mortar globbed between to fill the gaps covered the bottom part of the walls. The upper part was paneling, but not like what Griffon knew back in his world.

Real wood planks every few paces had crossbeams running across the ceiling. A shorter beam created an angle where the ceiling met the wall. Iron-forged hooks hung there, an oil lantern with low wicks dangling from each, creating a homey feel.

Thick planked picnic style tables with benches lined the center of the room. Square tables with ladder-back chairs were against two of the four walls. High-back booths lined the third wall, and behind them a staircase ascended to rooms above.

The fourth wall was glorious and dominated by a mahogany bar polished to a high sheen. No bar stools were present, but a wooden block ran the length underneath for people to prop their feet on. Behind the bar was a mirror with glass shelves in front of it, lined with various decanters and bottles. On the right were shelves and racks for glasses, steins, and mugs. On the left were large casks with wood-burned words delineating which were brandy, whiskey, rum, and so on.

Aiyana and Reggie headed for a booth on the far wall, sliding in and smiling.

Griffon felt it was weird that his friends looked so comfortable here, like they were returning to a favorite hangout spot. The gnome felt the same, and that alone was enough to make him worry. Nothing in this world had made him feel comfortable like this, and that immediately set him on edge.

Moving through the room, the gnome looked at the gathered patrons. There were a dozen locals scattered throughout the tavern, some whom he recognized, and they raised a hand or a drink of greeting to him. But there were folks he didn't recognize.

A halfling fiddling with a flute sat at a table with a strapping man wearing a leather half cloak, a two-handed sword leaning on the wall beside him.

At the bar was an old man in wrinkled clothes, slurping from a foaming mug, his white beard and moustache gathering as much ale as his mouth. The bartender was dressed to the nines and had an enormous head. He spoke with a massive worker standing next to the bar. The worker—wide shouldered and tall—slouched like they were having the worst day of their lives.

It surprised Griffon when he spotted another gnome. Dressed in dark navy robes, with a tall, pointy hat sitting at a jaunty angle on his head, the other gnome sat cross-legged on the polished bar top. He was chatting with a man who looked like his parents had been a giant and a cabbage, and the doctor bashed him with the ugly stick the moment he came out.

Ogre, Raven Stealer supplied. *Well, half ogre. Wouldn't ask which parent was the mother, human or ogre. It's generally impolite to inquire of such things, though that one may not care. On the other hand, he may just mush you to a paste for asking.*

"I wasn't going to ask." Griffon's tone was pouty and told the sword that he'd been considering doing exactly that.

He straightened up, squared his shoulders, and sauntered to the table where his friends were. Both grinned, amused by Griffon's reaction to the Traveller's Inn.

"The first time is always an experience," Reggie said.

"Shut up, Kazzek," the gnome said to the swashbuckler, using his 'weird name.' "Who should I sit next to? The mouthy know-it-all, or the hot chick?"

"Him," Aiyana pointed at Reggie, shifting her staff to lean against the bench on her side of the booth, making it almost impossible to squeeze in next to her. "But please, stop calling Reggie 'the hot chick.' It makes his head swell."

"I've got a swollen head for you right here," Griffon muttered, climbing onto the bench beside Reggie, shifting Raven Stealer on his back to sit.

"But it's gnome-sized," Aiyana quipped, "so large is a matter of perspective."

Griffon shot her a sour look, unable to come up with an appropriate comeback.

"Maybe that's how he gets *ahead* of others?" Reggie suggested.

"Thanks for that *heads up*," Aiyana giggled.

"Puns are pemtie," Griffon mumbled, settling in.

A woman walked up, took their order for drinks and meals, and headed off.

"What are we doing here, anyway?" Griffon asked. "I don't like this place. It gives me the creeps."

"We're eating," Reggie said, "then at some point, Jack will come over to talk to us."

"And generally, he pays for the meals," Aiyana added, "so that's a big plus."

The drinks arrived first, along with a tray of breads, cheeses, and thin sliced roast beast.

Griffon had ordered the first thing that had come to mind, which was a soda, burger, and fries. He'd had to explain what each thing was. The woman had brought him an ale, told him he could make a sandwich of meat and beef, and assured him that his spiced, fried potatoes were on the way.

Aiyana held her glass of wine, swirling it, and waited for a bowl of fruits to arrive. She'd asked for strawberries, melon, and grapes.

Reggie had asked for a bowl of stew and a Velentian brandy—a gnomish spirit—and grinned at Griffon's surprised look.

When the rest of the meal was delivered, Griffon stared at the spread.

"How do they have all this fruit, Aiyana?" he asked. "It's winter. None of this is in season."

"This particular inn has resources other establishments do not," she said with a shrug, inspecting a large, plump strawberry before biting into it.

She moaned in delight, rolling her eyes back as she drew the little green crown of leaves from her lips. A light dribble of pink juice ran down her chin.

The gnome made a pile of bread, rare meat, and a thick slice of cheese into a sandwich, and bit into it.

"Wow!" he said around the mouthful of food. "This is great! I think the bread is fresh baked, and cheese is so rich. And this meat…"

The gnome gestured pointedly at the tray on the table.

"…it's delicious," he continued, chewing as he spoke, "like seasoned, but not too much, but just enough."

The aeifain held up a hand to deflect the bits of food flying across the table from the gnome's mouth.

"Stop, you cretin," she said. "Chew with your mouth closed, then talk when you're done! Were you raised in a barn?"

"Why?" Reggie smiled. "Did he *cow* you, or just get your *goat?*"

"Stop *horsing* around," Aiyana said. "I can *barley* understand him!"

"*Hay*," Griffon interrupted, "I know *wheat* I'm doing. I ain't *chicken*. No *bull*. This conversation is *cheesy*, and I don't even know *rye* I think that!"

The other two stared at the gnome, shaking their heads.

"He's new to this," Reggie grinned, "You can't expect him to potato, carrot, green bean the first time out!"

The human and aeifain laughed.

"That didn't even make sense!" Griffon complained. "You can't do that!"

"The pun war rules are very specific," Aiyana explained, "and you can't just throw unrelated puns into the mix. You can transition by using a single related pun, thus shifting it to a new line of *pun-ishment*."

"Thus *o-punning* the door to a new topic, knock on *wood*." Reggie finished.

"This is dumb," Griffon complained.

"You *wood* think so," Aiyana grinned, "but the *oak* is on you. But you can't just *ma-hog-any* all the jokes for yourself."

The gnome looked back and forth between the two.

"I think he's *pining* for a reply," Reggie added, pausing to give the gnome an opening to work with.

"As much as I *cherry-ish* these sorts of conversation, and don't want to be an *ash*," Jack said from beside the group, "can we *table* this conversation? Just *bench* it for a while, and *chair* some insights with one another?"

"Well done, Jack!" Reggie said, looking up at the proprietor with a smile.

"That's didn't even make sense," Griffon grumbled. "Chopping off any response we might have is just wrong."

"See that?" Jack said, clapping the gnome on the shoulder. "Well done. You're getting it now!"

"No, I'm not." Griffon muttered. "I don't even know what I said."

"Okay then," Jack smiled and looked over his three guests, "may I *axe* you a question?"

"I don't like the *timber* of your tone," Aiyana smiled, "you sound like some kind of pun *hack*, trying to *cord-on* off the topic."

"Well," Jack said, "if I can side *rail* this topic, then maybe we can talk about what comes next."

The group fell silent, searching the statement for further puns.

Growing serious, Aiyana looked up at the plain man standing beside the table.

"Is it time for the question?" the wizardess asked, running her hand along her staff leaning against the bench beside her.

"It is," Jack nodded. "Would any of you like to go home?"

They exchanged glances, meeting one another's eyes.

"So," Griffon said, "is this like a save point finally?

"No, Griffon," Reggie said, putting a hand on the gnome's forearm. "This isn't a game. But he is offering for one or more of us to go back to Earth. We'd go back to the exact moment that we died."

"I'm ready to go," Aiyana slid off her bench, standing up.

Jack stepped back to make room for her.

"Oh, no," Griffon said, "I can't handle this. Chuz this. If you're going back to die, I'm leaving. Good luck, and all that bidj."

The gnome hopped off his bench and stomped towards the bar, bee-lining for the other gnome.

"Aiyana? Donna?" Reggie's words were tense.

"No, don't," the aeifain said, holding a hand towards the man without turning towards him. "I know you like your words, but it won't make a difference right now. I've made up my mind. Besides, I don't think we die, do we, Jack?"

The wizardess pulled her staff to her side, looking at the proprietor of the inn accusingly.

"When we entered these bodies," she went on, "they were dying. The magic, or whatever, revitalized and healed the body, though. And our spirits, or whatever, had a new home. I'm betting it would be the same when we return to our former selves, our original bodies. Am I right, Jack?"

She said the man's name with disdain.

Jack smiled, a soft expression full of compassion.

"I never said anyone would die if they went back," the ordinary man said. "I just said you always had a choice in the matter."

"Just one more game," Aiyana spat, "from the man who pulls the strings of the puppets."

Jack shrugged, not looking uncomfortable or upset.

"And I'm taking the Key of Aiyana with me," the wizardess held up her staff, "it's too powerful to leave lying around here for anyone to use. I think it's better to remove it from this man's game."

"I knew it was a game," Griffon cried, pattering back over, "even you agree, Aiyana! I knew it!"

"It's not the kind of game you think it is," Aiyana reached down and tousled the gnome's hair, "but you're still a pemtie."

"Stop that," the gladiator slapped at her hand, "you're not my grandmother. Though I guess you're old enough to be my grannie in the real world."

"I wouldn't put it past this man to pull in multiple generations," Aiyana said.

Holding up her staff, Aiyana's eyes went unfocused, and the artifact shrunk down to the size of a pin or broach. She attached it to her collar and nodded.

"I'll take this with me," she glared at Jack in challenge, "if he lets me make that choice."

"Of course," Jack nodded, "it is yours. You made it, and you can do with it as you see fit. Did you want to say your goodbyes?"

"Goodbye, Reginald," she threw a quick glance over her shoulder at the swashbuckler, "be well. Griffon, don't be a pemtie, and get a grip."

"Wait," Reginald said, sliding from the booth to stand. "Can I have a hug?"

The woman heaved a sigh, her shoulders slumping.

"Fine," she growled, turning back to the man.

He held out his arms, took a step towards her, but waited for her to meet him halfway.

She sighed again, and stepped into his arms, wrapping hers around him and thumping him on the back twice in quick succession.

He pulled her tight, putting one hand on the back of her head.

"You're going to be alright," Reggie whispered, "you'll see. You're an amazing, strong woman."

"Shut up," she said, her voice cracking.

Aiyana pushed her friend back and turned away, her hair falling to hide her face.

"Let's go," she said tersely, "I'm ready."

"Of course," Jack said, turning and gesturing to a door they hadn't noticed before. "Right this way."

"Oh," Aiyana said, turning back to the table and setting something down, "this is for you, Reginald. It's a portal stone so you can get back to that damned temple you're so obsessed with. I figure you'll be going back there. And take care of The Citadel, you'll have more use for it than me."

"Thank you," Reggie said, reaching for the stone.

When he looked up again, stone in hand, she was already walking through the door that Jack held open. It closed behind the pair.

"I guess that's it then, huh?" Griffon said. "You get more magic items, and I get nothing. Wait a minute, don't you owe me a magical item?"

The gnome looked up at the human, fists on his hips.

"Oh yeah, about that." The swashbuckler looked down at the gladiator, his voice rough and eyes wet. "I already gave it to you. Your translator earring works again, and I think that Al—before he wandered away for parts unknown—may have upgraded it as well. I think you can even use it to speak to others now."

"What? That's it?" Griffon complained, sliding into Aiyana's abandoned but still warm seat. "I was hoping for something flashier, like a wand of fireballs, or a polymorph charm. You know what else would've been cool? I was thinking that I could get a..."

Reginald sat back down, the gnome's chattering fading from awareness as he stared at the door Aiyana had passed through.

Donna stood on a dirty street in Denver, staring at a rundown jeweler's shop. Cars trundled past as she watched the door and thought back across the years of her life. She'd loved, married, had children, and went on to do the things in life she'd set her mind to do.

In the three long decades after her accident in the civil rights march in Chicago in the late 60s, she'd lived life to the fullest. She'd died that day, at least that's what the doctors said, but she remembered things differently, though. She remembered other places and friends like no one else she'd ever met. Therapists suggested trauma. Psychologists thought it might be PTSD from the riots. Medical doctors whispered about brain damage, causing delusions.

But she remembered the other place.

She fingered the odd silver pin—about three inches long—of a skeletal hand clutching a blue crystal adorning the collar of her cream-colored turtleneck. Brushing at her brown, ankle-length skirt, with one hand she checked her platinum blonde hair—once the deep rich color of mahogany—pulled into a bun. Her thick Italian locks had lost all their color after her injury, leaving her with hair so white it was almost silver.

Grinning to herself, she thought, *Oh goodness, I'm nervous. I look so different from the last time he saw me. Will he even recognize me? I look so much older now.*

She was in her early fifties but didn't look it, even with her hair losing all tint. Her skin was milky white, even though it had been naturally tan when she was younger. Slim without being skinny, she moved with the grace of a movie star from the Golden Age of Hollywood.

At least I can treat him to dinner, she thought. *That shouldn't be too much to ask, right? Hell, I'd buy him a house if he asked. Ugh, I'm being as silly as a schoolgirl.*

She invested in computers as soon as they hit the market. Her husband—an ivy league lawyer she married in 1970—wasn't happy about her taking control of the finances. None of that mattered now, though. She divorced him in 1990 after their second child turned eighteen.

The guys from her 'lost time' talked about computers, and she couldn't remember which computer company she'd heard about from them. But she remembered a big guy named Torrence—*No, it was Torrents, wasn't it?*—who looked like he'd just stepped off the cover of a Harlequin romance novel, mentioning things machines could do in his time. He once told her to invest in anything that looked like something from Star Trek.

She swore she remembered that happening. It was as real as the birth of her children, Kara June and Trinity.

And the little guy, Gary? Griffon? Grayson? Something like that. He was annoying, but he couldn't shut up about video games. But she made a mint investing in every computer and video game company she could. She would live comfortably for the rest of her life, however long that might be.

Reggie was another memory. He was young, but in her head, he was older, like a favorite uncle with a pipe and gentle, encouraging words.

But the person she remembered best was Nathan, and he never spoke about computers and games. He enjoyed working with his hands. When he talked about anything else, it was about family and pets. The man adored his family but wasn't close to them for reasons Donna couldn't remember.

For the past dozen years, she'd tracked the man she remembered from another world, trying to figure out if he was real or a medical delusion. She watched from afar as he built his business, waiting for the right moment to introduce herself. She'd waited for this day for a long time and was here to meet him for the first time…again.

Fingering her odd, skeletal broach, her guided meditations came to her mind. The little pin was with her when she woke in the hospital after the civil rights march. No one questioned it, most never even noticed it. Occasionally someone would comment it was a little weird. That's how she met Jack about ten years ago, in 1987. He was a life coach and saw the pin when she was at a tavern with some friends, saying how unique it was. He suggested she use it as a focus for meditation.

She'd worn it everywhere since she came back from the dead. It never did much, but she felt it helped her, guiding her intuition when she sought about what to do or where to go next in life. She'd drop it on a list of stocks to buy and choose the one it landed on, things like that.

But it had led her here on this day. Using a dry erase board with the months, it landed on this month and day. She repeated the process with a list of years. And here she was in Denver in the autumn of 1997, watching the shop of a man she'd only met in a delusion.

A little while ago, she'd seen an angry employee leave, slamming the glass door behind him. Now she watched three men approach the door. They entered the shop, and she crossed the street, dodging traffic. Pausing at the door, she heard shouting from within.

Drawing a deep breath, she reached for the handle and pulled the door open. Stepping inside, no one noticed her. It was like she was invisible, or their minds couldn't discern her in the room. She smiled, rubbing the pin on her collar, and took in the scene.

Two men with pantyhose over their heads were sizing up the glass cases lined up around the perimeter of the room. The third—who had a ski mask covering his face—held a double-barreled shotgun and was yelling.

"Give us all the money in the register and safe!" the man shouted.

"I'm sorry," Nathan, a man of medium height with no outstanding features, apologized. He didn't have a huge bushy beard like Donna expected, was taller, and his voice was different. But she knew him.

"I only have the hundred dollars in the register," Nathan continued, "minus the $17.38 it was short last night."

"I didn't steal the damned money!" the man in the ski mask screeched.

Nathan paused, tugging at his Christmas themed sweater.

Tilting his head, he asked, "Austin?"

The sound of shattering glass made Nathan turn towards the two men snatching various things from the displays.

"Stop," Nathan said, holding up his hands, "you can just reach behind them. The cabinet doors are open!"

Donna raised her hands, instinctively tapping into energy through the pin on her collar, and the shotgun jerked up, going off and blowing a hole in the ceiling tiles.

Nathan spun back to the man in front of him, his eyes going blank, his hands flying to his midsection. Then his focus returned to the present moment, and his eyes went wide.

"I'm…still alive," Nathan said. Raising his hands in front of him, he turned them this way and that, staring at them with wonder. "And I have both of my hands again."

Taking two steps forward, Donna punched the attacker in his kidney from behind. She kicked Austin's knees out from under him, and he went down. The man's hands, still holding the gun, flew up, and she snatched the weapon from over his shoulder.

She reached down, pulled two more shells from the young man's back pocket, broke the gun—ejecting the spent cartridges with a jerk—and slammed two more into the barrel. Snapping the gun back up, she spun to face the other two at the display cabinets.

"Reach for the sky," Donna growled, "you don't have the *stones* to face me down."

Nathan focused on the new arrival, as if seeing her for the first time.

"Who are you?" he asked.

"A friend," she whispered, her eyes clouding with tears, "from a long time ago. And I'm *aiming* to take a *shot* to be a friend again."

"Are you…" Nathan licked his lips, "*shell shocked?*"

"You *hit the target, dead on*," Donna nodded.

"Aiyana?" Nathan whispered, his voice cracking.

"You protected me," she said in a choked voice, "so many times. It's my turn to give you a *hand*, Nathan, priest of Jonath, and my hero."

Travis I. Sivart

End of Towers & Trolls, Portals, Book 5

Portals: Book 5 – Towers & Trolls

Sneak Peek: Legions & Liches, Portals, Book 6

Chapter 1

Reggie—swashbuckler and gambler—slapped the wooden bench he straddled, causing the silver coins between him and Dandy Rym to bounce, then looked up at the man. His opponent glared back, his eyes slitted and his mouth in a tight line.

The six men around them called out support for their boss. Reggie wasn't a house favorite in this arena.

"You can't win them all, Kazzek," Dandy Rym sniffed, calling Reggie by his nom de guerre, "sometimes you just have to know when to walk away. At least, if you don't want to lose everything you got."

The larger crowd in the arena stands, surrounding those surrounding Reggie, gasped. Reggie opened his hand, revealing what he held, and the crowd cheered.

Dandy Rym's eyes went wide, and his hand went to his hip.

Reggie dropped his five playing cards on the bench, showing the winning hand, and smiled.

"Parsay loves you, and I'm paying for that now," Dandy sighed, dragging his coin pouch from his belt. "But we still have the bet on your little friend below."

Reggie glanced to the blood sands below where Griffon, the gnomish gladiator, faced off against a rhinoceros beetle larger than a horse. Fingering his necklace of dozens of holy symbols, Reggie muttered a prayer to Parsay, asking for luck, and to Torr to help Griffon in combat.

"The town of Arena," Dandy Rym sighed, "one giant arena, surrounded by smaller arenas. People tell stories about how a trading post grew up around the original structure, and once merchants started putting up permanent structures, someone dug a new fighting pit."

The tall man put a hand on Reggie's shoulder, and Reggie wasn't sure if it was out of camaraderie or to make sure he didn't run. The rough men—surrounding the frontier fop and the swashbuckler—snickered and tightened their little circle.

"Sometimes it was for dog fights," Dandy Rym continued, "or cockfights, but there's always room for men to fight. They don't settle nothing in this town without someone fighting. And this is the second part of the bet you made with me, your old crew mate."

"Well, I always liked you—" Reggie said, but Rym waved him to silence.

"You won the first part, the card game," Dandy went on as if Reggie hadn't spoken. "You know, I always wanted to beat you when we ran together, doing heists and second story jobs, but could never do it. This second part, the fight in the gladiatorial arena, and Griffon being something of a legend, is quite the thrill."

"Well, the gnome volunteered." Reggie licked his lips, wondering what his host was getting at. "And the little guy is something of an attention whore. Griffon is an incredible fighter, but also an annoying and obnoxious bastard."

He's been that way since we met, Reggie thought, *shortly after Griffon came to this world from Earth.*

Even though Reggie and Griffon were from the same country in the same world, they were from two different worlds. Reggie was from the 1930s and had retired from being an archaeologist during the golden era of archeology, dying in his bed. Griffon was a twenty-three-year-old kid from the 2020s who lived in his parents' basement and played video games all day.

In this world, they knew Reggie as Kazzek Tel Virian, a twenty-something, blonde swashbuckler who once was a Robin Hood sort, but in the cities. Griffon inhabited the body of Auric, a famous gnomish gladiator who was twice the boy's human age, half his height, and ten times his skill in anything except snacking.

"I didn't want to make the bets," Reggie said, "but I need information about this disease. People are dying and it's getting worse now that the spring trade routes have reopened. After leaving Elda's Rest as the last of the winter snows melted, we followed clues about the disease, traveling west through the Wandering Hills until we reached Arena."

"Right," Dandy Rym nodded, patting Reggie's shoulder, "people are turning into the walking dead without being dead first, right? What did you call them, the 'lost folk'?"

Reggie nodded and swallowed as Griffon went down underneath the charging insect.

"And you'll get the information." Dandy Rym grinned, and it felt predatory to Reggie. "It's just a matter of you keeping that magical blade. If your little friend loses, and I think he will, I get his legendary weapon and yours. And after everything I've heard about you two and these artifacts, they'll change my world."

Griffon had already died twice, in two different worlds, and he didn't plan on doing it again. He rolled to one side, running his blade—Raven Stealer—along the underside of the immense beetle.

He called upon the cursed magic the witches had sacrificed him for and flung his hand towards the beast's head. A series of sparking explosions went off like a dozen fireworks, and he hoped it would blind the creature.

It didn't work.

Coming up from his roll outside the cage of legs, Griffon stood and the massive head of the rhinoceros beetle knocked him back. The gnome landed on his butt three paces away, but still held on to the ivory horn handle of Raven Stealer.

It's a bug. I could have told you that an illusion wouldn't work on an insect, even a giant one. Raven Stealer said in his head. *But you're very graceful when landing on your ass.*

"Bite me," Griffon retorted.

And your words are just as eloquent, the sword laughed, *you should write books.*

Griffon didn't have a chance to reply, dodging another charge from the beetle. The monster left a trail of white guts behind it from the wound, but didn't slow.

Waiting until the last moment, Griffon stepped to the side and swiped through three legs on one side.

The beast crashed to the ground, sliding along the red sands.

The gnome used one of the flailing stumps as a step and launched himself onto the back of the insect. Running along its shiny carapace, he stopped at the neck and rammed the sword down and into the monster's head.

You do know that beheading it would be more effective, don't you? Raven Stealer asked.

"Yes," Griffon grunted, "but not as good for the showmanship side of things. Listen to that crowd!"

The gnome held one hand up to the cheers of the audience, and the other on the hilt of the sword, using it to steer the massive bug as it tried to escape.

He jerked the makeshift tiller, guiding the beetle to trample the three men he'd fought in the first round of combat. The crowd loved it.

Grabbing the pommel with both hands, Griffon jerked the blade back and forth, decapitating the monster. The beast went down into the dirt and the gnome flew forward, ducking into a roll and coming up on his feet, his sword held high.

"See?" Griffon said through his wide grin. "I know what I'm doing!"

Great, Raven Stealer said sarcastically, *let's hope you know how to handle the third challenge.*

The gate in the arena's side opened and a gangly man ran out onto the sands, falling to his knees beside the beetle. He wailed, a long mournful sound, and threw his hands to the heavens.

"Aw," Griffon muttered, "now I feel a little bad."

No one is ever alone, wee one, the sword said. *Someone will always mourn, or avenge, the death of another.*

A sad, slumped goblin limped towards Griffon, head down and hands holding a water skin out.

The gladiator drank, the goblin kneeling at his feet, while arena workers came out to drag away the corpses from the first two battles.

Horns sounded once they'd cleared the field, and the goblin snatched the drained waterskin and bolted for the exit.

Six dark, sleek, low-slung forms darted out of the gate the goblin was heading for, and the goblin backpedaled and fell on his butt. Two circled the wall, moving out of the goblin's circle of vision. One creature turned towards the defenseless prey.

Iridescent scales covered the new beasts, with triple ridges running down their backs. Pointed snouts—bracketed by two smooth tentacles on each side—showed a prehensile tongue ending in short, cilium-like tendrils sliding over dozens of teeth.

Leaping on the goblin, claws pinned him to the ground, and the beast tore out the creature's stomach.

The crowd rose to its feet, cheering.

"People are so finicky," Griffon grumbled. "They did that for me a few minutes ago. What are these crocodile-wolf things, anyway?"

Vunteres, Raven Stealer gave an impressed mental whistle, *pack hunters who are armored, smart, and single-minded in the kill.*

Griffon didn't have a chance to say anything as three of the vunteres shot towards him, two angling to each side to flank him. The third one came straight down the middle.

The gladiator inside Griffon came to life, not so much in his head, but in his actions. This was something the gnome became used to since inhabiting this body. Sometimes he was all Griffon, and other times the body of Auric, the gnomish gladiator, took over. Usually in fights, and sometimes when dealing with plants. The previous soul—or spirit, or whatever—was a hardcore anthophile, and loved flowers and botany.

Pack tactics threaded through Griffon's awareness, and he knew the center one was a distraction to allow the other two to close for the kill.

"Two can play at that game," he muttered, throwing out more illusionary fireworks.

Blue, yellow, and green lights shot from his open palm, and Griffon threw himself into a roll to one side. He came up gripping his sword—pointing forward—and planting his feet, bracing for an impact.

The left flanking vuntere impaled itself on his blade, and Griffon danced to the side, turning the beast as the right flanking predator came down where the gnome had been a moment ago.

Pulling his weapon free, Griffon continued the momentum and beheaded the second foe. The third stood where he had started, shaking its head to clear its vision.

"Two down," Griffon giggled, reveling in the feel of battle, "and four to go."

He looked at the one over the goblin, and the beast was staring back at him, its meal forgotten. It arched its back and slunk forward, head low.

Taking advantage of the blindness of the closest one, he ran forward and hacked at the beast, cutting a line across its ribs and foreleg.

It hissed and lurched backwards, snapping at where the gladiator had been a breath before.

The goblin slayer ran at him, leaping over the injured vuntere, and Griffon readied his sword to impale it. The beast twisted in the air, landing an arm's length away, and then something hit the gnome from behind.

Griffon went down, flipping to his back and bringing his sword across his body. He gripped the blade in his free hand and jaws wrapped around the blade.

Claws raked at his midsection, his leather cuirass protecting his exposed stomach, but barely.

Jerking the blade left and right, Griffon cut into the cheeks of his foe, then twisted the blade, dislocating the creature's jaw.

The beast fell back with a gurgled screech. Griffon pushed to his feet, only to be knocked over again as the last two healthy monsters jumped on him.

The wounded two hung back as their pack mates savaged the gnome, clawing and biting at flesh exposed between pieces of armor.

You're the one who insisted on a 'classic gladiator look', Raven Stealer pointed out in his head, *saying that sandals, greaves, bracers, pauldron, and cuirass was enough protection.*

"Oh, shut up!" Griffon shouted, stabbing a vuntere in the throat with the spiral horn guard of the sword.

Grabbing a fistful of sand, he threw it into the eyes of the last uninjured one and followed it up with a sparkly light show. The fireworks refracted off the crystalline grit and Griffon imagined it must look like a fiery explosion to the watching crowd.

The beast fell back, and the gladiator leapt to his feet, laying about him with his sword, taking out the remaining monster.

Griffon was bleeding from a dozen places, his armor hanging in tatters. He limped in a circle, taking in his surroundings. The vuntere with the injured ribs and leg retreated, followed by the one with the broken jaw.

The gladiator stalked towards the injured animals, the crowd roaring, though Griffon couldn't tell if they were cheering him on or booing his magical antics. He didn't bother with showmanship this time, dispatching the one with the shredded mouth and throat first, then the limping one.

"I didn't think they allowed magic in the arena," Dandy Rym whined, "but your friend used it, anyway."

"There wasn't anything said about it being against the rules," Reggie shrugged, "so will you be honoring our agreement?"

They were in a small tent, a private room in what passed for an inn for in the tent-town of Arena. It was attached to a larger tent that was the common room, and a half dozen similar tents jutted out from the main one. These smaller areas served as private eating and sleeping quarters, and Dandy Rym had joined Griffon and Reggie in theirs.

The gnome lay in a hammock, having discarded his armor, and was rocking back and forth, clutching Raven Stealer. The myriad cuts were closed and little more than angry lines of welts.

"I first heard about this…affliction," Dandy's eyes shifted left and right, and he lowered his voice, "happening in Akar, just north of the Great Desert on the shores of the High Tarn. It's spreading from there, I think. I'd suggest going to Allendale."

"Why Allendale?" Reggie asked.

"Allendale was once well known for having many mind mages," Dandy Rym explained, "and I figure if anyone could resist a disease that turns you into a zombie when you're not dead, it's a mind mage."

"That's damn fine of you," Reggie said, holding out his hand to shake the other man's, "and I'm sorry you lost the bet."

"Oh, that's alright, Kazzek," Dandy laughed, taking Reggie's hand, "I bet good money on you and your friend. I didn't get your blades, but I'm about to be a rich man!"

"Raven Stealer healed you up nicely," Reggie gestured at Griffon's sword once Dandy Rym had left.

"Yup, old man," Griffon giggled, "my girl takes good care of me."

"Well, food is coming," Reggie said, rolling his eyes at the gnome's bravado, "and then we need to get a good night's rest. We have almost a week's travel to get to Allendale."

"Think we'll find the disease this time?" Griffon asked, pushing up on one elbow to look at Reggie.

"I hope so," Reggie sighed, "because I'm hearing more reports about this from all over."

"And you really think this is our fault?" the gnome asked.

"Yes," Reggie nodded grimly, "I think it's the disease we released when we opened that tomb in the desert before we went to the Nine Towers of Magic. You saw the warnings, and so did I."

"I didn't know it was this dangerous, or this important," Griffon said defensively, "otherwise I would've said something. I swear!"

"I know," Reggie nodded again, his face neutral, "so you say, and so you've said many times. Just eat up and get some rest. We leave at first light and hope we're in time to put that specific genie back in the bottle."

"In time for what?" Griffon mumbled quietly. "How do we put a genie back in a bottle? I think it's a bit late to do anything except for saving ourselves."

Calendar

The basic calendar is a lunar calendar. There are thirteen months in each year. Each month there are twenty-eight days. There is a new moon on the first day of every month. The first day of spring is on the Equinox.

Seasons	**Months**		**Days**
Spring	Loen	1.	Ginof
	Hapok	2.	Bestuf
	Axara	3.	Midā
		4.	Therin
Summer	Surem	5.	Uthr
	Santara	6.	Dunwith
	Xaco	7.	Lasin
Autumn	Harton		
	Thon		
	Ault		
Winter	Witen		
	Maleo		
	Frear		
Thaw	Milwen		

Portals: Book 5 – Towers & Trolls

Glossary

Aborgas: Small hamlet near Red City.

Aeifain: Willowy race of beings with almond eyes, pale skin, and slightly pointed ears. Often more advanced in arts, culture, and magic than the lesser races.

Akar Lake: Body of water near Ruger Whitley Estates.

Ault: Ninth month of the year, and the third month of the autumn season.

Axara: Third month of the year, and the spring season.

Bestuf: Second day of the week.

Bidj: A swear word meaning waste or offal.

Binaple: a fruit that grows on binaple bushes used for making red, orange, and yellow dyes.

Changing Wheel, The: The god of cyclical change who all the other gods bow to.

Chuz: A harsh swear word.

Dangrazio: Subterranean metropolis and trading post.

Dasism: A race who follow the path of elements and nature. Physically, they are slighter than humans, with olive skin, pointed ears, and almond eyes.

Dioneze City: A broken city on the eastern part of the continent run by slavers. Known for its gladiatorial ring.

Dragon Estates: An ancient castle rumored to have a dragon residing in the caverns below it.

Dargaon's Hole: Ancestral home of dragons in the Wandering Hills.

Dunwith: Sixth day of the week.

Durgan's Keep: A city-state in the far east that was founded by a rokairn and his adventuring companions.

Edgewater: Medium port town on the coast of the Sea of Seron.

Everyway: Largest city on the continent of Teurone.

Ez'rainia-fromton: City of the dead located in the Great Desert. Was the city in which Verl'zen-luk had been imprisoned before his rise to godhood.

Fate's Run: Dockside gambling hall in Tarnish. Run by a woman named Fate.

Frear: Twelfth month of the year, and the third month of the winter season.

Ginof: First day of the week.

Glass Valley: A valley made of glass in the slim desert that was formed when a stone dragon fell from the heavens.

Gray Lands: Home of the Aeifain.

Great Desert: A large desert east of the southern Rolling Mountains, which is home to Rogen the Plague and the Great Desert Empire.

Great Desert Empire: A civilization built by Rogen the Plague and his nation slaves, located in the Great Desert.

Hapok: Second month of the year, and of the spring season.

Harton: Seventh month of the year, and the first month of the autumn season.

Highest Spire: A structure that is fifty kilometers at the base and spirals upward. Doors that lead to other places in time and space are spaced every six meters. The height of this tower is unmeasured.

Hope's Hollow: A small village on the on the borders of the Black Wood and the Wandering Hills.

Humbrey: A Kingdom of thirteen houses that embodies nobility and honor.

Icon Hall: Aeifain home on the eastern portion of Teurone.

Jonath: God of justice, protection, strength, and earth. His symbol is a trident and balanced scales.

Kez'et-dual: A demon enslaved by the Troöds.

Khelikian: God of Insects.

Kord: A twisted gold wire that is the standard currency.

Land's End: A demon-ridden peninsula on the south-eastern most portion of the continent.

Lasin: Seventh day of the week.

Ley lines: Elemental energy currents, invisible to the naked eye, from which wizards can draw energy.

Loen: First month of the year, and of the spring season. It begins on the spring equinox.

Mage, Mind: Practitioner of the art of psychic magics such as body alteration, telekinesis, telepathy, etc.

Maleo: Eleventh month of the year, and the second month of the winter season.

Malvor: Duchy in the Kingdom of Trysteria, south of the Kingdom of Humbrey. Run by Duke Malvornick.

Midā: Third day of the week.

Milwen: The thirteenth month of the year, and the transition month between winter and spring.

Nine Towers of Magic: Abandoned during the Wizard Wars, this secluded and elite university was dedicated to teaching magic. Located east of the Black Wood.

Nomed: A demon-human-aeifain hybrid.

Northwood Community: The largest city in Northwood, founded by humans, dasism, and other races.

Obsidian/Onyx: God of Magic who came to power when the Talisman appeared in the sky.

Obsidian/Onyx Towers: Black towers raised by the God of Magic to distribute magical tools, goods, and weapons.

Ocean Wood: Lands reclaimed by the Dasism from humans under Kala the Black.

Olde Kingdom: A fallen Kingdom in the southern portion of the Everyway Plains.

Oracle Plain: Grasslands north of the Common Wood, east of the Slim Desert, and west of the Rolling Mountains. Home of the mystical order of the Oracle.

Pantageas: City run by mages and wizards in the northern Everyway Plains, just south of the Kingdom of Humbrey.

Paradise Island: An island created by a dead volcano. Now a refuge for pirates and seagoing folk. Run by small governments and individuals, known for its waterfalls.

Parsay Gevies: God of Luck, Chance, and Dreams. Referred to as Parsay by adults, who pray to him for luck, and as Mister Gevies by children, who pray to him for dreams to come true.

Pek: A silver coin, worth one-tenth of a gold kord.

Pemtie: A moron, ignorant, or stupid person, idea, or event.

Phaz, Day of: A day that happens once every four years. Shrouded with myth and superstition.

Promethene: Goddess of Song and Light. Her clergy is almost always women. Wife of the Walking God, Mother of Chanian and Senaria.

Pyridom of Power: A landmark on the east coast of the continent that focuses magical energies.

Red City: Run down city once plagued by lycanthropes and undead. Located on the coast of the

Red Wind: Located in the Red Plains, this city is known for its crime lords and drug trade.

Rock Crag Wastes: a rocky area geographically located west of the Great Desert and east of the southern Rolling Mountains.

Rogen the Plague: Rokairn slave master and lord of The Great Desert Empire.

Rokairn: The Stone Folk. A short, stout race known for their attention to detail, organization, and dedication to fine craftsmanship. Both sexes are known to have beards.

Rolling Mountains: An immense mountain range east of the Oracle Plain, and west of the Northwood.

Rondarius the Foul: Insane Necromancer

Royale Bay: A bay north of the Sea of Seron and east of the Everyway Plains.

Rugber Whitley Estates: A small community known for the mind mages born there.

Rumay Bay: A shanty town on the shores of the Broken Sea that was once a hub of trade before The Downfall.

Runsk: A warlord-controlled city nestled between the Grey Forest and Diaz Wood.

Santara: Fifth month of the year, and the second month of the summer season.

Sea of the Great Plague: A body of water south of the Great Desert.

Sea of Seron: A body of water south of the Everyway Plains.

Seawall City: A fortified city run by spellslingers in a military fashion, located on the east coast of Teurone on the Eastern Ocean.

Senaria: Goddess of nature, innate honor, and woodlands. Daughter of The Walking God and Promethene.

Sharp: A brass coin, with one one-hundredth of a gold kord.

Shuglak (shug-lak): Horse-sized herd creature with large round ears, a single nose horn on a flat hog-like snout, and two tusks jutting from the bottom jaw of males.

Shulyar City: Dasism name for Silver City.

Silver Castle: One-time home of the god, Jonath, who built it.

Silver City: Also known as Shulyar City, a city built by the god Jonath.

Sinking Swamp: A swamp that hides the Library of Time, west of Trysteria and north of the Everyway Plains.

Slim Desert: A thin desert between Everyway Plains and Oracle Plain.

Spellslinger: A generalized term for a wielder of one of the five types of magic; alchemy, mind magic, holy, conjuring, and elemental.

Stadia Isle: A pirate island in the Sea of Seron.

Surem: Fourth month of the year, and the first month of the summer season.

Talisman: A comet that returns on a regular basis, but now is in orbit around the planet.

Tarnish: Run-down desert city on the coast of the Sea of the Great Plague.

Tarra: Goddess of water and healing. Twin of Torr.

Teurone: Continent detailed in this book.

Therin: Fourth day of the week.

Thon: Eighth month of the year, and the second month of the autumn season.

Torgoth: God of Trade and Commerce.

Torr: God of fire and combat. Twin of Tarra.

Transvartius: A wise and benevolent man sometimes known as the Traveller, the Hidden Diplomat, and disciple of the Walking God.

Traveling God, The: God of innate magic, such as mind mages and wizards. Also known as the Walking God.

Troöd: A race from another dimension, that are reptilian in features. They have two distinct species, greys and greens. The former deal in summoning magics, and the latter are chameleon like soldiers.

Trysteria: Kingdom in the northern portion of the Everyway Plains.

Uthr: Fifth day of the week.

Vallenwood: a wood harvested from Vallenwood trees that is strong and beautiful.

Velentian Brandy: A strong alcoholic drink.

Verl'zen-luk: God of ritual Magic.

Witen: Tenth month of the year, and the first month of the winter season.

Wizard: Practitioner of elemental magics which tap into the energy of ley lines.

Xaco: Sixth month of the year, and the third month of the summer season.

About the Author

Travis I. Sivart writes Fantasy, Steampunk, Cyberpulp, Social DIY, and more. You can find him live streaming the writing and editing of his latest project from his home in Central Virginia, surrounded by too many cats.

You can find Travis on Amazon, Barnes and Noble, Books-A-Million, and other literary retailers.

Travis I. Sivart